Also by Mike Woodhams

Paths of Courage

FRANK RYDER RETURNS

RUN WITH THE BRAVE

MIKE WOODHAMS

Matador
9 Priory Business Park
Kibworth Beauchamp
Leicestershire LE8 0RX, UK
Tel: (+44) 116 279 2299
Fax: (+44) 116 279 2277
Email: books@troubador.co.uk
Web: www.troubador.co.uk/matador

ISBN 978 1784622 459

British Library Cataloguing in Publication Data.
A catalogue record for this book is available from the British Library.

Printed and bound in the UK by TJ International, Padstow, Cornwall
Typeset by Troubador Publishing Ltd

Matador is an imprint of Troubador Publishing Ltd

To my sons, Stephen, Matthew and James

I fled, and cry'd out Death;
Hell trembl'd at the hideous Name, and sigh'd
From all her caves, and back resounded Death.

MILTON

CONTENTS

Principal Characters   xi

Prologue   xiii

PART ONE – Into the Abyss   1

PART TWO – Treacherous Journey   55

PART THREE – Retribution   205

About the Author   297

PRINCIPAL CHARACTERS

British
Frank Ryder, Omega Unit
George Conway, Head of Omega Unit
John Watson, Omega Unit Chief of Staff
Sarah, friend of Ryder

American
Colonel Jake Hamilton, Green Beret Special Forces
Captain Cane, Green Beret Special Forces
Lieutenant Owen, Green Beret Special Forces
Master Sergeant Jed Brady, Green Beret Special Forces
Sergeant First-Class Clint 'Bear' Kellar, Green Beret Special Forces
Sergeant Oscar Sicano, Green Beret Special Forces
Admiral John Martin, NSA Director
Admiral Harry Peters, Chief of Naval Operations
Admiral Bill Johnson, Commander-in-Chief, Pacific Fleet
Captain Allen Jackson, Navy Commander, Fort Meade
Lieutenant Davis, Navy Analyst, Fort Meade

Iranian
Afari Asgari, insurgent
Tariq Vari Awad, insurgent
Fehed Al Wan, insurgent
Saad Amer Abdulla, insurgent

Qatak Nasir Ali, insurgent
Massoud, insurgent
Naveed, insurgent

Israeli
Ariel Barak, Prime Minister
Binyamin Marok, Minister of Defence
Benjamin Mitsa, Foreign Secretary
Major General Nemen, Navy Commander-in-Chief
Captain Ben Lehmann, Submarine Commander
Lieutenant Joseph Levi, Submarine Executive Officer
Meir Dagan, Mossad Chief
Captain David Yoman, Sayeret Mat'kal Special Forces
Sergeant Yari Shiron, Sayeret Mat'kal Special Forces
Corporal Daniel Hellmann, Sayeret Mat'kal Special Forces
Colonel Yabin, Sayeret Mat'kal Special Forces commander
Colonel Rosenthall, Air Force Special Operations
Captain Dakar, Special Forces Adjutant

PROLOGUE

The man hung, feet several inches above the floor, naked from the waist down. With head slumped on to his chest and arms stretched upwards, he swung gently on a rope suspended from the ceiling; a large, wet stain spread below him on the concrete floor. Two cables ran from his rectum down to the floor and over to a small electric generator in one corner of the windowless room; the smell of sweat and urine dominated. One of the four men interrogating leaned forward, lifted the man's chin and, once again, asked in Farsi, accent thick, "Who sent you?"

No response.

"Who sent you?" he repeated, this time with a sweeping back-hander to the face.

The man recoiled from the blow, opened his eyes set deep in puffed features, and looked intently at his tormentor, then spat into the Iranian's face.

Viciously punching the hanging figure in the stomach, the interrogator wiped the spittle away and signalled to the generator operator who immediately pulled at a lever firing an electric pulse through the wires.

The man screamed, bucked and swung violently on the rope before passing out.

★ ★ ★

He came to in his 6 by 10-foot cell, crouched against the wall under a yellow glare cast by a single bulb fixed to the ceiling; the stench of urine and faeces permeated the air. He was thirsty and his body ached. Taking in the cell, a sanctuary between interrogations, he saw rough prison overalls laying by the door and painfully put them on. Surrounded by dank, windowless walls, the only way he could tell night from day was by the temperature, which stifled when the sun's heat penetrated the prison block and plummeted during the darkness hours. His only comfort: a stained, straw-filled mattress easing his bruised and battered body and giving some relief from the cold, hard concrete floor. He had been given little to eat and drink: stale bread, water and thin, tasteless soup. Losing track of time he guessed he'd been in this godforsaken hole maybe three to four weeks, during which time his mind drifted, imagining at intervals his pain-racked body floating serenely over blue lakes and lush green meadows when it became too much to bear. He knew when he was hallucinating and tried desperately to bring reality back. The pain inflicted by his tormentors had almost broken his spirit; he was not sure how much more he could take. Days were filled listening to the screams of others, the sound of clanging metal doors and the dragging of bodies along the corridor outside. He remained in constant fear waiting his turn – not transient fear, but deep fear that penetrated his very soul. The dreaded journey to the room at the end of the corridor and the nightmare events which occurred within were definitely taking their toll. The anguish and suffering was almost unbearable. At first it never occurred to him to give anything to these bastards, but now he knew under the extreme pressure he would soon break and be forced to admit who he was and who had sent him. It was only a matter of time.

PART ONE

Into the Abyss

1

In a nondescript warehouse situated in an industrial zone south of the city of Jerusalem, Captain David Yoman, along with several others from Sayeret Mat'Kal's Unit 269, entered the tactical briefing room at 2030 hours. The captain sat in the front row of chairs facing a dais. Next to him sat Sergeant Yari Shiron, and next to him, Corporal Daniel Hellmann, the rest spread themselves out behind. The team, led by Yoman, had been called to the briefing still wearing their black battle fatigues on return from flushing out a suspected Hamas hideout in the central city. Slightly built, muscular, with dark close-cropped hair and intense brown eyes, Yoman attempted to relax, still coming down from the 'killing house' operation, but found it difficult in anticipation of why they had been hurriedly summoned. Awaiting them on the dais behind a desk, sat the commander, Colonel Yabin, together with his adjutant and a colonel of the Israeli Air Force.

"You know Captain Dakar here," opened the commander, gesturing towards the adjutant, "and this is Colonel Rosenthall of Air Force Special Operations."

The Air Force colonel nodded and looked intently at each man with dark, penetrating eyes and grizzled features.

On the wall behind the dais were detailed maps, together with photographs of the Middle East, in particular that of the Zagros mountain range in south-western Iran.

"I apologise for calling this briefing at such a late hour, but necessity requires it," said Colonel Yabin, his tall, thin frame looking a little awkward as he spoke standing at the desk. "I will come straight to the point. You men have been selected to undertake a mission into Iran to recon for a possible missile base here in the Zagros Mountains." He turned and placed his pointer on the southern area of the range. "We have reason to believe the base is somewhere in the vicinity of Kuh-e Mohammadabad – a 3,600-metre high peak. SAT coverage indicates nothing, nor does heat imaging, but we are assured the information source is highly reliable."

"Until we can produce evidence that it does exist," added Colonel Rosenthall, "the Americans will not use up valuable SAT time to lock-in, which we can understand, with the increasing turmoil in Iraq and Syria, knowing how many they have to cover the whole region at any given time. This mountain is in a blind spot to our SAT coverage." The colonel referred to Israel's military satellite surveillance system, Ofek (Hebrew for 'horizon'), covering the Middle East and most of Iran.

"We need to know quickly if it is a missile base. All our cities will be in range of Shahab-5s, which we suspect they now have. They can carry a big payload, conventional warheads, or warheads capable of mass destruction."

"And, if it is?" Captain Yoman asked without invitation, familiar with the informal and candid manner with which his commander preferred to conduct briefings.

"Take pictures and do whatever you can to disable," Yabin replied.

"We'll need high explosives," said Sergeant Shiron, piercing hazel eyes set in smooth, dark aquiline features fixing the commander. A livid scar ran from his left eye down to the corner of his mouth; legacy of a motorbike accident when he was eighteen.

"The demo boys have already put together compact devices using C4 powerful enough at least to damage silo heads, if any. Just set the timers and leave – fast," said the commander.

4

"When do we go?" asked Captain Yoman, feeling a little more relaxed now he knew what the mission entailed.

"Within the next forty-eight hours, subject to a favourable weather forecast over the Gulf and the southern part of the range for a night HAHO insertion," answered Colonel Rosenthall.

All the men looked at one another. HAHO (High Altitude High Opening) insertion was the ultimate means of clandestine parachute insertion and one of the most dangerous. From an aircraft flying above radar the parachutist would jump at high altitude using oxygen equipment and then effectively glide or parafly many miles on the thermals to eventually land accurately on or near the target. This form of insertion allowed silent penetration by lightly armed forces deep into enemy territory with speed and precision primarily for hit-and-run attacks, surgical strikes, or to form bridgeheads for troops following in on the ground.

"Not leaving much time to prepare," said Corporal Hellmann, a stocky, dark-haired man with brooding features and acned skin.

"The equipment and weapons, including the explosive devices, have already been assembled," said Captain Dakar, a small, slim man who looked completely out of place surrounded by these elite special forces' warriors but who could boast a successful term in the field combating counterterrorism within the State of Israel. "In the next twelve hours you will be required to check and recheck the equipment to satisfy yourselves everything is okay. Let me know if there is anything else you need," he finished.

The commander pressed a button on the desk and a white screen slid down over the wall maps and photographs. The lights dimmed and a projector at the back of the room shone through displaying several satellite pictures of Kuh-e Mohammadabad on the screen. "Now, before we get down to the details," he said, purposefully, "I want you to look closely at these satellite shots of the mountain. These were taken less than a week ago by the Americans and show the south-western side." He turned and ran a pointer over the high-resolution pictures, stopping at various areas giving the co-ordinates at the same time. "As you can see, nothing but rock, tussock and scrub. However these points do have some interest in that we cannot see beneath what appears to be rocky outcrops. We want you to check these areas first, then the remaining mountain side between here," he pointed to a small town called Kahbar on the south-western flank, "and Javazm on the south-eastern flank. It's a big area to cover – fifteen to twenty miles long by about five deep.

"If you find nothing, move to the northern side; cover the whole area and then start moving upwards if necessary." He paused for several seconds looking at the screen then said, "The search could take weeks, so you'll be living rough off the land. Keep on the move. The small town of Abbasabad, on the western flank, has an army garrison. If a base exists the area will be patrolled, so be more than watchful; keep the search pattern simple. Use the GPS to check off your position against the co-ordinates before moving on. Don't leave any sign of your presence – bury everything. Communications are to be kept to a minimum. Zip out only to confirm the existence of a base and when you are able to RV for extraction." He paused. "Okay, any questions?" He waited a moment or two. "None? In that case I'll pass you over to Colonel Rosenthall."

As the lights came back on and the screen retracted, the Air Force colonel stood up and pointed to a large map of the Middle East. "You'll leave Ovda at 1900 hours, fly direct to the Gulf above Jordanian, Saudi and Iraqi radar, and commence the HAHO at 30,000 feet on the Iranian coastline at approximately 2100 hours. If the wind and thermals are right you should be able to penetrate maybe fifty to a hundred miles inland," he pointed to the south-western side of the Zagros, "which should land you somewhere here." He moved the pointer to the foothills rising from the coastland plains. "From here you will make your way on foot direct to Kuh-e Mohammadabad about 200 miles further inland using

GPS." The colonel paused, running the pointer back down to the Iranian coast. "When the job's done you'll make your way back to the Gulf, set up a RV somewhere along the coastline and we'll heli you out."

"What happens if communications fail?" asked Sergeant Shiron.

"You make your way to co-ordinates we'll give you before you leave, between here and here," answered the colonel, pointing to the two Iranian coastal towns of Nay Band and Bandar-e Shui. "We'll have a cruiser waiting in the Gulf monitoring the position constantly to lock-on to a homing device once you arrive. Individual homers will be part of your equipment."

"How long will you wait?" asked Captain Yoman, anticipation mounting at the thought of a mission in the land of Israel's arch-enemy, Iran.

"As long as we can."

Silence descended for a few moments before Colonel Yabin spoke, "Captain Yoman will lead the eight-man team with Sergeant Shiron and Corporal Hellmann as number two and three. He will select the other five and the remaining four will be on standby." He paused looking at each of the men then said, "The operation will be code-named Tehome."

'Abyss'! Yoman hoped that was not to be an omen of things to come.

★ ★ ★

Forty-eight hours later an Israeli Air Force MC-130H Combat Talon II transporter left the runway at Ovda, climbed steadily into a clear afternoon sky, and banked eastwards towards the Persian Gulf. On board were eight commandos of Israeli's Special Forces Unit 269 led by Captain Yoman, together with the nine-man crew. In a little under three hours they would be over the Gulf. The aircraft climbed beyond 35,000 feet and levelled off. The flight plan: to fly over Jordan, Saudi Arabia, Iraq and Kuwait above radar detection, release the commandos 30,000 feet above the coast of Iran, and then return home by the same route. The weather forecast for the Gulf region was good and the expected wind patterns and thermals over the drop zone would present perfect paraflying conditions for insertion into Iran's interior.

Captain Yoman sat in line on canvas webbing against the fuselage with seven other members of the commando team, immersed in thought, the loud constant drone of the engines filling his ears. He let his mind drift as he leaned against the French-made BT80 chute pack strapped firmly to his back, housing the oblong silk parachute which allowed flight through the high atmosphere unseen by radar or the human eye. He wore thermal black tactical assault gear with portable compact oxygen equipment and tight-fitting helmet to protect from the severe airstreams experienced on the dive. The pack strapped to the front of his chest carried a Sig 9mm automatic pistol, spare ammunition, Kaybar combat dagger and shaped C4 explosive charges, rations and maps. The higher the aircraft went the colder it became. The ear-shattering noise in the uninsulated fuselage made it impossible to make conversation other than through the internal intercom system. The loadmaster handed out chocolate bars and cocoa. In the dim light, each side of Yoman, sat Sergeant Shiron and Corporal Hellmann, both having served with him for more than three years on clandestine operations throughout the Middle East; however, this operation would be the first into Iran. Born in Jerusalem, he often wished Israel could be free of the prejudices, hatreds and intolerances shown by many nations against the State, especially by his Islamic neighbours and, in particular, the terrorist organisations they spawned. But as a realist he knew this was not to be, at least for the foreseeable future.

Two and a half hours after leaving Israeli air-space the aircraft arrived without incident over the Persian Gulf and proceeded to fly south-eastwards down the Iranian coastline as the sun caressed the western horizon to starboard, highlighting the sea below in a blood-red glow. Yoman began one final equipment check and prepared himself mentally for the jump 'go' in less than fifteen minutes.

Suddenly, an alarm in the cockpit blared.

The pilot shot a glance at the gauges and said calmly, "Fuel-pressure drop, number one," before he quickly shut off the fuel supply.

The co-pilot turned to look out the window and saw flames leaping from the outer starboard engine. "Number one's aflame!" he shouted.

Moments later the pilot and co-pilot watched horrified as the inner starboard engine also burst into flames; immediately the pilot cut the fuel supply. With both props gone the pilot struggled desperately to maintain control, decreasing power as much as he dare to the port engines and attempting to avoid the aircraft yawing sharply to the right and spinning downwards, completely out of control.

The plane quivered violently and began to drop. Yoman saw through one of the small circular windows slipstream flames trailing from the engines. His heart leapt; his mind weighing up the options at the same time. Could the flames be stopped? If they had to abort could they get back safely to Israel or at least land somewhere in one of the Gulf States? And, god forbid, if they had to bail out, could they reach dry land?

The pilot and co-pilot struggled and did everything they could to keep the plane from losing height, attempting to veer south to escape Iranian air-space but without success.

At 15,000 feet and well into Iranian airspace the electronic sensors suddenly registered a lock-on.

"SAMS!" screamed the warfare officer, slamming on every electronic countermeasure available.

Too late; the Iranian surface-to-air missile, inbound at the rear of the aircraft, ignored the aluminium chaff shrouding the front, grazed the tail port wing and sheared off part of the tail structure, but miraculously without exploding.

The transporter dipped sharply and the pilot struggled to keep the 130H from plunging vertically. He switched to the operation's emergency frequency, then in an even voice, "Mayday! Mayday! This is Tomahawk. Repeat! This is Tomahawk. Do you read? Over."

The response was immediate. "Roger that, Tomahawk. This is Red Indian. What is your location? Over."

"Red Indian; this is Tomahawk. Be advised, fatal hit received! Iranian SAM! Bailing out! Location: 27.55North; 51.54East. Over."

A few seconds silence then, "Copy. This is Red Indian. Instigate destruct procedure. Good luck. Over."

"Thank you. Over and out." The pilot swiftly set the destruct switches for all the specialist electronic equipment and weaponry systems. Then over the intercom to everyone on board, "Bail out! Bail out!" before he made for the exit.

With a mixture of desperation and frustration, Captain Yoman removed the pistol from his chest-pack and slipped it into his waistband, abandoned the forty-pound load and oxygen equipment, including the mask. The other commandos did the same. Then through the helmet comms he told them, "No way do we land on Iranian territory. Parafly towards the Saudi coastline! Clear?" He prayed the winds would allow them to fly west and reach the coast and not land in the sea.

All nodded and followed him to the side escape-hatch.

He watched the crew bail out then waited for his team to jump, one by one, before he too leapt out of the doomed aircraft.

With Yoman and the other commandos close together in a fairly tight formation, wind tearing at their bodies, the rapidly changing digits on his wrist altimeter told him he was now at 8,000 feet and dropping faster than anticipated. He worried too that the wind velocity and thermals at this point were in a strong easterly direction as predicted, taking them not towards the Arabian coastline, but into Iranian territory as feared. No matter how much he tried to change direction the mottled browns and yellows of the

Iranian coastal plains loomed large below. An explosion to the south told him the aircraft had finally hit the ground.

The crew of the ill-fated aircraft, using standard-issue parachutes, dropped almost vertically, rapidly descending at various rates in the fading light, spread over a distance of almost a mile.

At 1,500 feet, Yoman watched vehicles producing plumes of dust track his flight path while he fought unsuccessfully to maintain horizontal flight. As the ground came fast towards him, he searched for a place to land offering some form of cover. Everywhere was almost flat except for a few low-lying sandstone outcrops and dunes. Closer to the ground, he saw the dark, snaking line of a narrow wadi running parallel with the base of a string of linked outcrops. Without hesitation he tugged at the guides, followed by the others, and all dropped quickly towards the wadi gouged out by centuries of wind and rain.

At 1,000 feet he looked on helplessly as the two military vehicles closed in towards the wadi. Minutes later he landed in the dry bed, quickly shed his parachute harness and desperately searched for cover. Within seconds, to his left and right, no more than twenty yards apart, the other members of Unit 269 landed and did the same in the sparse terrain that was flat, littered with small rocks that offered little cover, together with sporadic clusters of boulders that did provide some semblance of protection. They scrambled for the nearest cluster against the base of the wadi wall just as the first of the two trailing vehicles came to a halt on the edge of the opposite side.

Heavily armed troops spilled from the rear and began to spread. It looked hopeless but the captain was not prepared to surrender without a fight.

"Fan out, make every shot count," he urged the others, each carrying a P226 pistol with a 15-round magazine giving a total of 120 rounds between them.

With backs to the jagged wadi wall 10 to 15 feet high, Yoman and his team spread themselves no more than several yards apart in a rough curve. Each man had chosen a boulder large enough to give a modicum of cover. None spoke nor moved once settled, waiting, pistols cocked and ready, for the onslaught to begin. The wadi at this point was some forty yards wide.

The second truck arrived and discharged more troops who, together with the squad from the first, scrambled down into the wadi and began to zigzag towards the Israelis' position.

Yoman steeled himself, estimating twenty to thirty heavily armed men now homing in, edging closer from all angles across the dusty wadi-bed using whatever cover available; shadows only in the twilight haze.

The Iranians opened fire first, spraying bursts of metal into the bank behind, sending sandstone and slivers of rock showering down on the commando's positions.

During the intense firefight that ensued, Yoman, on the outer stretch of the curve, caught a sudden movement to his left, swivelled, and as he rolled to another boulder close by, gunned down two soldiers in rapid succession about to shoot from close range. He picked off several more under a hail of bullets but it became increasingly difficult to line up a target the closer they came and the more accurate their machine-gun volleys became. Now with only a few rounds left and nowhere to go, he knew it was only a matter of time before they would be overrun.

Suddenly, an ear-shattering explosion followed by an agonised cry.

Yoman looked to his right and saw Sergeant Moshe Soch writhing on the ground, right arm shredded to the bone and left leg severed at the knee; the bastards were using grenades! With blood gushing from his wounds, the burly sergeant struggled up, retrieved his pistol, and continued to fire until the magazine emptied before he died, bullets churning the ground around him. He then saw Corporal Abir Yaakov at the other end of the curve. Under intense attack, the corporal broke cover, firing wildly at the oncoming shadows, downing three as he stumbled erratically over the short distance towards a boulder that looked to give better cover. He never made it, reaching only halfway before he was almost cut in two by a fusillade of lead smashing his broken body against the wadi wall.

Yoman, in despair, kept blasting away until he heard the click of the firing pin against an empty chamber. He could do nothing now but await the outcome; either to be killed or taken prisoner. With the ammunition of the five other surviving commandos expended too, return firing finally ceased.

For several seconds an eerie silence hung over the wadi, Yoman remained still, looking straight ahead, waiting to be mown down at any moment. 'Abyss' had been an omen after all; they were now about to face the void. Slowly, one by one, the Iranian troops emerged from hiding and edged menacingly forward in the semi-darkness, weapons cocked. When they reached the Israelis, now standing in line, a stocky little man in battle fatigues stepped forward from the pack in front of Yoman and barked in Farsi, "Which one of you is in charge?"

"I am," the captain answered.

In one swift movement the Iranian rammed the butt of his rifle into Yoman's stomach. "That is for my men you have just killed," he snarled as Yoman collapsed, reeling with the pain; another blow, this time to the head, and the last thing he remembered were the cries of the others as they suffered the same fate.

Bound hand and foot, the Israeli commandos were dragged unconscious to the nearest truck, thrown in and driven to an Iranian base. Operation Abyss had ended before it had really begun.

2

Ryder's heart missed a beat.

Out in the centre of the ring the lithe figure of the young matador, resplendent in silver and blue, high cheekboned and displaying all the arrogance of his gypsy heritage, took up position, unfurled the small red cape and walked to within ten yards of where the powerful black bull stood. He stopped, raised the sword in his right hand and proffered the cape with his left.

Under an autumn afternoon sun bathing Seville's Plaza de Toros de la Maestranza the sound of a rousing pasodoble competed with a 12,000 noisy crowd chanting: "*Tor-re-ro! Tor-re-ro! Tor-re-ro!*"

"What's he doing?" Ryder's companion screamed above the clamour.

Ryder couldn't believe what he was seeing; *the boy has balls.* "Not now, Sarah. Not now."

But she persisted.

In a taut voice he gave in, "He's going to kill *recibiendo,* the oldest and most dangerous method of dispatch – unbelievable!"

"For Christ's sake, Frank; what the hell does that mean?"

"Enticing the bull to charge from a distance; when it reaches him he'll hopefully guide it past with the cape, letting it run onto the sword high between the shoulders. If the bull raises its head at the very last moment, a horn will undoubtedly nail him in the chest."

"Oh my God; that could kill him!" she shouted amidst the clamour, equally fascinated and repelled by this ballet of death.

"He knows what he's doing, don't worry." But he couldn't help thinking: *he could well do that!* The moment of truth had arrived.

The music stopped. The crowd hushed. The bull pawed at the ground and snorted. The matador drew himself up, sighting along the sword then flicked the cape, *"Toro, ha; Toro, ha."*

The animal sprang forward. The man waited, feet firmly planted in the sand.

Seconds later he and the bull merged as one; the sword flashed in the sunlight, entered the bloodied shoulders and sunk deep up to the hilt. The lowered head and massive body followed the red cloth out to the right, its momentum carrying it well beyond the man, staggering, coughing; blood gushing from an open mouth before plunging to its knees and rolling lifelessly on the sand.

The plaza erupted.

"Ole! Ole!" Ryder shouted, jumping to his feet, caught up in the euphoria around him. For Sarah it was over all too quickly; the skill shown by the man had been but a blur. To Ryder, and to most of those packed in the arena, the animal had been dispatched with grace and with skill.

"Did you see that? Did you see that?" Sarah gushed amidst all the applause, holding hand to her mouth, "So quick… so horrible; yet so beautiful." The closeness of such a primitive, violent act gave her a vicarious thrill more than she cared to admit. Ryder ignored her, absorbed in his own emotions. He could not help feeling respect for this boy who had just stared death in the face. He did not consider himself an aficionado but he definitely related to the emotion it generated, understanding the technical and ritual aspects which led up to the death of the bull. Only in this life and death struggle could the most primitive and intense emotions be experienced both by the matador and by those watching. The whole thing appealed to his inherent sense of survival and to his own deep primitive instincts.

Unscathed, the matador, glittering, turned and smiled broadly up at the frenzied crowd in a sea of white handkerchiefs. Arms raised, he walked towards the barrier and began a triumphant tour of the ring to the roar engulfing the plaza. Sombreros, cushions, cigars and flowers rained down onto the sand; the bull's ears, tail and a hoof were awarded by the bullring president. When he had completed a full circuit a trumpet sounded, the ring cleared and the last bull of the afternoon trotted out into the arena.

To Ryder, this beautiful Moorish-style ring with its arched colonnades, whitewashed walls and yellow ochre trim, the spiritual home of Spanish bullfighting, provided the perfect setting for the deadly encounter between man and beast. Sitting in the shade, second row up from the passageway between the ring and the stands, they were close enough to feel the vibrant energy and smell the action on the sand below. Ryder was pleased to see that Sarah was holding up well to the violent nature of the spectacle, considering she had never been to a bullfight before.

The sleek brown beast with wide horns stopped, raised its huge head and sniffed at the air, great neck-muscle raised and taut. It then ambled around the perimeter, shying away when challenged by the peons stepping out from behind the barrier. To Ryder this was not a good sign; it seemed this bull did not want to fight. He glanced at the programme. The bull, 'Insurrecto' –'Rebel' in English (aptly named he thought) – was a five-year-old from the ranch of Miura and weighed 1,200 pounds. He understood enough to know it was unusual for Miuras to lack bravery; they were feared by most matadors, referred to as 'the bulls of death'.

"I'm no Hemingway," Sarah cried, "but that bull looks as if he's not interested."

Ryder looked at her in surprise. "You've heard of Hemingway?"

"You think I'm a dummy, Frank? You could say I'm widely read." She gave him a cheeky grin.

"You're right. He's what those in the know call a 'Manso' – tame and cowardly."

One of the matador's peons attempted to cape the animal but it stood its ground and bellowed. He tried again. The bull shied away and galloped towards the opposite side of the arena, turned and ran back again, this time at great speed. Then just before it looked as if it was going to crash into the barrier the inconceivable happened: the huge beast leapt at the 5-foot-high structure, reached the top easily and used the solid timber framework to launch itself with hind legs across the passageway and up into the stands scrambling awkwardly over the low steel cable railing before spilling onto the concrete terracing not far from where Ryder sat.

Sheer panic gripped the spectators in that section as 'Insurrecto' found his feet and ran amok along the tiered seating. The crowd scattered; some jumping down into the ring, others clambering upwards. The animal cut a swathe through the mass of bodies surging upwards and sidewards trying desperately to avoid the slashing, hacking horns. Many fell in the crush, trampled as they lay helplessly in the path of the beast. Ryder, caught in the wave of humanity, tried to protect himself and a terrified Sarah, punching and kicking those who attempted to overwhelm as the panic-stricken throng fought to get away. Before he knew it the bull was only yards away; a young woman was struck in the thigh and swung helplessly from one horn. Everything happened so fast. The matadors and peons had only just now begun to climb up from the ring below waving capes to distract the enraged animal which seemed determined to continue its rampage. Casting the unfortunate woman on the horn aside, blood gushing from her leg, the animal charged straight at Ryder along the narrow concrete terrace dividing the *Barreras* and *tendido* seating.

He did not hesitate. Grabbing Sarah's large canvas bag, he threw it hard at the on-coming beast to distract it. The straps caught the right horn and the bag swung down over the bull's eyes, blinding it momentarily, halting the charge. In those vital few seconds, Ryder jumped up to the next tier, dodged the slashing horns, and hurled his 6-foot solid frame against the animal's flank, catching the bull off balance and sending it crashing sidewards down to the first row. He narrowly missed the thrashing hoofs as it keeled over with him all but entwined between its legs and then unbelievably again as the beast struggled to regain its feet. Desperately he tried to roll away but was slammed against the step; it's bulk squeezing him hard against the concrete surface. He thought he was about to die.

Suddenly a peon rushed forward, jumped on the animal's back and thrust a knife expertly into Insurrecto's neck, severing the spinal cord, killing the beast instantly.

Ryder struggled to push the bull away, kicking madly at underbelly, genitals, anywhere to keep those deadly hoofs at bay and somehow managing to avoid the nerve-driven flaying legs. Finally, after what seemed a lifetime, its death throes ended and he scrambled to his feet, shaken and bruised, thankful no bones had been broken and grateful to still be alive.

Mobbed by the jubilant crowd, strong hands swept him off his feet, hoisting him high on the shoulders of two swarthy Spaniards who carried him in triumph along the concrete tier, attempting to get him down into the ring for a victory circuit. Once down in the passageway between the ring and the stands, he was besieged by journalists bombarding him from every direction.

"*Eso fue algo muy valiente. Que te hizo hacerto?*" shot one overly excited young man, pushing a microphone into his face.

Then another from a gaunt oldie: "*Arriesgando su vida de esa manero salvo a muchos. Como te sienties?*"

"*Estaba usted no tiene miedo?*" This time a young woman from the *Diario de Seville*.

How the hell did he know what made him do it, or how he felt at the time; he knew he was risking his life… Yes, he was afraid!

The questions kept coming, but he pretended not to understand, shaking his head and shouting, "No speak Spanish… No understand."

It was frenzied; he had to get away.

Pushing his way through the throng and flashing cameras with difficulty, he eventually managed to leave the plaza with Sarah in tow and hailed a cab to return to his hotel, eventually losing those journos who had attempted to follow. On arrival he made straight for his room, removed bloodstained clothes, showered, and put on fresh jeans, shirt and trainers before heading back down to the hotel bar where Sarah patiently waited. He ordered a pint of lager, another gin for Sarah, and they both went out to a table on the terrace.

"Brave thing you did back there, Frank," she said, sipping her drink and looking at him softly, big hazel eyes conveying concern, hair bleached by the sun falling seductively across her tanned features. "You could've been seriously injured – killed even. Those horns were lethal."

He liked Sarah, especially when she looked at him that way. From the moment they met at his local, The Prince Albert, only a week back, he'd taken to her. She was fun to be with, looked good and had an easy manner. Glad she had agreed to join him on this trip, he was looking forward to the next few days shopping, sightseeing and attending more bullfights with her – amongst other delights.

He shrugged.

"Seriously; it might have killed you," she finished, concern melting away.

"Does that mean I get a reward for still being alive?" A grin creased his angular, swarthy features; alert brown eyes glinting under a shock of dark, wavy hair.

A saucy look crossed her face. "Hey, hero, don't get your hopes up. Keep doing stupid things like you just did and one day you could run outta luck."

With adrenaline still pumping he glanced at the long tanned legs folded opposite him. Suddenly he felt the urge to take her to his room.

She threw him a knowing look. "You married, Frank?"

That was a kick; bringing him swiftly back to earth, "Divorced."

"Oh, really," she seemed a little surprised, "How long?"

"Ten years. She didn't like army life." Instantly he regretted saying that. The less people knew of his army connection the better.

"Sorry to hear – kids?"

"No," he shot back; adrenaline dissipating. The break-up had been traumatic. He'd tried to make his marriage work but barrack life and youthful expectations got in the way.

"So, you're in the army; guessed you might be."

"Was…" a short pause, then inquisitiveness took over, "What makes you think that?"

"Not sure really, just something about you: precise, authoritative – well-toned, and the way you handled that bull – wow!" she gave him a wicked grin. "You're quite a mystery, Frank," she paused to sip her drink, "Anyway, if you're not in the army, what do you do to pay the rent?"

"Government courier."

She looked at him sideways.

Definitely time to move on. "You married?"

She didn't answer straight away and reached into her bag. "Like a smoke, Frankie?"

"You smoke?" He was surprised, then, "No thanks. I've given up."

"Don't normally, but I need a special now – want one?"

"Special?" *Whoa! Who is this lady?* He looked at her in astonishment. *Who would've thought?* He'd not indulged in a joint for over a year but felt tempted after today's escapade. "What you got?"

"Dro," she smiled.

Hydroponics stuff, normally good he had to admit. *One wouldn't hurt – would it?*

"Pass, but you go ahead," he replied with a half-smile, softening boyish looks that conveyed a Mediterranean heritage, although both parents had been born in London from Irish and West Country stock.

She lit a pre-rolled and took a long, hard pull. "To answer your question, Frank: no, I'm not and don't have anyone special either – do you?"

"No," he replied firmly, savouring the smell of the weed with the feeling coming back to get her upstairs.

"Love the bike, great colour. What is it?" she asked, changing the subject, recalling the pillion ride he'd given her when they first met.

"You mean the colour, or the bike?"

"Both," she shot back with an impish grin. "Very impressive, I have to say."

"Harley Fat Boy is the name; 'Indigo' is the colour," he mimicked the song. The bike was his pride and joy. The roar of the 1584cc, twin cam, 96B engine at full throttle with the wind in his face, gave him a priceless feeling of freedom and excitement.

"You remind me of the guy in that old movie; what's it called?" She screwed up her nose. "Oh yeah: *Easy Rider* – a classic," pausing, then, "Fonda, that's his name, Peter Fonda," she giggled. "Hey, Easy Rider, Frank Ryder – Cool."

He gave her an indulgent smile – enough with the banter.

At that moment the hotel desk clerk came over to the table and handed him a note.

He read quickly and glanced towards the door leading to the foyer. *Fuck! What the hell was he doing here?* It was Johnny Watson, the unit's chief of staff.

He excused himself and headed for the foyer, wondering what was so important to personally bring him all the way down here. It did not bode well for good news.

"Johnny, how's things?" They shook hands. "Hope this is not business."

"Afraid so," replied Watson, his large frame decked out in a smart, lightweight cream suit with white open-neck shirt. "You're wanted back, ASAP." Green eyes in dark, gaunt features bored into Ryder.

"Why not page me?"

"Because, Frank: your pager is bloody well turned off."

"I'm supposed to be on holiday, you know. Anyway, how did you find me?"

"We like to keep a discreet eye on our operatives when on downtime overseas. Could be a few fanatics out there who would welcome the chance to do a number on you," he shot back.

Ryder was a little shocked by this revelation. The only way he could track his movements was if he'd been under continuous surveillance. "I thought the unit was supposed to be completely off the books?"

"It is. As far as Special Branch is concerned you're just another government employee they have been asked to keep tabs on and protect if necessary. Incidentally, that was a risky – if not damn silly – thing you did at the bullring; could've got yourself killed."

"I can look after myself," he shot back, miffed at the intrusion.

"When on downtime, Frank, you're supposed to relax, not put yourself unnecessarily at risk. We don't want you to worry about your back when you're supposed to be having a break otherwise you'll end up in a mental institution. We have invested a lot of time and effort – not to mention money – in getting you to this level, we expect you not to do stupid things."

True. Maybe he should spend more time in good old England instead of chasing abroad. "Why send you and not a messenger, or get one of the guys you have on my tail to tell me?"

"The boss thought it important enough for me to come and get you personally; make sure you responded in a hurry." Watson reached into his jacket pocket, pulled out e-airline tickets and waved them at Ryder. "We fly out in two hours."

"How important?"

"You'll have to wait and see."

Watson seeking him out personally made him more than apprehensive for what might be in store. If the chief of staff did know he would not say anyway. He went back to the terrace with a little regret that he would have to forsake Seville and Sarah.

"Have to get back?" she cried when he gave her the bad news. "And miss all the fun? We've only been here a few days! Do you have to?"

22

"Wanted at the office."

"Surely you're entitled to a break for Christ's sake; you're a government courier, not a bloody cabinet minister… or, or a bloody secret agent!" she shot, waving her arms in the air and laughing.

If she only knew… He shrugged, gave her a weak smile and said, "Have to leave straight away – like now, so you stay for a few days; do some shopping. Don't worry about the hotel bill, I'll cover it."

She sulked and said nothing. He'd been looking forward to spending time with this nurse from Clapham, but when the boss called…

With that, he left the terrace, advised the desk of the new arrangement, and went to his room. After quickly packing, he and Watson left in a taxi. During the journey to Seville's San Pablo Airport, Ryder reflected on the sacrifices made working for Queen and Country: time was hardly ever his own and lately there seemed to be less and less, even to prepare for operations. This hurried return to London had all the hallmarks of yet another. However, despite this, he accepted his lot. It was a far cry from the streets of Brixton; the drugs, the alcohol and street gangs that dominated his early life before the army took him on at eighteen and gave him the discipline he needed and a purpose to his life. He was proud he'd got off that dead-end road he was following. Days spent with the 1st Battalion Parachute Regiment and then 22 SAS were good, especially the times spent with fellow soldiers in the Hereford pubs and the gruelling training sessions in the Brecons and in the hot, steamy jungles of Belize. But it was in his current quasi-civilian capacity in the 'unit' that he was most proud of, finding fulfilment of a kind as a no-holds-barred paramilitary with this ultra-secret organisation, operating covertly in some of the world's most dangerous places.

3

At 0200 the chauffeur-driven Jaguar that brought them direct from Gatwick swept in through the gates and pulled into a dimly lit yard. Watson and Ryder stepped out and strode towards a plain entrance with a plaque on the side wall displaying 'General Commodities Ltd.' Underneath the plaque was a small circular glass aperture set into the wall into which both men stared. The iris scanner confirmed ID, the metal door clicked open and they entered.

Inside the darkened two-storey plain brick building, empty at this late hour apart from several security personnel patrolling the corridors, they headed towards a lit staircase at the rear. The building, in the shadow of the redundant Fulham Power Station, had once served as a factory/warehouse but was now the headquarters of the off-the-books arm of the British Secret Intelligence Service. The unit, code-named 'Omega', had evolved within the SIS to primarily combat the ever increasing terrorist threat and to carry out necessary lethal and unpalatable activities to protect the nation without the constraints of the law. Working for the unit, after selection from the SAS, Ryder had finally found his niche. He liked to work alone, knew the risks, and fully understood that the Establishment would deny all knowledge of his existence. Only the chief of the SIS and a handful of others knew of Omega and the operations it carried out.

Ryder and the chief of staff climbed the stairs to the first-floor offices, showed security passes to the two guards at the top and were escorted down a short corridor to an office at the end. Knocking, the guard ushered them in.

George Conway sat at his desk but did not look up from the report he was reading.

"Take a seat." He gestured towards the two chairs opposite his desk. The rectangular office with the large mahogany desk, Conway's black leather recliner, the two Queen Ann chairs and a long credenza adorning the wall behind the desk would be considered sparsely furnished. The cream-coloured carpet together with cream walls gave the room a rather bland flavour. The only relief on the walls: a large, flat TV and a few original landscape paintings. A large green pot stood in one corner housing a tropical plant that looked to Ryder like a cascading waterfall. The room was windowless.

He finally looked up. "Sorry for the lateness of the hour. Good trip back, gentlemen?" Then, staring directly at Ryder: "Hope I didn't drag you away from anything important, Frank?"

Good sign. Called by his first name and not by his official designation, O3 (Omega 3), confirmed whatever was coming was not going to be heavy. The boss did not stand on ceremony with the agents he controlled and Ryder appreciated the familiarity; it made him feel like not just a number. "No, sir; quite boring really."

Watson stifled a smile; went to say something, but refrained.

"I trust you are fully recovered from the last job?"

The shoulder wound Ryder received in North Korea had now fully healed but it had taken longer than anticipated. Maybe the assignment had taken more out of him than he cared to admit.

Conway removed his horn-rimmed glasses and placed them on the desk. Looking intently at both men with steel-blue eyes he said, "Sorry I can't offer tea at this hour; perhaps a whisky?"

"Love one, sir," Ryder replied. This was a rare opportunity not to be missed.

Watson declined.

An almost imperceptible smile crossed Conway's features as he opened the credenza, took out two glasses and a bottle of Macallan single malt, poured one for Ryder and one for himself.

"Cheers," he said, raising glass. This thin, middle-aged man, softly spoken with a mop of white hair, could be mistaken for a college professor instead of a high-ranking officer in the SIS. As deputy head of the Special Operations Directorate he ran the unit and its several agents with a no-nonsense attitude and a respect for the operatives he controlled. From his many years operating alongside the nefarious activities of global espionage he understood better than most the murky and evil aspects of the world in which he and his agents operated. Experience told him and a few others in the hierarchy of the Secret Service that killing was the only thing understood by fanatical terrorism, and that legal niceties and international protocols should not be allowed to stand in the way of the defence of the realm.

Conway sipped at his drink and leaned back in the recliner.

"Okay, Frank. No doubt you are wondering why you have been recalled so suddenly, and as I don't want to keep you here any longer than necessary, let me get straight to the point," he said, opening a file in front of him.

"Do you need me to take notes on this one, George?" said Watson.

"No, not on this occasion; but thank you. We have a job for you, Frank. This one I can only describe as a working holiday to make up for the one you've just been dragged away from."

"Don't tell me; watching Russian spies on a Caribbean beach," said Ryder, savouring his malt.

"Not quite, but how does babysitting an American Special Forces team grab you?"

"It doesn't. The Yanks don't need to be babysat. Their SFs are almost as good as our own."

"Maybe so, but they need us for what they have in mind."

"And what might that be, sir?"

"Apparently it's a somewhat sensitive operation. At this stage they want to keep it under wraps – a 'need-to-know' basis – keep things close to their chests."

"So much for the so-called 'special relationship'," Ryder fired back.

Conway ignored his remark and moved on. "The operation is to be undertaken in Tehran and our network cells are needed to assist in what it involves. That's why you have been called in urgently."

"Why not use their own?" Ryder looked askance at the boss, then at Watson, baffled.

"Apparently they were all ready to go from a base in Turkey when the mission was suddenly aborted due, by all accounts, to their own network in Tehran being seriously compromised to the extent it's now almost non-existent. In one big hit seventy per cent of the network was either killed or arrested. To avoid standing down the mission they have asked us if they could use our cells to get their people in." Conway gave Ryder a wry smile before continuing, "We believe in the 'special relationship', so of course we agreed. They are aware our networks have grown in strength and quality in recent years, especially in Tehran."

On Conway's cue, Watson spoke next, "Iranian security is cunning and brutal as you well know, Frank. The Tehran networks are stable at the moment, but the whole political scene is very fluid. We continue to lose some cells through infiltration. They need to know they're dealing with someone they can trust. You're known through your efforts to help organise them last year, that's why you have to go and no one else. We have already made initial contact and they are prepared to help, on condition you're part of the team. You'll accompany the Americans to Tabriz, then on to Tehran. Once they're in safe houses you are to return via the usual route back into Turkey."

Ryder was now definitely intrigued by the whole business. "Do we not even have an inkling what they intend? I'll need to have some idea if I'm to get them in, sir."

"You will be told everything you need to know once you arrive in Turkey." Conway glanced at his chief of staff. "However, from our point of view, at a guess, we suspect they intend to disrupt Iran's nuclear programme somehow. Although the IAIC have access they feel they are not being allowed to see the full picture; the Americans are not prepared to go to war over that – not yet anyway."

"Sir, with the Israelis wanting to destroy the known facilities, why are they being prevented?" asked Ryder, taking another sip of his drink.

"Because with everything else going on in the Middle East, particularly the ISIS problem who they believe is being secretly backed by the Iranians despite the overtures they want to help; the so-called Arab spring; political aspirations of the many other terrorist groups, and, of course, the stirring of religious tribal differences. If the Israelis did that it would probably be the last straw and all-out war would erupt involving all the Arab nations, Iran itself, and, eventually, sucking in the big four. The Cousins firmly believe, and we do too, that the Iranians are definitely trying to build a nuclear arsenal despite the current president's conciliatory rhetoric. They have not stopped forming sleeper cells and encouraging terrorism and instability in the Yemen, Oman and in Africa and the Middle East in general. Forecasters also reckon they're attempting to encircle the whole Arabian Peninsular and eventually take over, which will include wiping Israel off the face of the earth. Once they have sufficient stock of nuclear warheads, their intention, no doubt, is to rebuild the Persian Empire and be on a par with the big four. It is only a matter of time before they strike and Israel will be the first to go."

"Sir, what about the current softening of relations between the two?" asked Ryder. "As I understand it the Iranians have already started to decommission existing centrifuges and stop building new ones, thus 'neutralising' their stockpiles of twenty per cent enriched uranium."

"Twenty per cent is within several steps of reaching weapons-grade, the Americans want that down to below five, suitable only for domestic purposes. After months of haggling they believe, and so do others, that Iran is just stalling for time, both for relief from the crippling sanctions and to achieve weapons-grade fission material. The Americans believe the regime can never be trusted with the means to enrich uranium. They've had enough of their huffing and puffing. The Iranians cannot be trusted even with a treaty in place and will say and do anything to achieve nuclear parity and at the same time reduce the pain of sanctions. Once they achieve it that'll be it; the Iranians will have leverage and the means to seriously threaten the rest of us: there will be no going back after that."

Ryder had to agree. Of the Iranians he'd encountered, most were devious bastards.

"When do I leave?"

"Immediately; you're on the red-eye to Istanbul, departs from Heathrow in less than four hours. You'll be fully briefed when you arrive in Turkey." The chief of staff handed Ryder all the necessary travel documents. "Once in Istanbul the Cousins will contact you and airlift you to the starter base."

Conway fixed Ryder with a confident look and a half-smile. "That will be all, Frank. Enjoy the holiday. Good luck."

The chauffeur dropped Ryder off at his flat in Battersea, waited whilst he gathered some clean clothes and packed bare necessities, then drove him to Heathrow. Once again no time to prepare, but at least he thought it would be a relatively soft assignment. This time his involvement would be minimal and hopefully he could expect to be back in London in less than two weeks.

4

Ryder nodded at the group of Green Beret commandos as he entered the makeshift briefing room at the partly disused Turkish Air Force Base at Bajirge near the eastern border with Iran. *Tough looking bunch,* he thought. 'Rambos' and 'Snake Eaters' some called them, but most of those he'd worked with were good, honest warriors; team players accustomed to dirty, unconventional warfare. Taking a seat behind a desk on the raised dais beside Colonel Jake Hamilton, commander of C Company, he waited for him to open the briefing.

"Good evening," the colonel said, shuffling papers. "Gentlemen, you already know you're going into Iran, but I can now give you the targets and their specifics. These have been held back at the insistence of the top brass for the sensitivity of the operation and for other reasons I'm not even prepared to guess at." He glanced at each of the twelve men before him. "But first, I would explain briefly why the delay in getting the mission underway. The reason: our networks in Tehran have been seriously compromised, so much so, we could not proceed as planned. But I can now confirm we are back on track and the mission has the go, thanks to the Brits and, in particular, this man here." He motioned towards Ryder. "This is Frank Ryder from British intelligence. They have agreed to let us use their networks instead. Frank's knowledge of the lingo, his experience of the local cells and the operational area will be invaluable."

Ryder nodded again at the group. He felt surprisingly alert after the long flight to Istanbul, the hurried transfer through the American military reception and then the uncomfortable flight straight here to the base in a C-17 Globemaster. Ushered into this briefing as soon as he had touched down and eager to find out what this operation was all about, he nevertheless had every intention of hitting the sack once it was over.

The colonel continued after a short pause and came straight to the point, "Your mission: to knock out two dams on the Jajrood and Karaj Rivers in the Elburz Mountains north of Tehran."

Murmurs of surprise rippled around the room.

Ryder was stunned.

The colonel, in his late forties, stood and moved his tall, rangy frame to the wall behind. Pulling back a curtain, the wall displayed regional and local maps of the Tehran area together with coloured photographs of hydro dams. Using a laser pointer on a large scale map showing the Jajrood and Karaj Rivers, he highlighted the targets. "The plan is to hit both dams simultaneously. Normally we would use two detachments, one for each target, but in the interest of security – 'need-to-know' syndrome – and to keep numbers down, we've decided to divide Detachment A into two groups. Captain Cane will lead the group to hit the Latyan on the Jajrood and Lieutenant Owen, the Amir Kabir on the Karaj."

He placed the pointer on the map approximately twenty miles north-east of Tehran. "Blowing the Latyan will do the most damage." He moved the pointer to the huge reservoir lake behind and then to an aerial shot of the dam itself. "As you can see the dam holds back a lot of water." He then turned and pointed to a detached blueprint of the dam. "The dam itself has seventeen intakes. Thirteen are used to generate power, the other four are flow-control gates. The maximum flow is 250,000 cubic feet of water per second. 125,000 watts of power can be generated through the turbines into the grid. The dam is approximately 385 feet high." The colonel turned to face the group. "Your objective is to release specially designed explosive devices into the lake where the currents should take them down through the penstocks to explode when reaching the turbine level. If only one of the devices enters a penstock and explodes, the experts think it will be enough to cause progressive deterioration and hopefully destruction of the majority of turbines, plus partial collapse of the structure. You'll be taking two to each dam. Until activated they're harmless."

"What are the devices and how can you be sure they'll float to the target?" questioned Captain Cane: muscular, of medium build with short, dark hair, whose suntanned, weathered features suggested a life spent mostly outdoors.

"The devices will be modified Mk-54 SADMs – very low yield and clean."

"Holy shit!" exclaimed Sergeant First Class Clint Kellar, his big frame, broad shoulders and long arms giving him the nickname 'Bear'. "You telling us we'll be humping nuclear bombs through hostile territory?"

Ryder recalled the US having developed various types of SADMs (Special Atomic Demolition Munition): a lightweight, nuclear, one-man portable device, designed late in the last century mainly to destroy power plants, bridges and dams. To his knowledge they had never been used in actual combat.

The colonel ignored the sergeant's outburst; it was normal in Special Forces' briefings. "It's calculated that 10 tons of payload in each – the equivalent of 20,000 pounds of TNT – set to explode in the bowels of the dams will disable the system enough to grind everything to a standstill. I'm told the force of the blast inside all that mass of concrete will be controlled and only affect the immediate area. If the external concrete lining fails, it's hoped the Iranians might think natural causes, or a blown turbine. I understand the Latyan was constructed in the early 1960s and Amir Kabir around the same time.

"How're they activated?" asked Master Sergeant Brady.

"Manually – timer switch – just before releasing into the water, then automatically short-fused on passing the intake grilles." The colonel turned to Cane. "Now, to answer the second part of your question: a computer-controlled flotation device within the casing will determine the downward path in relation to the currents and flow patterns by releasing compressed air from compartments welded inside the casing."

"Are they heavy, and how will we get them to the water's edge?" asked Lieutenant Owen, a lean, upright man, strong featured with fairish hair and a clipped moustache. He reminded Ryder of a typical British Army officer – a Rupert in fact, who'd been with 22 SAS.

"Each is circular, a foot in diameter and weighing 40 pounds, light enough to carry on backs in a specially designed harness. How you get them to the water's edge will be for you to decide after assessing the local situation."

The lieutenant nodded then looked at Ryder. "Hopefully the cells will guide us on that one."

Ryder acknowledged. He was beginning to feel the enormity of the task; he did not envy these men at all.

The colonel continued, "As you can see, both rivers skirt the city. Should both of the dams break, the surge created by the combined failure would cause major havoc in these low lying areas to the immediate south." He moved the pointer around the triangular area formed by the Amir Kabir Dam, approximately thirty-five miles to the north-west of Tehran and the Latyan Dam some twenty miles north-east of Tehran. "These areas will take the full brunt of the devastation expected. Even if only one fails it will cause some degree of havoc."

"What are the main industries in those areas?" asked Sergeant Oscar Sicano, clean-cut, dark features staring intently at the colonel. He was not that far behind the size of the man they call 'Bear'. To Ryder, these elite warriors seem to get bigger every time he has the occasion to join them.

"Cement, petrochemicals, oil refining, textiles, food processing. It's also an area for livestock products: meat, milk, etc."

"What are the estimates on loss of life?" Cane asked.

"The rural population is pretty widespread, so it's not expected to be high – if any. Tehran and surrounding areas have around ten million inhabitants crammed into less than 15,000 square miles. It's the country's most densely populated region. However, the capital is a bit too far away to be seriously affected by a burst. Even if they clean up quickly the general opinion is it will take years to recover. The dams provide the region's drinking water and most of its electrical power. Denying the population these basics on a large enough scale will hopefully frustrate their nuclear research facilities and other associated activities for a long time. Langley predicts resources and energy needed to put everything right again will deter any thoughts of nuclear parity for a while, at least. They also want to do it before the Israelis take matters into their own hands and bomb the known facilities. The powers that be don't want another regional war."

"How far away from the intakes would the SADMs be released?" Lieutenant Owen questioned.

"Half a mile hoping the drifting mechanism works, otherwise they'll drop to the bed. The most effective way would be to release from the top of the dams, but that would have a big risk factor. You'll need to gauge that risk once in place."

"Not much time to clear if we did, I guess," said Master Sergeant Jed Brady, angular, acned features looking hard at the colonel.

"As I said: the resulting explosion would be confined to the bowels, depending on when the devices blow and the extent of a chain reaction. You should clear the immediate dam areas as soon as you release the devices."

"Latyan looks to be almost a 1000 yards across. We'd have to move fast to clear in time," said Kellar.

"I would strongly recommend against releasing the devices from the top of this dam," said the colonel, moving the pointer to the aerial of the Amir Kabir Dam. "Somewhat less in length, but the same applies."

For a few moments there was silence.

Ryder could not help but wonder, why undertake what could turn out to be a very risky operation when the Americans could use the Stuxnet virus. This 500-kilobyte malware computer worm had infected the operating software of a number of high-profile industrial sites in Iran, including the Bushehr power plant where uranium-enrichment was reportably taking place.

Colonel Hamilton walked back to the table. "Once the devices are released it'll probably take an hour, or so, before the dams are breached – if they breach. During that time the local cells will hopefully have you well on the way to the extraction point – the same place you were dropped."

"The insertion point?" asked Captain Cane.

"Forty miles south-east of Tabriz and 200 miles east of here; the heli will fly low at night over the Urmia Valley, hugging the ground all the way."

"How reliable and secure are these cells?" asked Sicano.

Hamilton looked at Ryder for a response.

"Very, they desperately want democracy," he answered. "Events in the Middle East have spurred them on and they'll do anything to achieve it. I helped set up some of the cells but security is always a problem. Even though they operate separately we continue to lose some through infiltration. Tehran is an extremely dangerous place. However, we've never had a problem, those guys have big balls; they know their stuff."

"I trust we'll avoid another 'Desert One' then," Sicano said, referring to the failed mission to recover American hostages from Tehran in 1980 when the rescue helicopters crashed on landing in the desert south of the Iranian capital, killing several Special Forces operatives and causing a great deal of embarrassment to the Carter Administration.

"We have learnt from that unfortunate episode," Hamilton replied.

"Good to hear, Colonel."

The colonel looked around, "Any more questions on Latyan?" Silence.

"Okay, let's move on." He turned back to the wall and pointed to an aerial photograph of the Amir Kabir Dam. "The concrete structure has a crest of over 700 yards long, has ten intakes to generate power and three to control flow. The height tops at almost 600 feet. The maximum through flow is around 120,000 cubic feet per second."

"Will two devices be enough?" questioned Owen.

"Yep, as with Latyan, only one will need to explode to cause progressive destruction."

"Does it matter from which side of the lakes we release?" asked one of the team.

"No, I'm told the currents will guide the devices into the centre anyhow."

Another silence; the colonel turned to Ryder.

He took the cue and cleared his throat, "Thank you, Colonel. The important thing is to make sure you blend in with the local scene, work closely with the cells. Trust them, do what they tell you; it could be the difference between life and death. First contact will be with one of our Tabriz cells who will transport you by road to a safe house in Tehran, a journey of some 300 miles. From then on you will be in the hands of several separate cells. I'll remain with you until the last phase before you head directly for the targets. Oh, and brush up on your Farsi." He paused, not sure how his next comment would go down. "It will also be advisable to be only lightly armed."

"Why? What happens if we're blown?" Brady asked.

"The need is to blend in so you won't have to use them. Weapons must be concealed. No RPGs and the like."

Nervous laughter; Ryder knew full well Special Forces like to be adequately armed. It lessened the risks.

"Unless it's at the RV you won't stand a chance of escape. Even heavily armed you can count on there being too many," Ryder finished and referred back to the colonel.

"As soon as you release the devices don't hang around, get the hell back to the RV. Should the structures fail there'll be major chaos. Make sure you get out fast." He paused to look at each man in turn. "You leave in twenty-four hours. Until then study the information packs you'll be given shortly showing detailed maps of the terrain around the dams, including roads in the surrounding areas, etc. Study them thoroughly. You'll remain in your designated quarters. You are now in total lock-down until we leave." He paused, then, "Any further questions?"

Silence again.

"None…? Good. The code-word for the operation is: Overflow. That will be all for now."

Ryder stood, left the dais and followed the others out, still a little shocked by the intended operation, glad his role was non-offensive and would end on reaching the Iranian capital. Not exactly 'a working holiday' as the boss had put it, but close enough he supposed. It was now time to catch up on some badly needed sleep.

5

The MH-53M Pave Low helicopter took off in darkness from Bajirge and swung east. On board, huddled in the fuselage, sat Frank Ryder with Captain Cane and the eleven-man team listening to the throb of the twin-turbo engines as the helicopter gained speed and headed towards the Iranian border. Operation Overflow was underway. Each man wore typical Iranian working-men clothing: battered jeans, loose cotton shirts, cloth caps and old leather shoes. Concealed beneath the shirt, a M9000S Beretta automatic compact pistol together with Kaybar knife tucked into the waistband. The crew, part of the USAF's elite 160th Special Operations Aviation Regiment (SOAR), commonly referred to as Night Stalkers, were trained to infiltrate and operate in the hostile territory they were about to enter. With its array of electronic jamming devices, radar detection systems and computers, the MH-53M, even on the darkest of nights and in the worst kind of weather, could closely follow the terrain using the most sophisticated navigational aids available.

The Pave Low eventually flew over the border and into Iran only 80 feet above the ground and a 100 feet below standard radar cover from most of the land-based systems. As they hugged the rolling hills between the surrounding mountain peaks at almost 140 knots, the pilot and co-pilot, wearing the latest night-vision goggles providing excellent peripheral vision and wide field of view in sharp hues of green and black, checked and re-checked the GPS and radar, relying solely on the scopes and instruments to guide them accurately in the low cloud conditions which now prevailed. Fifty miles into the journey they reached the western edge of Lake Urmia, Iran's largest salt-water expanse. Ryder watched through the windows as they skimmed over the dark waters, guessing at no more than 10 feet above the surface, hoping too that the Tabriz network had had time to organise at such a short timeframe. Visions of no one meeting them at the RV plagued him but he managed to push them to one side. For the most part, the flight so far had been one of silence as the men mentally prepared for the insertion. The next twenty-five miles over the salt-laden water went swiftly; the helicopter eventually reaching the far side, hurtling over salt-flats then on over empty, undulating, rocky landscape; hills, valleys and marshland covering most of the remaining 125 miles to the RV without incident.

Soon the helicopter's inertial navigation system, computing velocity and movement, informed the pilot the distance to the RV point was now less than ten miles.

In the distance, Ryder could see through the windows traffic headlights moving along the main Tabriz/Tehran highway and again the worry as to whether or not they would be met flooded his mind.

Shortly an irregular curve of green smudges came up on the terrain-following radar and the map co-ordinates indicated the insertion point lay only minutes ahead.

"RV, bearing zero-eight-zero," called the co-pilot.

"Roger that. ETA: two minutes," the pilot acknowledged, turning the Pave almost 90 degrees due north and flew directly towards the landing point.

Heat images of two parked vehicles and four humans standing close by filled the radar screen and instantly the coded signal came through.

Relief washed through Ryder – plus a surge of exhilaration.

"Contact, RV signal confirmed," voiced the co-pilot.

"Roger. Prepare to land," replied the pilot.

Seconds later, the Pave hovered 20 feet above the ground for several seconds in a swirl of dust and sand before landing not far from the parked vehicles and the waiting men.

The helicopter engines powered down but kept ticking over as the back ramp came down. The flight crew wanted to be airborne as soon as possible; Iranian jets could swoop down at any time.

Ryder quickly disconnected himself from the aircraft's comms system, sprang down the ramp, and immediately recognised the leader of the main cell in Tabriz running towards him. They embraced and after a short exchange, Ryder signalled okay to those in the chopper. The Americans quickly emerged, carrying two wooden crates housing the nuclear devices. Short introductions and the crates were then hurriedly placed into a prepared false-floor compartment in the back of two battered, canvas-covered Mercedes trucks. Captain Cane and five of his team then clambered into the nearest; Ryder and the rest into the other.

After less than three minutes on the ground the helicopter's engines powered up and the Pave rose into the air and veered westwards into the darkness.

With headlights turned off the two diesels accelerated towards a highway not far in the distance. They reached the smooth tarseal strip in minutes and swung eastwards, merging in with the fairly light traffic, headlights now on full beam. Through the open back of the front truck, Ryder sat tensely watching the second truck and other vehicles further behind following as it gained speed along the straight open road. Nobody spoke, remaining deep in their own thoughts accompanied by scratchy Arab music emitting from the driver's cab.

After almost an hour into the journey an unexpected checkpoint came into view at the junction with the main Tabriz/Tehran highway heavy with traffic. Ryder, in the front truck, looked though the hatch at the rear of the driver's cab and expressed alarm. Trucks only were being directed into a checking lane, other vehicles were being waved on through.

He reached for his Beretta, as did the others.

"Put them away," the cell leader shouted over the roar of the diesel, "Do not be concerned. These makeshift military checkpoints are frequent due to the sanctions imposed by your governments. Smuggling is rife from Turkey. Powerful mullahs and generals openly set these up to control the flow; lining their own pockets, you might say. Few of us are able to gain access to Western domestic technology, so they make the most of it."

"Fuck, we've hardly arrived," shot Lieutenant Owen. "If they search us we're gone." He injected a bullet into the Beretta chamber.

"You heard what he said, Lieutenant. Put it away," Ryder shot back, not impressed. "The devices are well hidden, unless they remove the floorboards we'll be ok. If they do, then you can start shooting."

The Lieutenant looked hard at him and, for a moment, Ryder thought the American was going to challenge him, but the cell leader intervened, "Have papers ready and say as little as possible. Leave everything to me," he said, cooling the situation, as they pulled over into a line of several trucks. He then moved and sat by the tailboard, and the American put the Beretta away.

Ryder's truck, followed closely by Cane's, edged towards the checkpoint. Five long minutes later four soldiers, semi-automatics slung over shoulders, sidled up to Ryder's vehicle, two either side, the one nearest to the driver demanded to see his papers. On presentation the soldier took time studying the documents and, finally satisfied, handed them back and he, with the others, strolled to the rear. Ryder nervously fingered the grip of his Beretta under his shirt. He became more alarmed when, through the cab hatch, he saw in headlights further up the line, soldiers mingling about and two heavy army vehicles crammed with troops out to one side. The cell leader threw a worried glance at the others and ranted at the soldiers for the delay they were causing. The four soldiers, ignoring him, lowered the tailboard and displayed their disappointment in a string of epithets and rude gestures once they saw it was empty of merchandise. They ordered everyone out and demanded to see papers whilst two of the soldiers clambered up into the back. Ryder felt the adrenaline pump as the two inspected the wooden floor; he prayed they would overlook the concealed compartment.

To the throb of diesels and sound of Arabic music, four more soldiers sauntered arrogantly up to Captain Cane's truck and demanded to see the driver's papers. Two detached themselves as the papers were handed over and went to the rear. They lowered the tailboard, the occupants were ordered out and papers called for. Once this had been done, and they seemed satisfied, one soldier climbed up and began to tap the floor with the butt of his rifle.

Suddenly a shout, then another – much louder this time.

Ryder knew instantly the hidden compartment in Cane's truck had been discovered. Without hesitation he drew the Beretta, turned, and shot out the headlights of Cane's vehicle. At the same time, Kellar put a bullet into the soldier inside the truck and another commando dropped the man standing beside him.

Before the two soldiers by Cane's truck, and the soldiers with Ryder, could react, they too were swiftly gunned down.

One fast-thinking soldier, however, managed to fire off a few rounds, killing Lieutenant Owen instantly before he took a bullet to the head from Ryder.

Up the line, soldiers rushed towards the trucks, crouching and weaving between the vehicles, firing erratically as they advanced.

Hurriedly stripping the dead of weapons and ammunition, at the same time returning fire at the approaching troops, Ryder, Cane and the remainder of Detachment A then scrambled into the two Mercedes. In the rear of the front truck, Ryder and those with him readied themselves for a firefight whilst Brady jumped into the cab, pushed the driver aside and took the wheel, powering the diesel forward. Cane and Kellar did the same in the truck behind, Kellar at the wheel.

Ignoring other traffic coming both ways and causing mayhem as vehicles careered off the highway to avoid collision, they swung the heavy vehicles out of the line, across the broad expanse of tarseal and roared on into the surrounding barren landscape followed not long after by the two parked army trucks hard on their heels.

In the desert darkness, Ryder's truck veered away from Cane's as they raced, zigzagging madly over the shale-strewn, uneven terrain. Ryder, using rifle and ammunition taken from the dead soldiers, kept up continuous fire at the headlamps and black mass of the pursuing vehicles. The vehicles were closing rapidly, issuing heavy fire. The commando next to Ryder jerked and screamed as half his head was blown away, and another beyond him threw up his arms and toppled over the side head first onto the sand. Even in these most desperate of times, his thoughts were on the nuclear devices; they could not be left to the Iranians. He rushed to the shattered rear window of the driver's cabin, bullets zipping through the canvas cover and off the metal all around.

"The code – quick, give me the code to disable the nukes!" he screamed at Brady.

"Negative! Negative!" Brady screamed back, desperately trying to keep the bouncing, swerving vehicle under control.

What the fuck! Is he refusing?

He tried again, "Give me the fucking code, soldier; we ain't got time to play games. The bastards find these nukes we'll pay with our lives!"

"I told you, Negative," the American spat, turning quickly and giving Ryder a wilting look, "It's NEGATIVE! NEGATIVE!"

Ryder got the message, felt foolish, then turned and, with the help of one of the commandos, ripped up the floor and broke open the casings to expose the smooth, dark grey metallic spheres, so small yet capable of such devastation once armed. He flipped open the lids on top of the two spheres, entered the required code and pushed down the red button marked: 'Destruct'. Within seconds the contents, including firing mechanism, miniature computer and flotation devices melted away. Then, in the darkness, with the help of the others, he tossed each as far as he could away from the careering vehicle.

Over the roar of the truck, engine revved to the max, and the crackle of machine-gun fire filling his ears, Ryder hoped Cane would do the same in the bouncing, zigzagging truck not far ahead. He need not have worried; the American had systematically destroyed the spheres and cast them out into the darkness at the same time as Ryder.

Minutes later, under a fusillade of fire, he watched Cane's vehicle, peppered by machine-gun fire, suddenly veer out of control, all tyres on the rear wheels completely shot away. The big Mercedes careered on for several hundred yards, skewing and throwing the captain and the others all over the rear making it impossible to return accurate fire before it hit a rock, flipped over on to its side and screeched to a halt in a shower of steam and sand.

The pursuing truck quickly caught up and skidded to a stop alongside. Troops piled out and surrounded the crippled vehicle. Amidst shouting and brutal treatment meted out by their captors, Cane and the others were quickly disarmed, rounded up, bound and herded into the Iranian truck.

Ryder's Mercedes sped on hotly pursued, Brady straining to maintain control. Ryder lay flat to the boards returning fire protected only by the low metal sides and tailboard. Bullets whined and ricocheted everywhere off the framework. The vehicle swung hard right down into the protection of a flat, shallow wadi and raced along its bed for less than 200 yards before the engine finally gave out and the battered truck rolled to a halt.

Leaping from the wreck, Ryder and the remaining Green Berets ran for the edge of the wadi in a desperate attempt to escape, but it was futile. No sooner had they reached the base when the two pursuing trucks, headlights blazing, raced towards them and skidded to a halt. Heavily armed troops disgorged, fanned out and clambered down into the wadi. Sporadic fire ensued and incoming rounds sprayed the ground all around where they sheltered. They were quickly surrounded.

Ryder, still dazed from the impact, considered, for a brief moment, to make one last stand and take as many with him as possible, but with only a little ammunition left saw it was hopeless. He felt despair; the going from this point on would be tough if he lived through this; he feared for his life. All he could do now was hope for a political exchange, but even that was a remote possibility. Throwing down his rifle he stood and raised his arms, expecting a bullet at any moment. The others followed and soon all were brutally rounded up, bound and frogmarched to join Cane and the rest. With Lieutenant Owen dead, together with the two commandos who died in the fleeing trucks, only Ryder and nine of the original twelve-man American team were now left.

Operation Overflow had come to a premature and ignominious end.

6

Under a clear blue sky, Afari Asgari watched with a mixture of hate and fear as the late model Mercedes turned into the local market place; a wide street teeming with people and lined with colourful stalls. Her hate burned fiercely from the death of her parents by the brutal ruling regime and her fear from what might happen if she failed to succeed at what she was about to do. These emotions were mitigated a little at the thought her actions might, in no small way, help to destroy Iran's ambitions to become a major nuclear power. Her target, the vehicle with a police motorcycle escort, which slowly pushed its way through the noisy throng; in the rear sat the leading scientist controlling Iran's nuclear weapons programme. The current president, although seemingly wanting better relationships with the West, was unable to thwart these ambitions coveted by the opposition and the hawks within his own party. But most importantly, he did not have the backing of the supreme religious leader – the ayatollah. These factions wanted beyond all else to exert total power over the region, and Afari, along with many others in the MEK (People's Mujahedin of Iran), wanted no part. Today the scientist would pay for his role in these ambitions.

Controlling her fear, she stepped out from her vantage point into the milling crowd and headed towards the vehicle, praying the others were ready. Concealed within her *jilbab* she carried a small but powerful pre-set magnetic charge. The vehicle slowed; she got closer – heart pounding.

Suddenly, the Mercedes halted to avoid the lead police motorcyclist from being bowled over by melons cascading in large numbers from a collapsed stall. Fellow conspirators had done their job; now it was her turn. The rear police escort pushed his motorbike forward to help his fallen colleague, leaving the rear of the vehicle unguarded. In the confusion, Afari jostled her way to the side of the vehicle. Here, amongst the pressing humanity, she quickly removed the compact bomb through a slit in her robe, glanced around to see if anyone had noticed, and then, in one swift movement, placed it up inside the rear wheel rim. She felt more than heard the solid clunk of metal adhering to metal before hurriedly stepping away, turning and vanishing into the throng. The shaped charge would direct the explosive power to inside the vehicle which would hopefully kill the occupants but theoretically leave nearby people and traffic unscathed.

She walked briskly away through the narrow alleyways of District 10, and headed for her small apartment in Qazvin Avenue. She knew the area well having been brought up in the teeming alleyways of this southern part of central Tehran. Petite and attractive with soft, rounded features and piercing hazel eyes, she was only fifteen years old when her mother and father died. Resolved to avenge their deaths she joined the MEK at eighteen and had been involved in guerrilla warfare against the oppressive regime ever since. Now twenty-five, she had become a hardened insurgent in her native land. She believed the ruling elite ignored the people at their peril and had hoped that by now the Israelis would have bombed the nuclear manufacturing plants out of existence, finding it hard to understand why they continued to hold back. In conjunction with Israel's Mossad, the MEK's focus was on destroying the current regime's nuclear ambitions, and the assassination of one of its scientists would help to make that possible.

Afari eventually reached her apartment building and was about to enter when she heard above the noise of the traffic, a dull boom someway in the distance. She smiled. Arriving at the first floor, she entered the apartment and suddenly froze. Standing in the small lounge were three men. One held a silenced pistol levelled directly at her chest.

Fear and panic seared through her – VEVAK, Iran's secret police. She had dreaded this moment, knowing one day it had to come.

The man with the gun asked for ID; the hardened features of the other two held her firmly in their gaze. She raised her handbag and was warned not to do anything silly. She handed over her driver's license.

The man glanced at it and then threw it on the table.

He flicked the gun up and down indicating for her to empty the rest of the contents of the bag onto the table. She did so.

One of the men sifted through the jumble and indicated nothing of interest.

Then the third said abruptly in a thick accent, "You are a terrorist, accused of crimes against the State."

Fear seared through her like a knife. "Who says this of me?" she shot back, inwardly trembling, almost unable to stop it showing.

The one who had rifled through her bag said in a cultured voice, "We know you are MEK and involved with recent bombings."

Three pairs of eyes bored into her, making her want to vomit, "That is not true!" she blurted, mind racing to think of a way out.

"Do not deny; it will make it worse for you," he spat with a cold smile, then turned to the others.

They smirked, running eyes over her body.

Oh my God – rape!

She spun and lunged for the door. But not quickly enough and they were instantly upon her.

A short struggle, before they dragged Asfari kicking and screaming back to the table. Quickly removing her *jilbab* and underclothes, they pressed the top half of her naked body face down on the table with feet on the floor and arms stretched out across the veneer, held at the wrists.

Would she survive this? She feared for her life.

The cultured voice, laughing, spread her legs whilst the other two pulled on her outstretched arms. He dropped his trousers and thrust into her. She sobbed as she felt his groping and brutal penetration and his rough hands running all over her upper body. When he had finished the other two followed, taking their time, revelling in her torment. The violation completely overwhelming, she tried to blank out the pain and anguish thinking of her mother and father and of the good times she had spent with them; but most of all she thought of revenge.

When the last one had satisfied himself she was ordered to dress. Hurting from the brutalization of her body and weeping with shame and revulsion, she wanted to die. One of the men handcuffed her and the three, laughing and joking, led her out of the building and into a waiting car which took them to the Ministry of Intelligence and Security HQ in downtown Tehran.

7

Suddenly, Frank Ryder was jolted from his stupor at the sound of clanking cell doors, shouting and scuffling, as men were dragged out of their cells and along the corridor outside. He felt bile rise in his throat. He had coped with the beatings but had only just held on when the grinning brown-faced interrogators had used electric probes. Thank God he'd listened to the techniques of blanking out pain taught by the psychologists and trainers at Hereford. He thought of home, even his wild youth in the Brixton streets, absent parents, and fishing for big carp in the Kent lakes, anything to take his mind away from the brutality, not allowing the agony to penetrate and overcome his resistance. He questioned himself time and time again. *Why the fuck not tell them what they want to know? Who the fuck cares if they know? Hey! Hey! Who gives a fuck!* But he did not give in; instead he lost himself in memories and mind over pain. He believed the more you showed suffering, the more you would be brutalized. Fear seared through him at the expectation of what was about to come.

What fucking game were they now going to play?

His cell door swung open and two guards entered. They roughly wrenched him up from the mattress, dragging him unceremoniously into the corridor and frogmarching him once again down to the end and into the large, windowless interrogation room. Lined up against the stark grey walls in the dim light were the remaining members of the American team, plus several Iranian prisoners closely watched by more than a dozen armed guards; Captain Cane stood dignified and upright, as did the other Americans. Looking at them strengthened Ryder's resolve to resist, but this bringing everyone together in the same room was a first and it heightened his fear.

The interrogators entered, led by a tall, middle-aged officer they had not encountered before. Positioning himself at the central table, the officer, dressed in a neat green uniform, stood for a moment before he strode over to the Americans and walked down the line, eyeing each man intently. When he reached the end, Ryder held the officer's chilling gaze before the Iranian returned to the table. Moments later he spoke directly to the commandos in perfect English. "Gentlemen, I know you clearly understand me therefore I shall not repeat what I have to say, nor shall I elaborate in any way. It will be up to you to answer your own conscience and come to what I hope will be the correct decision." He paused to light a cigarette, drew deeply and blew smoke towards the ceiling, then continued. "We have broken your imperialist network in Tabriz. We know your purpose here was to attempt to disrupt our economy and food sources by destroying two of our most important dams. We will, however, eventually extract everything we need to know about each of you and you will confess to the world what you have attempted to do to the Iranian people." He blew another column of smoke upwards. "You have been most stubborn in resisting so far, but we are not prepared to wait any longer." He stared coldly at Ryder, who suddenly felt an overwhelming sense of foreboding. *How did they know about the dams? Had any of the others talked? If so, how much did they give away?* These questions and many others flooded Ryder's thoughts, overriding his fears.

The officer turned and nodded at the interrogators, two of whom then manhandled the nearest Iranian prisoner to the table. A small pair of bolt cutters was produced. Utter fear showed on the man's face as he struggled to resist.

Fuck! What do they intend to do with those? Ryder felt rage and revulsion at the prospect. He wanted to turn away but was inexplicably drawn to the table where the unfortunate man's right arm had been outstretched and held with fingers splayed.

The brute wielding the cutters stood poised, the officer nodded, and he slowly moved the shiny curved blades downwards and, without hesitation, sliced off the Iranian's thumb.

A primal scream of shear agony filled the room, piercing Ryder's very soul.

The officer looked at the Americans and lingered on Ryder. "This man will continue to suffer unless you confess to the world who you are and what you intended to do."

He remained silent but raged inside, wanting to kill this psychopathic officer.

Again the officer signalled to the interrogator wielding the cutters.

The cutters went to the index finger of the sobbing man who let out another almighty scream as that finger came off too.

"Do I have to take them all before you do what I want?"

The poor man, hand in a pool of blood, looked beseechingly at Ryder who turned away, forcing his mind to block out the scene.

The officer waited, the tortured man's gulping sobs filling the room. After a minute or two he turned again to the interrogator and nodded.

This time the cutters came down and, one by one, sliced off the remaining three fingers. With each severance, the room was filled again with nerve-shattering shrieks ending only when the officer drew his pistol with suppressor attached and put a bullet through the unfortunate man's head, splattering blood and grey matter across the table and over the floor.

Ryder screeched in protest and lunged towards the table, unable to take any more, followed seconds later by the Americans. All were beaten back mercilessly with rifle butts by the overwhelming number of guards. The smell of blood and fear filled his nostrils.

"That has set the tone nicely, don't you think?" said the officer with a cruel smile when things had settled down.

Ryder was nowhere near prepared for what happened next.

The officer, green uniform spattered in blood, strode over to the line of the six remaining Iranian prisoners, placed the pistol against the head of the nearest and pulled the trigger. He then moved to the next, and the next, and shot them too, continuing along the line in quick succession without a shred of emotion, until all were dead.

The room was now in total uproar. The remaining captives, unable to control their emotions, screamed obscenities at their tormentors whilst brutally restrained by the guards.

"Confess! Confess!" the officer shouted, rushing towards the line of Americans, ordering the guards to take Brady to the table.

Ryder's mind reeled at the horror, the dead bodies, the psychopathic interrogators, and the even more psychopathic officer now preparing to mutilate or kill an American. He would probably kill them all eventually in his frenzy, unless a confession was made. Ryder felt nausea and rage as he surveyed the carnage, smelt the blood and fear, then he finally broke.

"Stop – stop! You fucking shits; stop it!" he screamed in English.

Sudden silence, then, "Well, that is much better," voiced the officer, breaking it, calmer now after the killing spree. "At last you have come to your senses, as I knew you would. This method always encourages men to be – how shall we say: more forthcoming? Yes, that is the term." He smiled coldly, letting dark eyes linger on Ryder like a snake. "Now we shall talk and you will sign confessions."

At that moment the door flew open and in strode a short, grey-haired man wearing a general's uniform. The interrogators and guards snapped to attention. The general glanced disdainfully at the blood and gore and ordered the interrogating officer to step outside the room.

Heated voices soon came from the corridor and, minutes later, the officer returned, features taut and flushed, looked angrily around the room and said, "You are to be transferred immediately to another centre. There you will tell us all we need to know and inform the world how you have attempted to violate our beloved country." He then stormed out, followed quickly by the three other interrogators. The guards menacingly closed around the prisoners. Ryder shuddered; a further prolonged, painful time lay ahead. How much more could he take?

Not long after the ordeal in the interrogation room, Ryder and the nine Americans, together with a group of Iranian prisoners, were herded out into the compound. In the bitter November wind, Ryder dug deep to overcome his despair and resist making a break for it; reason told him it would be futile. Eventually, three large canvas-covered army trucks entered the compound and drew up alongside the shivering company. They were then hurriedly manhandled into the back of the middle vehicle already occupied by a number of other emaciated prisoners, including women. Once all tightly packed in and the tailboard bolted, the guards hurriedly dispersed into the front and rear trucks and the three vehicles left the compound, heading east.

PART TWO

Treacherous Journey

8

As the convoy of three trucks merged with the bare, rugged terrain in the snow-sprinkled northern foothills of the Zagros Mountains some 100 miles south of Tabriz, Ryder lapsed in and out of awareness but could not wash away his own miserable world of defeat and despair. He tried to squash the negativity but his thoughts left him wondering how all this would finally end. Packed tightly in the middle vehicle, the journey so far for him had been traumatic, travelling over potholed and rutted dirt roads causing extreme discomfort from the continuous jolting and bouncing on the hard metal floor. His personal misery ebbed and flowed as the vehicle weaved its way through wooded valleys and climbed up and down steep inclines of barren mountainsides coupled with the continuous throaty roar of the engines and crashing gears. Muffled English, Hebrew and Farsi conveying the despair of those around him did not help the mental pain and anguish he now suffered, which almost matched that experienced in the filthy Iranian cell and the room at the end of the corridor. The khaki camouflaged vehicles strained slowly up a steep incline, engines grinding at full power over the narrow, dusty road. It was late afternoon and a watery sun had dipped behind the peaks, casting long shadows over the rough and jagged windswept ground. The convoy crested a ridge in the rapidly rising foothills and began its descent into yet another deserted valley of rock, scrub and scanty trees.

Patches of pristine snow grew in size the higher they went.

Suddenly, a thunderous roar blotted out every other sound, then a rumbling from deep within the ground. Seconds later this was followed by a series of short, sharp cracking noises which echoed down the valley and shook the entire mountain and the road cut into its side.

Earthquake!

The truck lurched violently and was thrown hard to one side. The ground under gave way, sending the lead truck plunging off the road and down into the valley to the right, engulfed in a torrent of collapsing rubble and dust. Ryder's middle vehicle rolled; bodies collided with one another and smashed against the metal framework as the vehicle rode down on a river of earth, dust billowing into the rear almost choking everyone within. The vehicle behind immediately followed and all three careered uncontrollably down on top and partly beneath the moving mass of earth and rock, eventually coming to a halt half buried on the valley floor some 100 feet below.

An eerie silence engulfed the valley. Before the dust could settle, Ryder crawled from the debris, dazed but unhurt, amazed to still be alive, followed by a jumble of others from his truck. He recognised only Sicano, Brady and Kellar. All had suffered minor cuts and bruises.

Survival instinct immediately kicked in and without a word, Ryder, the Americans, and others who were able rushed over to the nearest vehicle, its crushed rear protruding from the rubble. It was clear no one had survived inside the mangled wreckage. They removed what weapons and ammunition they could retrieve and sprinted to the next.

Inside the twisted mess of the second truck some of the occupants were horribly injured and barely alive. Weapons and ammunition were again removed but not before the Iranian prisoners shot those that were still breathing, not out of compassion but out of revenge for what they had suffered.

Hurrying back to their own vehicle, less damaged than the other two, Ryder and the three Americans checked the sprawled occupants amongst the debris. Captain Cane was clearly dead, half buried, head smashed to pulp; the other five Americans were somewhere beneath the pile of rubble; frantic digging exposing their crushed and lifeless bodies. Out of the nine who left the prison only Sicano, Brady and Kellar had survived. Seven Iranian prisoners, one a woman, had also survived. Most suffered cuts and abrasions, one had both legs broken, another lay in a pool of blood from a crushed leg. In the failing light the survivors looked at one another. Ryder knew they would not get far with the seriously injured men and the Iranian authorities would show little mercy to those left behind.

Shocked by the swiftness of what had just happened, he tried to come to terms with the situation, acutely aware of the urgency to get away without delay. Providence had set them free, but in this vast, hostile mountain range, with hardly any food or water to speak of, he knew the situation was nothing short of desperate; the odds of escape and survival almost nil. The trucks would soon be missed and they would be hunted down. No choice but to run and put as much distance as possible between the valley and themselves before the sun rose. Ryder thought about making his escape alone but decided it was probably best to stay with the survivors – at least for the time being. In this environment there could be strength in numbers.

"Okay, who's taking command?" he shot at the Americans. It had been their operation; he was only support.

They each glanced at one another. The lengthy silence that followed prompted him to think that perhaps without their officers these men might be losing a little of their nerve.

Then Master Sergeant Brady said quietly, "I will." He did not sound convincing.

Ryder could hardly believe it. "How much do you know about this part of the world, Sergeant?"

"Not a lot. Overflow would've been the first op here."

"What about you two?" He looked at Sicano and Kellar who both gave blank looks and shook their heads.

Fuck! Am I going to risk my life following these guys? – Don't think so.

Ryder came to a decision; glancing at each of the remaining survivors, "We've been given this chance to escape; I suggest we take it and go our own ways. Grab what you can and split."

"Wait!" shot Brady, "You've been here before, come with us."

"No disrespect, Sergeant – but I prefer to make it alone. You guys know what you're doing. Just head west."

Brady hesitated, glanced over at the other two Americans then said, "Look, we have to be practical here. If it's a question of who leads; I understand you're ex-Brit Special Forces, you take command."

Sicano and Kellar nodded in agreement.

Ryder was a little surprised at that. These men were toughies and not in the habit of relinquishing leadership; he could only reason they had weighed up the odds and concluded more chance would be had of escaping Iran with his knowledge and experience than if they tried it alone. And, like him, probably thought there would be strength in numbers.

Having operated in northern Iran before, Ryder knew enough of that part, at least to maybe get them as far as the Turkish border. He did not hesitate. "Right, if that's what you want, let's go." He now had command. First priority: sort out the injured, second: get away from here fast, and as far as possible.

"What about the bodies?" Brady asked. "We need to bury."

"No time," he shot back. "It'll take too long to dig out then bury."

"We can't just leave them like this," pressed Kellar. It was standard practice for Special Forces, especially Americans, to never leave their dead to the enemy.

"You'll have to if you want to survive; leaving ASAP must be the priority. Iranian troops could be swarming any time. We need to put as much distance away from here as possible."

The three Americans stared at one another.

Ryder was not prepared to waste any more time. "Okay, you do what you have to; I'm outta here."

Suddenly, from inside the truck, the raised voice of the Iranian with the broken legs averted their attention. He spoke rapidly and passionately to the man with the crushed leg alongside, "Massoud, my legs, I cannot move them… the pain… it's unbearable!"

Massoud pointed to his own left leg. "I cannot help. I cannot move. Look, Naveed, my leg is smashed too. The bleeding will not stop." He tried to move but gave up. When he eased the makeshift cloth tourniquet, blood from the severed femoral artery spurted out.

Naveed turned to one of the surviving Iranians looking on with a pistol tucked into his belt and demanded, "Give me the gun."

The man hesitated, suspecting what he intended to do.

"Give it to me!" Naveed pleaded, "Give it to me!"

The man reluctantly handed it over.

Naveed rolled sideways, tears filling his eyes and, without a word, shot dead his haemorrhaging companion. He then immediately placed the end of the barrel into his mouth and pulled the trigger.

Shocked by what they had just witnessed, no one spoke for several seconds, the echo of the gunshots reverberating down the valley.

The first of Ryder's priorities had been resolved and he prepared to leave; the Americans reluctantly doing the same, Brady saying quietly, "We're with you."

One of the three men Ryder suspected of being Israeli military, due to the way they handled themselves, stepped forward and said, "We want to join you."

Another who believes in the strength of numbers. "Please yourselves," he replied.

One of the surviving Iranians also asked if they could join.

Ryder agreed; *more the merrier!* Ordering everyone to hurriedly gather up weapons, clothing and equipment they were able to carry, together with what scant food they could find from the wrecked vehicles, he led the bedraggled, defiant band up the valley west towards a setting sun – hope renewed.

9

Snow began to fall as Ryder, leading the file of eleven men and one woman, weaved silently through the trees up the rising ground, swirling snow hampering progress and branches swaying overhead in the wind affording little protection from the growing storm. However, the more snow, the more their tracks would be covered. They travelled through the night and well into the next day. Now almost totally exhausted and acutely aware of their vulnerability in this wilderness more than 3,000 feet above sea level, Ryder looked for somewhere to rest, get warm and eat some of what little food they had. Survival depended on adapting to the extreme conditions. Ryder knew he and the Americans would be able to, but would the others have the fitness and endurance needed for what they would have to face?

Wearily, they trudged on until stumbling upon a depression surrounded by bush, offering protection from the wind and large enough to accommodate all below the general level of the ground. A shelter of branches and brush was quickly built and a fire lit. Anyone searching would have to get close before detecting the flames. The risk, however, had to be taken; hot food and warmth was now the priority.

Although close enough to the fire to keep warm, the separate groups kept largely to themselves; Ryder and the Americans, the Iranians a little further away, and the others on the hollow perimeter. Most of the meagre food scrounged from the trucks was soon devoured. Snow was scooped up into tin mugs, heated, and drunk with relish. Finally, cigarettes taken from the dead guards were shared out within the groups, lit by embers from the fire and savoured. Having given up smoking for less than six months, Ryder fought hard to resist the temptation, although desperate for a nicotine hit.

Kellar's voice distracted his thoughts. "Reckon they've found the trucks yet?"

"More than likely," Sicano replied, drawing deeply on a cigarette. "We've been moving now for maybe fifteen to twenty hours."

The Iranians spoke rapidly amongst themselves, then one calling himself Tariq Vari Awad spoke to Ryder in broken English. "They had radio contact. The alarm would have been given," he said, shifting his short, stocky frame and looking intently at him with brown eyes set in smooth, round features.

"Not much time if they did," shot Kellar, before Ryder could answer.

"Hope you're right," he said to the American; the smell of cigarette smoke almost making him give in.

The conversation around the flames was a mixture of Farsi, Hebrew and English, depending on what group you were in. Ryder understood Farsi well from his army tutors and from his time in Iran. He knew a little Hebrew too, from joint operations with the Israelis when with the SAS.

"How far we come?" Brady asked.

"Twenty-five, maybe thirty miles," Ryder replied.

"Heading west?" questioned Kellar.

"Last time I checked."

"Where are we?" the American pressed.

"Zagros Mountains," the Iranian cut in again.

"Anywhere is better than where we were going," said Brady. "Hey, you speak good English," he said to the Iranian.

"I study," Tariq replied, sadness to his voice.

"How far to the Turkish border?" shot Sicano in Farsi, looking across the flames at the nearest Iranian naming himself Fehed Al Wan.

"Approximately 200 miles north-west," the tall, thin, menacing man with a large hooked nose replied. No translation was necessary as all the Americans could speak Farsi well. Ryder was impressed.

"The Iraqi border must be close," said Kellar. "We should go for it."

Ryder replied, "We could face real problems taking that route. First, the Peshmergas." He referred to Kurdish guerrillas, literally 'those who face death'. "I know they're on our side at the moment against the ISIS crowd, but you can never be sure; secondly, ISIS themselves or Ansar al-Islam militia. All three operate on the north and east borders fighting for independent states. If we're captured by the Peshmergas I'm not sure what our fate would be – probably okay – but if by the other two we'll be beheaded for sure with our dicks shoved down our throats. And thirdly: many other fanatical terrorist groups are fighting for power in Iraq with no telling what they would do. No, we'll head for Turkey, it's safer." He definitely did not want to encounter terrorists if it could be avoided. To him Turkey was the nearest safe haven where he had connections.

"They will expect us to run for Turkey," offered the shortest of the four Iranian men, muscular with piercing eyes set in hawk-like features who said his name was Saad Amer Abdulla.

"That's a risk we'll take," Ryder replied.

The three men furthest away from the fire talked quietly amongst themselves.

Ryder threw a log on the fire then shouted over, "You with us?"

All three glanced at one another before the leader firmly replied, "No."

Ryder was taken aback at the curt reply. "You wanted to join us; why the change?"

The man stared hard at him for a moment, appearing to struggle inwardly before glancing towards the Iranians and asking Ryder, "Can I speak with you privately?"

He nodded and joined the group out of earshot of the others.

"I am Captain Yoman, Israeli Special Forces, and this is Sergeant Shiron and Corporal Hellmann." He paused whilst handshakes were made, then, "You are Special Forces?"

He was not surprised at the captain's revelation; everything about the three screamed military. He replied, "Ex."

"SAS?" pressed the Israeli.

"Again, ex." He wondered where this was all going.

"Are they Special Forces?" Yoman nodded towards the Americans. "Why are they and you here?"

"Long story; you'll have to ask them." It was not for him to say; besides, it was none of his business anyway.

"You Sayeret Mat'kal?" he questioned, holding Yoman's gaze, attempting to divert the line of questioning.

The captain nodded, surprise registering. "Unit 269."

Ryder was impressed. He knew from his SAS experience with this top secret anti-terrorism organisation that members of Unit 269 were considered the best of the Israeli Special Forces.

The Israeli captain glanced at the other two then back to Ryder. "What I have to say is for you only."

Ryder nodded, not sure if he would be able to comply with that.

The captain proceeded to tell him briefly about the failed Operation Tehome, finishing; "So, we have decided, now that we're in the Zagros, to try and complete the job we came to do."

Ryder stared at the Israeli in disbelief. "You're kidding, that's one big fucking ask, Captain – you crazy? How the hell do you expect to locate that base without compass, maps, co-ordinates?"

"We'll know the mountain when we see it. The image is firmly imprinted in here," he pointed to his head, "As are the co-ordinates."

"No good without GPS. You're talking 800 miles or more over rugged country in extreme conditions – unprepared. If a base does exist how will you disable without explosives?"

66

"I'll worry about that at the time. It's important to know if a base exists."

"Why are you telling me this?"

"If you make it safely to the Turkish border you can inform my people that Tehome is still active."

Ryder shrugged; the man seemed determined. "Okay, have it your way." He turned and walked back to the fire.

Ryder said little to the Americans, other than explain who Yoman and his men were; not mentioning what they intended to do. Like him, none was surprised.

The watches were arranged. Ryder wondered if he would ever get out of all this alive until finally exhaustion overcame him and he dropped into a fitful sleep. Soon, one by one, the others followed.

The night was crisp and clear and the stars shone bright during Ryder and Yoman's watch. Both crouched on the rim of the depression staring into the surrounding bush and up into the night sky so vast in its black richness and yet so personal to all who found comfort in its illusion of permanency.

"How long were you in that shit-hole?" Ryder asked.

The captain was silent for several moments then, without looking away from the sky, replied in a low voice, "Too long – four, five weeks. They worked us over good. The schmucks got nothing outta me, or them." He nodded towards the other two lying not far away. "That earthquake was a fucking godsend. I don't think I could have faced another stinking cell or sadistic schmuck." He winced like he was recalling and turned to look directly at Ryder, "You suffer too?"

Ryder nodded. He liked this man – tough and straightforward.

"Same." Like the Israeli, he was not going to give much away. "When you intending to split?"

"First light." Yoman looked back up into the sky and pointed to a bright star in the south-east. "That's Sirius. Tomorrow we'll head in that direction."

Ryder tried briefly once more to dissuade the Israeli. "To go south is a dangerous business, even fully prepared, but to attempt taking out a missile base, Captain, is pure suicide."

Yoman looked at him firmly and said with an air of finality, "That is the risk we will take. Nothing will stop us, so save your breath."

Rebuffed, Ryder refocused on the bush and both men lapsed into silence.

At dawn they prepared to move out. Ryder asked the Iranians what they intended to do and each said they wanted to head for Turkey with the rest.

"Can we talk?" Ryder said to the three Americans and led them out of earshot; they had a right to know the Israelis were intending to split and why. He came straight to the point, "The Israelis are going south in search of a missile base."

After a few moments' silence with only the sound of the wind whistling through the trees, Ryder explained what the Israeli captain had told him. When he'd finished the Americans just stared at him in disbelief.

"A missile base – that's crazy," broke Kellar.

"Longway to go not knowing what's at the fucking end," Brady added.

"Sure have to admire them though," voiced Sicano, looking intently at Ryder. "Maybe we should join them; compensation for missing out on the dams."

They all glanced sheepishly at one another; had Sicano hit a nerve?

"Turkey is the easiest and the most viable option," Ryder countered. "To join them is a huge thing to commit to – even to contemplate – in the situation we're in." A short silence. "And, if there's no base, we've risked all for nothing; a thousand miles of hostile territory unprepared, to find nothing!"

"Our mission failed," added Brady. "Oscar's right, we should join the Israelis; make something of this – regain some self-respect.

I'm thinking: will it let us sleep easy knowing these guys are having a go at the Iranians with limited resources and much less hope of succeeding? Anything we can do to help is, I believe, within our operational scope. We're allies after all."

Ryder could hardly register what he was hearing; he turned to Kellar. "You feel the same?"

He nodded.

"You guys crazy?" he shot. "We have to get outta here, not go fucking traipsing through hostile territory after a base that might not even exist. What the fuck can six of you do anyway, even if you found one?"

"At least we'll have tried," shot Sicano. "At least we'll be doing what we're trained for. I for one don't want to go back a failure. This could redeem us."

The two others agreed with Sicano.

Ryder felt a pang of guilt. These men were prepared to risk their lives for something they believed would help the brotherhood and for their own self-respect. He understood clearly where Sicano was coming from and he could not help but agree with the logic. Was his conscious pricking? The warrior within wanted to help the Israelis, wanted to get even with the Iranians for what they did to him. He knew his duty was to get back to the 'unit', but then again, he was here in the first place to support the American operation, and now they wanted to continue, only this time a different target; so, what the hell.

"Okay, we go south with the Israelis and God help us," he said with a mixture of determination, expectancy and a little fear at facing the unknown.

Smiles all round from the Americans. Ryder did not know whether to laugh or cry as they returned to the others.

"Captain, I've told them your intentions; they had a right to know." He glanced at the Americans.

The Israelis threw looks of surprise.

"We want to help if you agree, under your command."

"You sure you wanna do that, Frank?" said Brady, "We're happy with the way things are."

"It's their operation, Jed. Captain Yoman has all the background on what they're looking for. It's logical he take the lead."

Brady shrugged.

Yoman glanced quickly at his two colleagues then replied, hardly able to conceal his delight. "I accept. Like you said, we're crazy, but together we might just pull this thing off."

No turning back now, Ryder thought.

The Israeli captain looked over at the Iranians on the other side of the hollow, busy talking amongst themselves, and called, "I'm taking command. We'll not be going west. Here we part company."

They were visibly stunned. The one named Qatak Nasir Ali, who had hardly said a word since fleeing the trucks, rushed forward, pleading with Yoman, "Turkey is freedom, not to go west is madness. We must stay together, that is our strength. Where can you possibly go otherwise?"

Yoman stayed silent.

Qatak continued, "This is our land, we know it well. We can help you."

Yoman looked the Iranian straight in the eye and replied sharply, "No. We'll be moving fast. You're not trained for these conditions." He glanced at the woman, who, like Qatak, had hardly uttered a word, keeping much to herself.

"She's one of us," shot Saad.

"Do not speak for me, Saad!" she spat, "I speak for myself." Her dark, defiant eyes burned into the Iranian, then into Yoman.

Fiery, Ryder thought; she looked fit, but what they intended was no job for a woman.

"My name is Afari Asgari. I am with the underground."

"Underground?"

"MEK…"

"People's Mujahedin of Iran," Saad cut in, "enemies of our corrupt state."

She threw him a sharp glance then raised her head defiantly. "I fight and shoot as well as any man. Give me your pistol." She thrust her hand out to the Israeli.

Yoman hesitated, stared at her for a few moments then turned away throwing a surprised glance at the others, as if looking for their agreement, then slowly withdrew the pistol from his belt and handed it over.

In the growing light an eagle glided on the thermals above and gave a sorrowful high-pitched screech.

She expertly checked over the Russian Makarov then told Saad to set a small stone on the edge of the hollow some ten yards away.

Ryder gripped the butt of his pistol, taking no chances.

When Saad finished she waited for him to return, released the safety-catch and then let loose, hitting the stone with a single shot.

Ryder raised his eyebrows; *impressive* but she looked as if she had not the stamina to trek all those miles south.

Yoman echoed Ryder's thoughts, "Very good; you can handle a gun. However, where we're going is many miles away. It'll be a gruelling, dangerous and punishing journey. We're attempting it with little firepower and no preparation to speak of." He paused as if weighing his words. "You do not look strong enough to undertake such a mission. You will slow us down."

For a moment, Ryder thought she was going to strike the Israeli. Instead, she put hands on hips and looked daggers, then in a cold, clear voice, full of venom, replied in almost perfect English, "How dare you speak like that to me; you have no right. My life has been dedicated to overthrowing this malignant regime since their thugs killed my parents." She paused to control her emotions. "How the fuck you think I have managed since they left my life? How the fuck you think I survived?" She glared at the other Iranians. "We've had to survive in these mountains more times than I care to remember, mostly eluding government forces. To be fit and capable of handling all kinds of weapons is paramount. I have suffered more abuse and danger than you'll ever know. If you think a long journey fraught with uncertainty is beyond me then think again, *Captain*." She paused then in a calmer tone, "I will not slow you down. I want as much revenge as I can get and if that means more danger and hardship wherever you're intending to go, so be it, اد خ هب ما رهنماى."

'God will guide us'. Seemed appropriate to Ryder. *We'll need all the bloody help we can get on this one – even God's.*

"Oh, and one more thing, *Captain*: do not worry about me being a woman. When roughing it with men in these mountains there's no such thing as privacy. I've seen more dicks than you can count on your fingers. If for some reason any of you get a hard-on that's your problem. Just make sure you keep it to yourselves. And, by the way, I'll bury my own shit."

Wow, one tough lady. It reminded Ryder of an equally spunky woman he'd taken into North Korea on the last mission.

"You know these mountains?" Yoman asked, showing surprise, taking back the pistol.

She nodded, as did the other Iranians.

To Ryder, if they were telling the truth, the Israeli should take them, including the woman, despite the reservation of more mouths to feed and a larger group that would possibly be easier to track.

"How far to the south?" the captain shot, turning to the men and ignoring the woman.

"Down to the Gulf," Fehed quickly replied.

Ryder threw a glance at Yoman and indicated to move out of earshot.

"Captain, maybe you should reconsider," he said when they were. "It's going to be tough just surviving, let alone finding our way. They could be of use. Besides, if we find that base you're looking for we'll need all the firepower we can get. The woman handled the gun like a pro."

Yoman thought for several moments then nodded in agreement.

Both returned to the group.

"It's decided," said Yoman. "Those who want to tag along can, including you," he shot a glance at Afari.

"In what direction?" asked Saad.

"South to the Gulf."

"South!" exclaimed Tariq. "Why? You risk greater capture. You will pass through densely populated areas."

"Going south will be the last thing pursuers will expect us to do," said Yoman, a little impatiently. "We have to move right away; that gunshot could bring others. Now, who wants in?"

Afari showed her relief and immediately agreed. Then, one by one, the others did too.

Without wasting any more time the group quickly dismantled the shelter and smoothed the ground the best they could to hide their presence. They then followed Captain Yoman out of the hollow and up the slope southwards into the mountain wilderness of high peaks, tree-lined rolling hills and pastureland which ran for a 1,000 miles down to the Arabian Sea. Ryder, in the rear, wondered where all this would finally lead, and what the hell he had let himself in for, not daring to think he might never come out of this crazy venture alive.

10

A dense haze floated into the surrounding valleys as the column moved silently over the tree-covered terrain keeping to a gruelling pace. By midday the party had made almost fifteen miles across the foothills of the massive range. The slopes had now become steeper but the ground levelled off for long stretches in a series of gentle sloping plateaus, low ridges and shallow valleys. The trees had thinned enough to see well ahead, and large clearings were cautiously skirted to avoid detection from the air and exposure to the wind.

It was during one of these flanking movements that Captain Yoman, leading, suddenly stopped and raised an arm.

Ryder ran to his side.

"What is it?"

"Listen!"

They all strained ears, and then heard it too.

"Plane; take cover!" Ryder cried.

All scrambled for the nearest dense scrub.

Saad stumbled and sprawled in the snow.

Ryder grabbed him by the collar and smartly dragged the Iranian under a bush just as a light, single-engine aircraft came into view from the west and flew low over the clearing some 200 yards in front of where they hid to disappear as quickly as it came behind trees to the east.

None of them moved, until they could no longer hear the aircraft's engines.

"That was close, real close," said Brady, brushing himself down. "Think he saw us?"

"Doubt it," Ryder replied. "Not returned, so I guess we're okay."

"Maybe it has IRI," said Yoman, looking a little shaky, eyeing him intently.

"Again I doubt it. Heat-imaging equipment in a small plane like that seems unlikely."

"Should we continue south?" asked Fehed.

"It's our best chance, keeping to these foothills; scrub and trees will give good cover," said Qatak, staring hard at the Israeli captain.

"Where are we now?" Ryder asked, feeling anxious at being so exposed.

"Zanjan province," replied Saad. "Hamadan is not far, directly south."

"Densely populated area right down to the next major city of Esfhan," added Fehed.

"How far?" asked Yoman.

The Iranian shrugged, "Thirty, forty miles to Hamadan – 200 to Esfhan."

"We have to give both a wide berth," said Ryder.

"I agree," replied Yoman, turning to Saad. "You, what's the best way?"

"South-west into Kordestan for maybe fifty, sixty miles then turn south through the more remote regions."

"That would take us close to the Iraq border," said Ryder. "We could encounter troops, or worse, al-Islam."

"Don't see we have much choice," said Yoman. "Now that we could've been spotted, we must avoid populated areas at all costs." He looked firmly at Ryder. "Okay, move out."

Not long after leaving cover, Yoman sent his two men ahead to search for food with instructions to shoot only when certain of a kill. It was a risk that had to be taken; there was no other way of killing on the move, and without nourishment they would all die anyway in the severe conditions.

That afternoon the clouds came and more light snow began to fall. Wet, miserable, but relieved tracks would be covered, the column strung out in line, trudged relentlessly over the windswept hills, bodies willing themselves forward, aching from the exertion. Ryder was surprised the woman kept up without complaint.

The hunters returned just before dusk with two hares and a polecat. They made a camp sheltered in a depression, and over a quickly prepared fire cooked the hares and smoke-dried the polecat for 'jerky'. After eating, mostly in silence, deep in their own thoughts, the exhausted group smoked the last of the cigarettes, except Ryder; although more than tempted, he forced himself not to give in. The watch was agreed and finally, with Ryder and Brady taking the first, they all turned in totally spent.

As the first rays of light percolated through the trees at dawn the next day the camp was cleared and they continued south-west. Cold, miserable and hungry, Ryder struggled against an icy wind over gently sloping plateaus and across shallow valleys. Yoman led, together with Fehed as guide, with the rest bringing up the rear.

Three hours into the morning the sound of baying dogs suddenly came on the wind. Ryder and the others instantly scattered, gained cover in surrounding bush and pointed weapons firmly in the direction of the oncoming sounds.

The baying dogs came closer.

Shortly a small deer burst through the undergrowth, followed frantically by four long-legged, shaggy brown dogs, weaving in and out of the trees in hot pursuit. The deer was exhausted. Twenty yards in front of the hidden men, the animal turned and faced the dogs in a last desperate stand.

All watched the small hind ward off each dog, until finally it was brought to its knees by the persistency and ferocity of its attackers.

A shrill whistle and the dogs immediately backed away, circling their prey.

Attention focused towards the trees; Yoman signalling everyone to remain quiet and hidden.

Soon two men came into view running towards the dogs with rifles and backpacks, wearing long coats and fur hats with bandoliers crossing their chests. Reaching the deer, they shot it immediately.

Ryder looked across at Yoman; they needed that animal desperately. Signalling to the captain he was going to break cover, the Israeli nodded agreement and both men emerged from hiding to face the hunters.

The two men jumped back, startled at the sudden presence.

One of the dogs sprang at Ryder. He swung at it with the butt of his rifle and sent it flying, yelping in pain. The other dogs slunk quietly to the feet of their masters.

Yoman motioned the two men to drop weapons which they hurriedly did, fear showing on weather-beaten faces.

"Sergeant, get those rifles!" he shouted at Shiron, not taking his eyes off the hunters. He asked who they were in Farsi, but received only blank stares.

Sicano then asked the same question in Kurdish. They understood and quickly told the American they were Luri tribesmen. Ryder was surprised the American spoke Kurdish fluently.

The Israeli captain glanced at Sicano. "Tell them we want the deer."

He did and the cowering hunters eagerly agreed.

"Search the bags," snapped Yoman, "Take everything useful… and, Corporal, check those rifles."

Hellmann took one of the rifles, expertly slammed open the breech. "Russian made. Good hunting rifle," he said.

"Take them and the ammo belts," the captain ordered.

Hellmann obliged, giving one rifle and belt to Shiron and keeping the other for himself.

"Tell them to cut up the deer and put it in backpacks," said Yoman sharply to Sicano. "Make sure none is wasted, and don't take your eyes off them doing it." He turned to the Iranians. "You four, help," he pointed to the men. Then at Afari. "You included."

77

After the meat had been cut and packed, Yoman, levelling his rifle at the two men, ordered the rest to move out. Ryder knew then the Israeli intended to kill the hunters but understood; the two had been in the wrong place at the wrong time and to let them go would be a mistake.

The tribesmen glanced nervously at each other as the dogs jumped and barked at their feet.

Fifty yards on, all heard a short burst of gun fire and yelps confirming the fate of both hunters and their dogs. The captain soon rejoined the group and handed the Luris' long coats and fur hats to the other two Israelis.

Heading south had fooled the Iranians, Ryder thought; the longer that remained the better. The wind had dropped considerably and only light, wispy snow now fell in the open gaps between the thin stands of trees. The column, with Yoman in the lead and Ryder bringing up the rear, moved with reasonable ease through the tussock and shrub thinly layered with patchy, powdered snow. As the afternoon wore on the terrain became less hilly and began to slope downwards in a series of plateaus, ending in a broad, undulating plain with the white peaks of the Zagros, tinged in gold, rising high to the left in the distance. Mature trees became less numerous and eventually gave way to sprawling scrub, increasing in density as the ground levelled off. It was here, beyond a thick belt of high, swaying reeds, that the group came to its first major obstacle: a broad, fast-flowing river.

Yoman decided to follow it in the hope of finding a fording point but, after tramping several miles along the marshy bank without so much as a sign of shallow water, gave up and decided to attempt a crossing. Without rope or axes, it was impossible to form a sturdy raft to carry the group across the 100-yard-wide flow, but by using strands of reed as twine to form a lighter raft of larger reeds, sufficient at least to keep clothes and weapons dry, they could hang on and manoeuvre themselves to the other side. Luckily all could swim, and they began building a raft from the surrounding reeds.

One hour later the raft was completed. Afari insisted she would help in the water and began to remove her clothes.

Ryder stopped her and looked at Yoman. "We'll need to somehow keep the equipment on the raft should it get rough; she could hold it down. The additional weight will keep it more stable."

The captain thought about it, then agreed.

Not caring about their nakedness but shivering violently, the eleven men bundled clothes and belongings onto the raft with Afari on top. Lifting the 6-foot square of reeds they ran through the mud to the water's edge. Wading into the quickly deepening water, Ryder was almost paralysed by the bitter cold as the brown, murky liquid slid past his waist, chest and shoulders. Lunging forward on command, he kicked out with the rest, committed now for the opposite bank. The intention: ride the current, but at the same time, guide the raft and hope to land not too far downstream. He worried the longer they remained in the icy water, the less chance they had of surviving. The current proved deceptively strong, whisking the raft out into midstream. Kicking, pushing, pulling, the men slowly but surely manoeuvred towards the opposite bank, the strong, swirling water continuously threatening to suck them under.

During a particularly sharp spin, Qatak suddenly cried out. Ryder, the nearest, turned in time to see the Iranian's head disappear beneath the swirling waters. He lunged out, caught the man's flaying forearm and felt it snap as he disappeared again beneath the surface. Seconds later the Iranian broke the surface screaming. Ryder could not change arms without releasing his own grip on the raft; to let go would have proved fatal for both.

Moments later, Hellmann grabbed Qatak by his good arm and drew him closer to the raft. Ryder, releasing his grip, struggled to keep the now almost unconscious Iranian's head above water until he had revived sufficiently to manage himself. Desperately, Ryder fought to overcome the pull of the current, cursing and gasping as strength slowly ebbed away; body so numb, the cold no longer seemed to matter.

Spun and buffeted continuously, the raft gradually made headway across the surging river until finally it reached the other side. Feeling firm ground beneath his feet and relieved at making it to safety, Ryder helped drag the waterlogged raft up over the mud and into the reeds. Shaking from the bitter cold he and the others searched frantically for anything that would burn whilst Afari made Qatak as comfortable as she could, cleared a space for a fire, and soon had twigs, branches and dry reeds ablaze.

They hung damp clothes on the reeds enclosing the rapidly burning scrub and huddled inside as close as they could to the flames. The fire roared and Ryder basked naked in its warmth, unconcerned by the presence of Afari who busied herself gathering and checking the equipment from the raft. When the clothes had fully dried they all quickly dressed, doused the flames, gathered belongings and moved out, leaving the clearing as free of their presence as possible.

They trudged through the night. Come dawn, before them lay gently undulating, patchy snow-covered steppes sparsely populated by saplings and bush. Ryder could see Qatak was in considerable pain, his forearm connected to the upper arm only by muscle and sinew with the elbow joint almost completely split apart. Afari had tried to reset the grotesquely twisted limb, but the nerves and sinews were stretched and torn to such an extent all she could do was bind the arm tightly against the Iranian's chest, and hope for the best.

Beyond the river the landscape became much flatter and less gruelling in nature. Ryder moved easily, almost abreast of the others, across the open ground until they were about ten miles south-east of the river and less than 100 yards from tree-lined rising ground ahead. Suddenly, he heard the familiar sound of an approaching aircraft and froze. The others looked at one another in sheer panic and, without a word, began to run frantically with Ryder for the dark line of the trees. One minute later, a single-engine aircraft flew out of an overcast western sky and swooped low over the desperate, stumbling group. It banked sharply and flew mockingly over them once more, so close they could almost hear the whirr of the cameras, before disappearing westward as Ryder and the rest flung themselves into the belt of trees, breathless and cursing.

Fuck! This time, no escape!

"Shit! Shit! They've seen us, for chrissake!" Brady shouted.

"Motherfucker's so low he just had to see us!" cried Kellar.

Sicano emerged from cover along with the others and shook off the snow. "He saw us for sure!"

"Maybe," replied Yoman, brushing himself down too.

"How the hell did he get so close?" asked Brady.

"Hugging the ground," answered Ryder. "Definitely know where we are now; troops probably already on the way."

"We can't hang around to find out – move!" shot Yoman.

They left the protection of the thicket and headed as fast as they could towards the next clump of trees, half a mile away. They moved in column now, with Yoman at the head to reduce the number of tracks, keeping a steady pace despite the cramps that began to plague both Saad and Tariq. Travelling in this manner, from one thicket to another, for a further eight miles was covered without mishap; snow thankfully falling, obliterating their line of direction.

Late afternoon arrived and Yoman chose a place to make camp in a small but densely wooded area where they would stay until dawn the next day. Ryder quickly settled in, grateful to rest his aching limbs. The Israeli captain insisted on no fire so they made do with chewing what was left of the polecat jerky. Turning in as soon as a brushwood shelter was finished, Shiron and Hellmann took the first watch and the rest, so utterly exhausted, were soon asleep, oblivious to the cold and the light snow which fell, gently blanketing the ground around them.

Ryder and Yoman were called in the early hours for the fourth watch. Shaking off the cold and tiredness, Ryder huddled with the Israeli at the edge of the camp. The snow had ceased and sparse clouds now scudded across the sky regularly breaking the soft illumination of a crescent moon hanging low on the horizon.

Whilst he scanned the surrounding trees and dense bush, Yoman tried to get a fix on the stars through the silhouetted foliage of the forest canopy.

"Still a way to go, Captain?" Ryder asked.

Yoman turned and looked at him, sharp features pronounced in a shaft of light.

"I guess so, but we'll get there."

"Looking at those peaks, I have my doubts." Ryder nodded towards the jagged snow-covered peaks forming the heart of the Zagros range, just visible in the diminished light cast by the crescent moon through the tall stands of trees.

"We'll keep to the foothills and valleys; so long as we maintain a rough south-easterly direction, the target will be found."

"I admire your confidence, Captain – a big ask; we're going to need a shit-load of luck."

"Not luck, Frank – determination."

An hour passed uneventfully; the two men intermittently discussing survival problems, at the same time striving to keep warm, when Yoman questioned, "What the fuck's that stench?"

"I noticed earlier; much stronger now, though."

The captain sniffed the air; the smell seemed to engulf the whole clearing, pungent and penetrating.

Fehed awoke, the percolating stench filling his nostrils. He sprang out of the shelter and hurried over to where Ryder and Yoman squatted.

"Wolves!" he cried. "Quick! Rifles!" the Iranian shouted, hastily arming his machine pistol.

"Hold it!" shot the captain. "Wolves won't attack; too many of us."

"Wolves in these parts sometimes roam in large packs, especially during bad winters, and would not hesitate to attack humans if hungry enough and sufficient in numbers," said Fehed urgently.

Ryder felt uneasy at that, straining to see if he could detect any movement amongst the shadows. He turned to Yoman. "Start shooting and the sound of gunfire could have every fucking Iranian soldier homing in on us for miles around."

"I'm fully aware of that," he spat back.

"If you don't," Fehed snapped, showing raw fear, "you'll have the whole pack on us and there won't be anything to find! From the stench, there could be as many as twenty – and close," he pressed.

The acrid smell grew worse.

"It's only a question of time before they attack," he pressed again, highly agitated.

The three crouched, watching, waiting, Ryder trying to stem the fear that grew by the second.

"Wolves are cowards – we don't need to fire," Yoman suddenly hissed, jumping up to move forward.

Ryder tried to grab him but he was too quick; rushing into the bush, shouting at the top of his voice and waving arms frantically, the captain disappeared into the shadows.

Ryder made to follow but froze as a spine-chilling howl rose malevolently in front of them, followed by another to the side. Then blood-curdling screams amid a torrent of gut-wrenching snarls, growls and primordial screeching filled the air.

By now the others had joined them at the edge of the clearing facing the trees.

Fehed looked urgently at Ryder. "They have the taste of blood! Shoot now or all will be lost!"

Ryder hesitated, but only for a few seconds, before letting loose with rifle, followed by the others, spraying the surrounding bush.

Screams of animal pain, guttural snarling and scurrying came from all sides as the wolves fled from the hail of bullets; the undergrowth became a frenzy of movement as terrified animals fought to escape the onslaught of lead. When the frenzy finally ended, Ryder shouted for the shooting to stop, leaving the staccato sound of automatic-rifle fire echoing through the valleys and beyond.

Smoke and the smell of cordite mingled with the stench of wolves hung heavily in the air. Ryder stood transfixed, visibly shaken by what he had just witnessed; so many of them and so close. Then he followed Shiron and Hellmann as they rushed into the bush to find the captain. What Ryder came across sickened him. Yoman's torn body lay grotesquely against the trunk of a tree surrounded by dead wolves, his face almost unrecognizable with arms and legs shredded. He was still alive, but in a bad way.

The two Israelis tried to make the captain as comfortable as they could but he was losing a lot of blood and they could not stop it.

Brady turned and said to Ryder, "He's not gonna make it… do we carry on?" inferring Ryder was now back in command.

Ryder in turn looked at Shiron. "What do you want?"

The Israeli, scar livid on his cheek, glanced at Hellmann then said firmly, "We'll carry on… you take command."

Then to the Americans, "You okay with that?"

The three agreed. Brady pulled him to one side. "We need outta here – and fast." He glanced down at the captain. "He's too bad to travel."

Ryder turned to Shiron. "We have to get away. Can you carry him?"

The Israeli shook his head; it was obvious the captain did not have long to live.

Ryder looked at him intently and could tell Shiron knew what he was thinking, but before he could say it the Israeli turned, went back to Hellmann attending Yoman and spoke to him quietly. Moments later, the sergeant drew his pistol and, without hesitating, ended the captain's misery.

"Okay, bury him quickly and let's get away from here," said Ryder, tentative at being back in command.

As the first rays of light appeared dimly in the eastern sky they dismantled the shelter and gathered belongings. Pushing from his mind the shocking demise of the Israeli captain, Ryder led the file out of the wood and headed south, weaving a path through scrub and gorse towards the black mass of the horizon. The wind cut deep and more snow was in the offing. They made good progress through the undulating and often torturous terrain, until some fifteen uneventful miles later, forced by cold and fatigue, Ryder sought shelter in the late afternoon. Making camp in a shallow hollow he decided to remain there for the rest of the day and move out the following morning. After eating, the watch was agreed and a short while later, Ryder, and those not on watch, collapsed into fitful sleep.

11

Ryder lay cold and tense in the shallow hollow watching with growing concern as the twelve parachutists descended out of a clear morning sky and drifted down into the valley below. The small transport plane from which they had disgorged banked steeply at the end of the broad depression and made one more deafening swoop over the drop zone before rising rapidly again south-west to disappear out of the valley. No one spoke as Ryder, squinting against the sun's glare, tried to determine exactly where the parachutists had landed.

"Special Forces," Brady snapped, breaking the silence, releasing the safety-catch on his Kalashnikov.

"To be expected," Ryder shot back, doing the same.

"Yeah, but this soon?" said Kellar.

"Mountain troops," voiced Saad.

Hellmann pointed down into the valley. All looked and saw through the trees six men moving swiftly in single file up the slope towards the hollow, and to the left another six heading north-east away from their position.

"We need to move, now, Frank," Brady urged.

"I cannot go another step," pleaded Saad. "Nor can he," he glanced at Qatak.

"You move, or we go without you," shot Brady.

Ryder threw the American a look that said, "I'll make that call."

"Maybe we should take them out whilst we still have the strength?" said Shiron.

"We have to keep going," Brady pushed home, looking hard at Ryder.

"They can easily track us in this snow," Shiron pressed.

A short silence as both men stared at one another.

Ryder had to agree with the Israeli. A patrol so close held too many risks. "We'll take'em," he said firmly.

Brady threw him an angry look. "How do you propose to do that without alerting the others?" he countered.

"Bayonets," Ryder shot back, raising his machine pistol. "We'll use these only as a last resort."

"They're getting real close," said Kellar in an effort to ease the tension. "Gonna stumble right on us."

The six Iranian soldiers were now less than 100 yards away, and heading straight for the hollow.

Ryder glanced at the patrol, then at Brady. "You and your men take the first three and we'll take the rest," he nodded at Shiron and Hellmann. He turned to the Iranians. "You hide in the bush here. Don't move until it's over."

With that, he and the others hurriedly positioned themselves along the edge of the hollow concealed in bush. Ryder steeled himself for action.

The thud of footsteps, jangling metal and laboured breathing came closer.

The patrol reached the hollow and began to walk single file around the rim.

Suddenly, one of the soldiers turned, let out a cry and pointed down in the hollow at Fehed partly exposed in the bush, and raised his weapon.

Before the soldier could fire, Ryder leapt, his whole weight behind him, striking the man's mid-drift and sending them both sprawling over the rim and down the snowy slope. The bayonet, aimed at the heart, glanced off body armour and the soldier rolled away. Determinedly, he lunged again, aiming higher, but the man rolled a second time and he missed. Partly regaining his feet, the soldier brought his rifle up and in desperation, Ryder lunged once more, higher this time, and the bayonet sliced deep into the soldier's throat. Choking, he fell to his knees, looked at Ryder with terror-filled eyes as blood spurted from the severed jugular, before crumpling to the snow, dead.

At the same time, the others pounced. Shiron's bayonet hit body armour too and he rolled with the man partway down the slope to smash hard against a tree. Fortunately the soldier took the full impact against the trunk and was severely winded, allowing the Israeli to make another strike. This time he got it right, slipping the bayonet up under the armour, through the ribcage and deep into the heart.

Hellmann had little trouble with the last man in line dispatching him with a powerful fist to the face followed by turning him and swiftly slicing the bayonet deep across the soldier's throat.

Of the three American's only Sicano struggled to take out his target when he hit armour; the bayonet slipping from his grasp at the crucial moment forcing him to use all his strength and skill to break the soldier's neck; but not before the burly man almost overcame him with his tenacity to resist. The soldier was the biggest of the six-man patrol and, no doubt, the element of surprise had played a considerable part in the outcome. The two other Americans had swiftly dispatched their targets, having gone straight for the throats first time. The whole violent encounter was over in a matter of seconds and left a bloody scene of red-stained snow and crumpled bodies littering the slope.

Stripping the dead of everything useful, including field glasses, detailed maps, a compass and field rations but most important of all, a GPS strapped to the wrist of the soldier Ryder had killed, they shared out the spoils. Unfortunately, the maps only covered a small area, but at least with the co-ordinates shown and the GPS, Ryder could keep track of where they were for at least another twenty or thirty miles. After that they would use the compass and back to guesswork. The second in line had been carrying a radio transmitter.

"Anyone worked one of these?" snapped Ryder.

"I have," Hellmann replied.

"Good – get that working, and hurry. I want to transmit."

"Without call-code?"

"Yes Corporal, without call-code."

"What frequency?"

"You choose. I want to buy some time. Move those dials."

Hellmann worked his way through the frequencies until a high-pitched Iranian voice came through the speaker.

"Bear One to Bear Three… What is your position? Come in – over."

Ryder took the mouthpiece. "Bear Three to Bear One. Targets sighted and engaged two miles north-west of drop zone, pursuing. Radio damaged, attempting to repair… Over and out," he shouted in Farsi, fading the signal in and out with the dial.

"Will they buy that?" Sicano asked.

Ryder shot a glance at the American. "Put yourself in the commander's position; he receives a sketchy transmission confirming a sighting and targets have been engaged. The signal is confused, but coherent. What should he do? I know what I would do: send troops to the new location. The last scenario he would consider is us destroying his elite troops; and knowing the radio was damaged, he would not be unduly worried if no further transmissions were received either. Besides—"

The radio crackled again; a voice came through ordering all search patrols to head north-west of the drop zone.

Ryder smiled, white teeth glittering in the fuzzy blackness of a stubby beard. "Hold that frequency and keep open. I want to know every move they make." Then, turning to Saad and Qatak, "We're moving out now, with or without you." He felt sympathy for both men but they had to keep moving.

Both Iranians shrugged and struggled to their feet, as did the others. Afari helped Qatak, his pale and drawn features indicating he was in some pain.

Ryder checked the group's position with the GPS before he ordered the party to move out south-eastwards down the slope and into the valley below. Tired and hungry they traversed the valley as quickly as they could, trying to put as much distance between themselves and the dead soldiers as possible, keeping well to the bush and avoiding open ground like the plague. Ryder drove them hard until, by early afternoon, the party had cleared the valley and began to clamber up the rising ground on the other side.

Eventually, well into early evening and totally exhausted after covering many miles over rugged ground, they made camp in a rocky gully providing good cover. The radio receiver kept them informed of the movements of any pursuer. Sicano suggested maybe they should transmit signals, at least to let any friendlies listening know they were still alive, but this was quickly turned down by Ryder on the grounds any signal would not transmit far in these mountains and they would seriously risk discovery. After a hasty, meagre meal of field rations and water, Brady and Kellar agreed to take first watch and the rest finally collapsed in the makeshift shelter.

The Iranians, especially Afari, looked all in; less so the three Americans and two Israelis. Ryder himself felt totally drained and exhausted. The adrenaline that had kept him going was fast coming down leaving only a desperate tiredness and fatigue. All he wanted to do now was sleep, and he did the moment he laid down his head.

The night was long, cold and uneventful, and for most, the dawn could not arrive soon enough. Fortunately, for Ryder, he'd slept well and felt revived.

Qatak, in particular, had had a bad time. Afari, despite her fatigue, stayed close by to attend him as best she could, but could do little. When Ryder awoke he went over to the injured Iranian.

"Arm looks bad," Afari whispered; she pointed to the Iranian's fingers. "They're black; turning gangrene."

The others joined them.

She pulled back the loose cloth covering the arm. All winced when they saw the wound. The limb was certainly a mess and there was no mistaking the faint odour of rotting flesh.

Moving away, followed by the others, Ryder said, "He can't travel like that."

The Americans and Israelis nodded and glanced at one another.

Ryder knew what they were thinking: *He'll hold us up*. He did not want him to die like the Israeli captain. "It must come off," he said firmly. "If we don't do it he'll certainly die. I know it'll mean being holed up here for another day or so, but that's better than maybe having to amputate later out in the open."

Shiron voiced what Ryder had suspected, "He'll hold us back. We have a long way to go. He'll never make it." The Israeli glanced at each of the Americans for support; instead, they just shrugged.

"We do it now. He'll make it." Ryder hoped he was right, even though the odds were against them. If it had been a leg then it would have been different.

They went back to the Iranian.

Qatak lay, slight frame propped against a rock, staring at them with glazed eyes, his pallid olive skin drawn taut across gaunt features. He was obviously in great pain and trying hard not to show it.

Ryder began to speak, but the Iranian raised his good arm and looked at him with pain-filled eyes. "It must come off… do your best… make it quick."

Ryder nodded, turned to the others. "Any of you amputated before?"

Silence for several seconds.

"I have," said Afari, almost in a whisper.

She looked haggard and frail, but Ryder noted the fire in her eyes and steeliness about her.

The rest turned to her with looks of surprise but said nothing until Ryder told the other Iranians to prepare a fire using dry timber to avoid thick smoke.

Two hours later Qatak whispered he was ready. Afari had

prepared a place by the fire and had boiled water from a nearby stream. Strips of cloth were washed and dried for bandages.

She examined the wound carefully revealing the elbow joint completely shattered and joined only by torn skin, muscle and sinew. She turned to the others, "To remove the lower arm and gangrenous flesh it will be necessary to cut through the joint with a sharp knife then cauterise muscle and tissue left on the stump. I'll use the knife taken from the hunters."

They all nodded. Ryder put the broad blade of the knife into the fire.

Qatak was then carried to the fire and made comfortable. Kellar placed a tourniquet on the man's upper arm whilst Afari wiped sweat away from the Iranian's brow before carefully arranging the arm so that the inner elbow was fully exposed. Checking the knife blade glowing red in the embers and bayonet blade washed in boiling water, she reached for a piece of cloth, wrapped it around a short stick and placed it firmly between the Iranian's teeth. Qatak's eyes were wide conveying fear at what was about to happen. Afari looked tense and drawn. She glanced at Ryder; he gave her a short, reassuring smile. Kellar patted the Iranian on the shoulder and began to tighten the tourniquet.

Afari indicated to hold the Iranian firmly down. She took hold of the bayonet handle with her right hand, gripped the Iranian's upper arm firmly with her left, then made two bold sweeps around the limb, cutting right through flesh to the bone.

Qatak gave a stiff, muffled scream and writhed in agony, but was kept down.

Blood spread everywhere. Afari did not panic, but calmly told Kellar to keep the tourniquet as tight as he could whilst she found the joint and drove the bayonet in, severing the lower arm completely in two deft strokes.

The Iranian fainted.

Loss of blood had been stemmed by the tourniquet and the raw red stump of the upper arm was now fully exposed.

Afari reached for the hunter's knife in the fire, removed it and swiftly drew the broad, flat blade twice across the bloody tissue. The flesh seared as the blade cauterised the wound, fusing flesh, muscle and arteries together in a few hissing, hellish moments, before she threw the knife to one side and hurriedly began bandaging the stump.

Wrapping the severed limb in cloth as best she could, Afari told Kellar to loosen the tourniquet before moving away and slumping against the face of the rocky outcrop. The whole episode had taken less than thirty seconds but she looked mentally drained.

The two Israelis had moved away to keep watch whilst the amputation was taking place. The weather was good and they could see both ends of the gully. Both said little as they focused on the scrub and bush. In the background the sounds of the amputation could be heard.

Then, "See what you can get on that," said Shiron, looking at Hellmann and nodding towards the transmitter.

The corporal stood and went to the transmitter. Seconds later, "That's funny, I could've sworn I left it on channel and switched off before turning in," he said, shaking his head and looking inquiringly at Shiron.

"You probably unknowingly moved the dial."

"Maybe, but I doubt it. I made a point of turning off to save the battery," replied Hellmann, still shaking his head as he tuned in.

But all he got was a hiss and then the transmitter died. "Batteries fucked."

"You saying someone tampered with it?"

"How the fuck do I know?" he spat, then calmer, "But, maybe you're right; I could've forgotten to turn it off."

"Did you see or hear anything unusual?"

"Not a thing. Who the hell would do that anyway?"

Shiron looked thoughtful before barking, "Okay, Corporal, destroy that radio – *now*. Scatter the pieces; we don't want any followers finding it."

"What about the Brit? He won't be happy."

"Don't worry. I'll handle that."

The corporal removed the power-pack, sheared off the terminals with a bayonet, and threw it deep into the undergrowth. Then, with the help of Shiron, quickly dismantled the framework and scattered pieces into the surrounding bush.

When finished, Shiron stood and strode over to where the others were huddled around Qatak.

"We should be moving out," he said to Ryder, impatiently.

"Why? This man's in no fit state to move. He's just experienced a fucking major trauma, or haven't you noticed?"

"I would have thought that obvious, Frank. We wasted six Iranians less than a few days' march back. Another day here puts us at serious risk of being tracked down. Any competent commander would order searches in every direction within a ten to thirty mile radius of the hollow, particularly south now he knows our pattern."

"We're not leaving until this man is ready to," replied Ryder, angrily.

"If you don't want to leave; stay then. We'll go it alone."

The Israeli turned and began to gather his belongings, ordering Hellmann to do the same.

"Please yourselves," Ryder shot, pissed off at the Israelis; the Iranian needed rest after such an ordeal.

The three Americans exchanged urgent glances.

"You go; I'll stay until he can move," said Afari, still propped up against the rock face. "We'll catch up."

"Wait!" exclaimed Kellar. "Let me talk to him," he glanced at the Iranian, "see what he wants."

The American leant over Qatak, now conscious, and explained they had to move on. The Iranian, obviously in great discomfort, looked silently at him then, after several moments, said he was able to continue.

Kellar glanced up at both Ryder and Shiron, "One hour and we'll be ready to move."

Shiron looked hard and long at Ryder and the three Americans before nodding in agreement, "One hour."

Ryder wondered, under the circumstances, if the Americans wanted to continue; he looked at Kellar then at the other two. "Now these two are going it alone, you prepared to carry on?"

Silence for a moment then Kellar answered, "I'm staying."

"Count me in," said Sicano.

"And me," said Brady.

"Okay, Sergeant, we're with you," Ryder said to Shiron. "You want me to lead still?"

The Israeli nodded; white scar on his cheek showing strong through the stubble.

Decision made. *Onward we go.* "Where's the trani?" Ryder asked. *Time to find out where the pursuers are.*

Hellmann glanced at Shiron.

Shiron answered, "Fucked – batteries dead. We broke it up and scattered in the bush."

"That wasn't your call, Sergeant," shot Ryder, angry the Israeli had not bothered to tell him before doing it. "We could've maybe nurtured a little more out of them."

The Israeli shrugged.

Disappointed though he was, Ryder didn't want to push why this had happened after only a relatively short period of use. It was gone, nothing he said would bring it back; he had more pressing things to worry about. His thoughts turned to the woman. He was impressed by her loyalty. It took some guts to offer to stay in this harsh, hostile environment alone with this badly injured man. Would he have stayed if the circumstances had been reversed?

A cold wind lashed his body as he left the gully one hour later at the head of the file; a sense of foreboding washing through him at the thought of what the future might have in store.

12

It was early evening and the group, led by the Iranians, crested a low ridge and suddenly stopped in their tracks; below a shimmering stretch of blue-grey water lay before them.

"We are too far west," said Fahed. "That's Lake Darbandikan. We have crossed into Iraq."

Ryder shot a glance at the Israelis and Americans, then turned to the Iranian, "You sure? Why no border posts?"

"The border in these mountains is very blurred – hard to define," he replied. "The remoteness allows our troops to freely enter Iraq to pursue us with impunity without worrying about border controls, as we have learnt to our detriment."

"Easily get lost in this kinda terrain," Kellar voiced.

For the last two days they had slogged up and down sparsely wooded slopes broken by small plateaus, avoiding clearings and keeping well to the scrub. In the distance jagged outcrops of rock, violet and grey, rose against dramatic backdrops of snow-covered slopes and black sheer rock faces of the high, barren peaks. The Zagros continued to fill the whole horizon for as far as the eye could see eastwards, falling gradually in a series of lesser peaks and brown hills down to the yellow plains beyond directly south and west.

"We have to get back," said Shiron, anger in his voice. He looked at Ryder. "You don't have to."

Ryder turned to the Americans. "You want to continue west; chance Iraq?"

"And al-Islam," replied Sicano, looking intently at Ryder. "We agreed to help these guys." He swivelled to the Israelis then back again. "But, your call, Frank," he said, eyes boring into Ryder.

Ryder looked inquiringly at Brady and Kellar.

Brady responded first. "The choice has already been made. I'm staying."

Followed quickly by Kellar, "Me too."

He agreed; they had not come this far to turn back. Nodding towards the Israelis he said, "So be it. We head for Iran."

With that he led the group down towards the lake.

Ryder wondered how they could have tracked back into Iraq; local area maps taken from the hijacked patrol did not go this far south so the GPS had proved little help. However, his geographic knowledge told him that the Iran border must be somewhere not far beyond this lake. They moved on down to lower ground along the western side where they sought cover amongst bush on a narrow plateau overlooking the water. Below, between themselves and the lake, a road ran north-south parallel with the shore.

Focusing binoculars, Ryder scanned the scattered trees on the slopes that met the shoreline and then swept along a tongue of land jutting out into the water, half a mile to the right. At the end of the tongue he could make out a jetty, alongside which lay two grey-painted vessels. He passed the glasses to Brady, "Gunboats?"

The American scanned the sleek grey vessels, and a few moments later turned to the Iranians, "Gunboats – on a lake?"

Fehed replied, "Iraq and Iran jointly patrol the lake. The Iraqis cover the most; the Iranians: the eastern arm."

"Why?" shot Sicano.

"Keeping track of insurgents, but smugglers mainly – drugs, people. It is easier and quicker to transport large quantities of opium from Afghanistan and humans between Iraq and Iran by water than through the mountains. Both sides tend to be less than strict about policing. It's the insurgents the Iraqis are interested in; the Iranians: smugglers."

"How near are we to the border?" Ryder asked.

"About eighteen miles down the eastern arm, over there." Fehed pointed to a wide gap in the shoreline almost opposite. "The arm ends just outside the Iranian border. The main lake runs roughly north-south for about twenty miles; the average width of the arm is about two miles."

"Can we reach the border without crossing the lake?" he pressed.

"Yes, but we will have to cross either the fast-flowing Diyala River about fifteen miles to the south, or go back the way we came and go over the top."

Ryder indicated to the Israelis and Americans to follow him out of earshot. "We have to cross that stretch of water – hijack one of those boats; it's the quickest way into Iran." To go back up and around the top of the lake, or cross another river, did not exactly appeal to him.

"I agree," said Shiron, without hesitation. "We should ditch the Iranians here," he added.

"We need them," Ryder replied, quietly. "More equipment – ammo, weapons – can be carried by eleven. No telling what we'll need if we find what you're looking for."

"What about the injured one?" Hellmann asked.

"A problem, but we'll manage. He's still good to handle an AK. We're not leaving him, if that's what you're thinking." Ryder would rather put the man out of his misery than leave him to the mercy of the Iranians. "We stay here until dark before moving to the boats," he concluded.

They returned to the huddled Iranians where Ryder quickly explained the plan. He moved to where Qatak lay, tended by Afari. He was concerned how she was managing. What they were experiencing was difficult even for people trained for this kind of thing; but she seemed to be coping. He could not help but admire her fortitude.

"You did well on the arm. Where did you learn?" he asked, curious.

98

"Father was a surgeon. I read his manuals."

"You mean that was a first?" he said incredulously.

She nodded.

His admiration went up another notch.

"You said your parents were killed by the regime. What happened?"

She turned away, hand raised to her mouth. Several seconds later she swung back and levelled tear-filled eyes at Ryder then said bitterly, "Murdered by Pasdaran thugs – beaten to death."

"Can you tell me the reason?"

She looked at him in a way that indicated she was unsure she should tell him and looked away again. He sensed she wanted to talk.

He waited and moments later she whispered, "Accused of plotting to assassinate a high ranker in the IRGC."

He had briefly come across the Pasdaran in Tehran when setting up MI6 cells; they belonged to Iran's Islamic Revolutionary Guards Corps (IRGC) and were the custodians of its economy, its nuclear programme and for the protection and proliferation of the Islamic way of life. They were worse than the VEVAK when it came to brutality.

"And were they?" he asked gently.

"No, the IRGC wanted my father dead and they did not want a trial. The MEK found out that he and my mother were killed in America by Qod agents when attending a medical conference. The killing was made to look like a mugging so anyone in Iran could not be blamed," she replied, on the verge of tears again. Then defiantly, "But I've had my revenge in a way and will continue to do so, God willing," she finished.

Qod Force, Ryder knew, was the IRGC's overseas operations branch – Iran's equivalent to MI6.

"How did they treat you in prison?"

She looked at him blankly, raised hand to her mouth, stifling a cry, then turned away and proceeded to make Qatak comfortable.

He wondered if he had pushed her too far; better to leave it. He made to move away but she stopped him with a hand on one arm.

Without a word, she removed her heavy jacket and rolled up her shirtsleeves and trouser bottoms to reveal massive bruising to both her arms and legs. "You can imagine what the rest looks like; these were not caused by the earthquake… " She stared out over the lake, then after a moment or two, said in almost a whisper, "I was abused in every way, but never gave them what they wanted."

"For how long?" he asked, shocked at the extent of her bruising; it was worse than his own.

She then broke down and quietly sobbed.

He gently placed an arm around her and drew her towards him in an attempt to console but she pulled away, wiping the tears, "Several weeks… I would not have lasted another," again a soft sob. "I was prepared to die. I prayed so much to die. Thank God for the earthquake. Thank God providence has given me another chance at revenge."

She buried her head in her hands. He wanted to hold her, to comfort her but he could see she was distraught enough that no amount of consoling would help.

She turned back to Qatak and began to check his wound.

The conversation was over. Ryder understood and returned to the others.

Eventually twilight approached and they began to stir when Hellmann, on watch, suddenly shouted and pointed to the hills behind. In the fading light, less than 300 yards away amongst scrub and rock, a line of armed men descended towards them; how many could not be determined. Were they Iraqis, terrorists, Iranians? Ryder was not about to hang around to find out.

"MOVE! MOVE!" he shouted, grabbing weapon and gear.

Instantly, everyone swept up rifles and packs and scrambled frantically down the slope towards the lake as bullets began whining and ricocheting all around them.

Halfway down, Ryder feared the attackers were too close and, together with the Americans and Israelis, turned and fired rapidly forcing the pursuers to dive for cover giving the others time to widen the gap. From behind his rock cover he guessed, from the extent and source of the return firing, that probably only several were in pursuit.

Looking to see the Iranians were well down the slope, he ordered a retreat continuing to spray lead into the darkened ground above. Once they were clear he hoped to get some distance before the pursuers realised they had bolted. Finally at the bottom of the slope they breathlessly regrouped amongst the bush and trees.

Regaining his breath, Ryder ordered, "You five," he pointed at the three Americans and the two Israelis, "stay here and fight a rear guard. I've had experience with gunboats; I'll race ahead and hopefully get one of those boats ready to go."

"We'll all be in deep shit if you don't," shot Sicano.

Ryder ignored the American and turned to Afari and the other four Iranians. "You all come with me – move!"

Reaching the jetty they raced along the 200-foot long timber structure out towards the boats silhouetted at the end against the silvery gleam of the moon-bathed waters. Ryder selected the boat to the left and prayed it had enough fuel to get across the lake. They all leapt aboard, Qatak helped by Afari.

Whilst the others scrambled about the boat, Ryder headed straight for the bridge where he hurriedly checked the instruments, relieved to see the fuel gauge reading half full. Although the gunboat was old and Russian, it was in surprisingly good condition and he was confident he could handle her.

Tariq entered the cabin, diverted Ryder's attention away from the instruments, and pointed out towards the darkened horizon. In the distance, skimming over the water, he saw two powerful gunboats converging towards the jetty almost 100 yards apart on the port side. His heart sank; they had to get away soon or be blown out of the water.

Qatak had seen the two approaching vessels, too. Reaching for the nearest machine pistol with his good arm, he rushed to the side of the gunboat, jumped the short distance down to the jetty, and ran back towards the land.

In the bush and rock where the jetty met land, the rear guard kept the pursuers at bay. Qatak joined them and screamed for all to make for the boat; he would give cover.

Brady refused, until in desperation, the little Iranian tore away the folds from his arm and thrust the stump into the American's face.

Brady winced, the elbow joint was raw and bloody, puss oozing from the burnt, rotting flesh.

He looked at Qatak's pleading eyes, glanced at the others blasting away into the surrounding trees and without wasting another moment handed the Iranian his last magazine, telling the others to do the same. Then he, Sicano, Kellar and the two Israelis broke cover and ran as fast as their legs would carry them, zigzagging along the jetty towards the boats.

Reaching the gunboat breathless, but in one piece, the five men scrambled on board as bullets began to ricochet off the superstructure. Shadowy figures began to emerge from the darkness and run along the jetty. The Iranian had held them off just long enough and no doubt paid the ultimate price.

Brady quickly joined Ryder on the bridge as he opened the throttle; the throaty roar of the 2000 bhp diesels drowning out everything else.

"Hope you know how to drive this fucking baby?" shouted the American over the noise as they surged away from the jetty.

Ryder ignored him, concentrating on keeping the boat steady and watching the oncoming crafts. No point and no time to tell the American he'd had some experience of this type of craft training with the SBS (Special Boat Services).

In the meantime, Sicano and Kellar in the stern, reached for grenades, pulled the pins and hurled them as hard as they could at the other quickly receding moored vessel. Seconds later, one exploded on the bridge and the other ripped up the end of the jetty.

The stubby grey gunboat, visually similar to the classic Second World War British Royal Navy Vosper, but without torpedo tubes or depth charges, skimmed out over the darkening waters at twenty-five knots straight towards the lake's eastern arm leading to the Iranian border. Mounted in front of the bridge, a pair of 20mm cannons pointed towards the night sky, and on the stern, a 75mm gun sat squat and menacing behind its metal shield. Attached to the starboard side of the bridge an inflatable rubber raft, protected by a metal casing, banged hard against the superstructure to the bouncing rhythm of the powerful launch.

Brady, beside Ryder, trained glasses on the fast approaching identical gunboats bearing down on the port bow, powerful searchlights skimming the waters. A minute or two more and they would be in range of the guns on the pursuing craft and could expect the first salvos.

Sicano frantically checked out the cannon situated in the bow and fed in an ammunition belt whilst Kellar hurriedly primed and loaded the gun in the stern. In the small forward cabin, under the bridge, the rest of the men, except Hellmann tending the engines, searched for food and anything else that could be of use.

Ryder cursed a full moon illuminating the lake. Instead of losing themselves under cover of darkness they had no choice now but to try and outrun the pursuers.

Each of the closing vessels had turned off searchlights in preparation for action, and at approximately 1,500 yards, the two dark shapes veered away from each other to mount a two-pronged attack.

Ryder swore under his breath. He looked at the approaching craft now within range, felt the adrenaline pumping, and opened the throttle full out, at the same time shouting at Kellar to open fire with the 75mm stern gun.

The gun boomed and seconds later a small column of water

spouted up in front of the nearest vessel approaching on the port quarter. Almost instantly the gunboat on the port beam opened fire, sending a shell whistling overhead to explode in the water astern.

At less than 1,000 yards the craft coming straight for them on the port beam veered a few degrees, enabling her to use the gun in the stern; but before she could open fire, Kellar sent another shell over and scored a direct hit midships, destroying the bridge. The men cheered; one down and one to go. Ryder could hardly believe their luck.

A shell from the remaining gunboat landed just in front of the bows, drenching Sicano and the bridge. Ryder instinctively swung hard to starboard and then back again to port. The other gunboat, veering to port at the same time, now lay directly in their path.

With the stern gun unable to fire forward, Sicano raked the launch with cannon. Tracers found their target and he kept on firing until the boat turned away.

At that moment the disabled gunboat, wallowing astern, blew up with one tremendous roar, illuminating the whole scene and showering debris over the water.

Now on the port bow the remaining boat swung wide and came again, this time bearing down on the port beam, firing rapidly.

The water around Ryder's fast-moving vessel erupted every twenty to thirty seconds, and cannon shells and tracers strafed the port hull with relentless ease.

Suddenly a blinding flash, followed by a loud crack, and the boat lurched violently to starboard. When the smoke cleared the dazed men on deck picked themselves up and saw that a hit had been received midships completely wiping out the cannon. Miraculously, Sicano was unhurt and no one else had been injured.

Ryder quickly regained control and brought the craft round until the stern faced the pursuing gunboat; this reduced the vessel's profile and made it impossible for the following boat to use its stern gun, although cannon kept hammering away. They were now well into the waters of the eastern arm.

Suddenly, two white flares from the shore burst overhead, illuminating the sky and the two boats locked in mortal combat on the smooth silvery waters below.

The pursuing craft saw her advantage and swung to port, at the same time rapidly firing the gun in her stern. Ryder immediately veered to starboard, managing to maintain the distance, and the awkward firing angle between them, but not for long. The crew of the gunboat handled the launch well, gradually reduced the gap and kept firing no matter how hard he tried to evade and stay on their bow.

Ryder willed Kellar to score another hit before it was too late. If the pursuing boat got ahead the only remaining gun would be useless and they could be picked off at will.

The cannon fire on the port side was now so intense the men sought cover below deck or on the starboard side, cockpit and superstructure providing protection. Ryder guided the boat by secondary controls forward of the bridge. Kellar remained at the stern gun keeping within the protection of the 75mm's shield.

A shell hit the steel mast carrying the communications antenna and radar scanners, exploded and sent two-thirds crashing down onto the port side, midships. There it hung at 60 degrees, not quite severed and causing a definite list; the tip, which had bent on impact, cutting the water and greatly reducing the gunboat's speed.

The flares died but were quickly replaced by two more, bursting low in the space between the two boats.

Ryder came out of a sharp turn to port and swung immediately back again to starboard just as Kellar rammed home another shell and pulled the trigger.

A column of white water spouted up immediately in front of the bow of the attacking craft, now abreast on the port beam. Seconds later, an orange flash engulfed the bow and the whole boat seemed to rise right out of the water and crash back down again, before veering sharply away to port to abruptly stop, bow partly submerged.

Everyone cheered and those below came up on deck relieved at the sight of the stricken boat now well astern.

More flares burst overhead.

The whole situation was fraught with danger.

Fehed yelled at Ryder. "The lake, it's under radar scan; every move we make is monitored – they'll be waiting for us the moment we land. Soon Iranian gunboats will arrive!"

Suddenly, the sound of tortured metal rent the air as the broken section of mast separated away from the base and crashed over the side, causing the boat to surge rapidly forward, freed from the drag.

Everyone went below, except Kellar who remained at the gun in the stern. Ryder continued to steer at maximum knots down the eastward arm using auxiliary controls, keeping the gunboat in the middle of the two-mile-wide stretch of water.

The Americans and Israelis studied the shoreline maps as best they could in the bouncing vessel and dim red light of the forward cockpit, concerned what would happen once they reached the end of the lake. Brady turned to Ryder crouched over the controls. "A few more miles and we should abandon close to the south shore," he shouted above the roar, pointing at the same time to the dark shoreline on the starboard side.

"I'll reduce speed as much as we dare," Ryder shot back. "Set the controls and send her the rest of the way down the lake after we go over the side in the inflatable. Hopefully, they'll think we're still on board."

"The flares – they'll see us," was Brady's frantic reply.

"We'll go between flares – no choice."

Ryder focused back on the controls; he too had been worrying what would happen once they ran out of fuel – it was getting low. Immediately, he gave orders to check if the inflatable on the starboard side had avoided damage, praying it had as the attacking boats had been to port nearly all of the time.

Brady came back shortly with the good news that it was still intact; the central cockpit structure and a metal security casing had protected the inflatable from direct pounding and from flying metal. Relieved, Ryder ordered him and Kellar to make it ready and prepare to abandon ship at the first opportunity. This they quickly did by removing the casing and unhooking the black rubber raft from its frame and securing flat to the deck before retreating below to retrieve the outboard motor.

Back on deck they fixed the outboard in place and skilfully lowered the inflatable over the side securing it to the bouncing gunboat with ropes. Minutes later, within several hundred yards of the shore and at half throttle, the gunboat rounded a promontory and the flares suddenly stopped. With only moonlight now bathing the waters, this was their chance and Ryder did not hesitate. Reducing speed to eight knots, he ordered everyone on deck to abandon. Despite the low rate of knots it was a dangerous manoeuvre, even for those well practised. As they began to clamber in under the shadow of its hull, Saad, the last, suddenly slipped on the gunnel and fell into the turbulent water but was quickly grabbed and pulled out by Tariq and Fehed before he fully went under.

Meanwhile, Ryder, praying the flares would hold off a little longer, jammed the wheel in place with a metal crowbar to send the vessel straight up the lake, opened the throttle and made a mad dash from the cockpit. Out on deck, as the gunboat rapidly gathered speed, he leapt into the bouncing inflatable to only just clear the gunnel and almost capsize the raft before landing sprawled headlong amongst its occupants. Kellar hurriedly cut the rope securing the raft to the bow and Shiron did the same at the stern. Brady then opened the outboard throttle and steered straight towards the shore, now less than 400 yards away. The black silhouette of the gunboat raced away across the waters and more flares began to burst overhead, illuminating the speeding vessel. Ryder hoped it would be well down the lake before the fuel ran out and hoped those scanning the waters would be fooled into thinking they were still on board.

In the relative darkness outside the light thrown by the flares, they reached the shore, slid into the shallows and dragged the raft over gravelled ground to hide amongst thick bush. Then, with one last look at the empty gunboat in the distance, still surging its way down the lake, they struck out south-east into the rolling foothills of the Zagros Mountains, towards what Ryder hoped was the Iranian border.

13

Mist clung heavily to the trees and shrubs, undisturbed by a gentle breeze. Ryder hoped for more snow, but the sun rose high in a clear sky removing that possibility. For three days after leaving the lake they had trudged almost non-stop through forested hills and over rocky, snow-swept terrain. According to the GPS, together with using manual calculations, Ryder determined they were some forty miles inside Iran, heading south-east at altitudes varying from 3,000 to 5,000 feet above sea level. The terrain reminded him of the Brecon Beacons where he'd spent many hours training carrying heavy packs; this was a lot easier, but infinitely more dangerous. The Americans and Israelis seemed to be coping well with the extreme conditions, too, but he could see the strain was beginning to tell on the Iranians, especially Afari. Periodic sleet and high winds had increased the wind chill factor and despite all being adequately clothed, Ryder was concerned hypothermia could soon become their main enemy. Fortunately, shelters so far had protected them from the elements, but food had run low, leaving only what remained of the deer to chew. In these barren hills and steppes game appeared scarce and Ryder wondered how they would replenish what little they had. Unless they could maintain a supply of food their chances of survival were slim.

Since escaping the earthquake, they had been on the run now for fifteen days, travelling more than 250 miles averaging some sixteen miles a day. That was a good tab given the circumstances and Ryder hoped it could be maintained or even bettered. It was a small miracle they were still going after the condition they were in when the truck crashed and from what they had suffered under their captors. The stress of the journey so far had certainly sharpened him both mentally and physically; the damage to his body now mostly healed. Should they succeed and return safely he could at least retain some semblance of respect in that he had helped the Israelis to attain their goal. He wondered how long it would be before the four remaining Iranians, especially Afari, dropped off the gruelling pace and what their reaction would be once they realised the Gulf was not the objective. However, the longer they held on, the better. The more firepower available, the more chance there was of success.

Cresting a narrow ridge, the group began to descend into yet another valley when Ryder suddenly called a halt, pointing to a hut nestled amongst thick bush and scrub, 300 yards down the slope. He could just make out the circular earthen structure, easily missed had it not been for the wispy smoke spiralling from the centre of the dome.

"Dwelling?" questioned Shiron.

"Yeah, and that means food," Kellar replied.

Ryder didn't hesitate, ordering Saad and Tariq to go down and scrounge as much food as they could while the rest waited.

When the two men were within fifty yards of the dwelling, four large dogs came bounding out, followed by several men and a handful of children. After a brief exchange of greetings they were led inside.

Five tension-filled minutes passed before the two came out again, each carrying a small bundle, and made their way back up the slope.

"Did the best we could," said Tariq on reaching them, a little out of breath. "Some cheese, grain cakes, but that's it. Plenty of mouths to feed in there, including goats."

"What about a goat?" Ryder asked.

"No. We tried everything. They're Luri shepherds and the few in the pen are all they have left for winter. They'd probably let you have their women before the goats."

"Hey, make a deal pronto," Kellar quipped.

"If you saw the women, you'll probably prefer the goats," said Saad.

Afari threw him a withering look.

"We have enough meat for one more day, and that's it," Sicano announced.

"Then I say we go down and grab us a goat," shot Shiron.

"They have rifles. They would use them if they had to," said Tariq.

"Okay, we'll take one," Ryder said firmly, "we need a diversion to get everyone away and move in. Anyone butchered goat before?"

Tariq and Saad said they had.

Ryder turned to Brady. "We'll go with them. The rest of you will make noise over there," he pointed to the open ground sweeping away from the dwelling. "We'll manoeuvre round behind the dwelling and when the time is right, move in. You two," he glanced at Tariq and Saad, "grab the first goat you can lay hands on and get out fast. If anybody is still inside, no killing; silence, yes, but no killing. We want to be in and out quickly and without problems. Is that understood?"

Tariq and Saad nodded they understood.

"Good! Let's do it."

Ryder watched until the others were well down the slope before he, Brady and the two Iranians slipped silently away to the right under cover of bush, along a trench-like depression, arriving minutes later behind the dwelling. From here they could see and hear the others shouting and rolling in the dirt and patchy snow making a great deal of noise in the process.

Men, women, children and dogs burst from the dwelling and ran frantically towards the sound. Ryder waited until the Luris were well away from the dwelling then leapt up and rushed for the entrance.

The stench inside stung his nostrils, but eyes quickly adjusted to the gloom to see goats milling around in the open pen at the rear of the half-circular compartment.

Tariq together with Saad, lunged forward and fell determinedly amongst the bobbing, bleating beasts. Within moments Tariq waylaid a white billy, threw it over his shoulder and made for the entrance followed by Ryder and the others.

Suddenly Brady gave a cry of alarm.

Not 10 feet away stood an old man, propped against the door to an adjoining compartment, rifle levelled directly at Brady's chest.

A split second later the gun went off. Brady was thrown violently backwards and crashed heavily to the floor.

Panic gripped as the old man fumbled desperately to inject another bullet into the chamber of the .303.

Before anyone could react he swung the rifle up again.

In one swift movement, Ryder raised the rifle slung around his neck and fired.

The old Luri staggered backwards, a bullet between the eyes, and crumpled to the floor.

Sweeping Brady over his shoulder, Ryder hurriedly rushed for the entrance, staggered out and ran on up the hill, hotly pursued by the Luris alerted by the gunfire, themselves being chased by Kellar and the rest. The dogs jumped and barked loudly around the Luris, thinking the whole thing was a game. Catching up with the shepherds, Kellar forced them at gunpoint back to the dwelling.

At the ridge, Ryder gently laid the sergeant down and fell to the ground gasping. The American was bleeding badly and Afari did her best to staunch the flow using bunched cloth pressed tightly against the wound.

The rest arrived.

"What happened?" Kellar growled, looking at the mess that was Brady's right shoulder.

Ryder quickly explained.

"How bad is it?"

"Looks bad but only a flesh wound, bleeding heavily," Afari replied.

"Can he be moved?" Ryder asked, concerned at the need to get away quickly; the shooting would undoubtedly bring others.

Whilst Afari tended the American, Tariq quickly sliced the throat of the bleating, struggling goat and hung it on a nearby tree branch to bleed out.

Brady struggled to get up. "Put more pressure on the wound," he winced, "I'll be okay. Help me up. We can't hang around, for sure."

Afari applied more cloth and pressure to the wound and then put the arm in a makeshift sling before helping the American to his feet. But he was shaky.

Ryder turned to Kellar. "Can you carry him?"

The big American nodded.

"Okay, let's move," ordered a relieved Ryder.

With Brady slung across Kellar's shoulder and the goat on Tariq's they fled the ridge, Ryder acutely aware that distance was necessary for as long as strength permitted.

★ ★ ★

In the remote highlands, Ryder led the others in single file, trudging relentlessly through the scrub, tussock and stands of firs, negotiating slopes strewn with rocky outcrops and narrow, rippling streams. The goat was gutted and butchered at the first opportunity and the meat shared out equally. They covered many miles without encountering a single soul, not daring to remain long in one place to rest in the daylight hours and travelling only at night. Despite the hardship of the terrain they maintained a steady pace and Brady, after the second day, could thankfully manage unaided; his wound improving with the careful attention of Afari using lichen with medicinal qualities to stop infection, learnt from her father. The men looked like a bunch of brigands with weapons, scruffy, ill-fitting clothes and stubbly beards.

On the third day out from the Luri hut they came to a black tarsealed road that snaked through the centre of a narrow valley they would have to cross if to maintain a south-westerly direction. It was the first sign of civilization since the hut. In the distance could be seen a truck and a car travelling away from their position.

"Looks fairly new with those white line markings – even has crash barriers," said Sicano.

"Pretty open down there too," said Kellar. "If we're gonna cross, maybe we should wait till nightfall?"

It was early afternoon; Ryder didn't want to hang around that long. The two vehicles had vanished over the horizon and the straight road as far as the eye could see both ways was empty, although it did sweep behind a prominent bluff in the distance to their right. "No, we'll take our chances and cross now."

With that they followed Ryder down the slope.

When they were less than thirty yards from the road a truck suddenly swept round the bluff followed by another, then another. Although well in the distance on the straight road, those driving the front vehicle would easily see the group if they attempted to cross or tried to run for what little cover there was.

Ryder immediately fell to the ground and crawled to a shallow depression with the rest hard on his heels. The dip, thankfully deep enough, with clumps of tussock at the base and on the rim, gave at least some form of cover several yards away from the road. He slowly popped his head up between the long grass and, using binoculars, scanned the oncoming trucks. "Fuck. Military," he said, more to himself than to the others.

"How many?" shot Shiron.

"Three big bastards."

"Carrying troops?"

"Maybe, can't tell."

The Israeli swept his glasses over the trucks and moments later, "Definitely troop carriers."

Oh, shit. Ryder turned to the Americans. "If we're spotted, it's all over."

"What the fuck are troops doing in this remote area?" Kellar asked.

"Military exercise maybe?" offered Sicano.

"In these remote mountains?" questioned Shiron.

Ryder now clearly heard the roar of the diesels. "Maybe they're here to hunt us down?"

"No, I don't think so," said Fehed, "we are still not that far away from the Iraqi border. This road would frequently be used by the military. As you have seen for yourselves the region is rugged and roads are few and far between, using these highways is the only way to move troops and equipment fast between centres. They could be heading anywhere up north."

Ryder hoped he was right; he was about find out. "Okay, here they come. Keep close together; hug the ground." He prayed they would merge in with the mottled colours of the earth and tussock and that those in the vehicles would not be paying too much attention to the immediate surrounding land.

A thundering roar as the first of the three trucks came level to where they lay. Ryder gripped the butt of his rifle and awaited the sound of screeching brakes; it never came. The second truck swept by, then the third much to his relief. Ryder waited until the last had disappeared and all was clear before he stood and, with the rest, made a dash across the road, not stopping until they were well into the trees on the rising ground almost at the other side of the valley.

Twenty-four hours and some twelve miles later, after spending most of the darkness hours sleeping, another obstacle presented itself: a narrow bridge, some seventy-five yards long, spanning a deep gorge and guarded by troops on the far side. From a vantage point overlooking, Ryder scanned the metal structure and in particular the small complex of huts and a guardhouse on the far side.

"Why guard the bridge?" Kellar asked.

Fehed replied, "Because it is the only bridge going north from the military airfield at Dezful, and a likely target for insurgents. MEK have tried twice without success, as you can see."

"How far does the gorge run?" Ryder asked, hoping they might avoid crossing.

"Many miles," said Saad.

Ryder lifted the glasses and scanned the gorge both ways for as far as he could see; no likely crossing points, nothing obvious anyway. He swung back to focus on the buildings where the guards were. Two timber sheds, sat on a flat section of land beside the road with smoke coming from a central chimney, filled the lenses. Two canvas-covered army trucks sat behind the buildings and several soldiers could be seen milling around. Moving to the right he settled on a small guardhouse by the bridge with a lifting barrier where two soldiers in greatcoats stood watching the road. Pointing towards the buildings he asked Shiron, "What d'you make of those?"

"Bunk houses. Could house maybe fifteen to twenty men, and that guardhouse is probably manned every hour of the day and night."

"Won't be easy getting past that many," said Sicano. "Maybe we should look for another way."

"The gorge both ways is pretty steep and rugged as far as I can tell," said Ryder. "My guess is we'll have to travel miles out of our way over difficult ground to find one."

"We should cross the bridge," said Kellar.

Ryder, after viewing the ruggedness of the gorge, was now resigned to taking the bridge. He looked at the others, "What do you think?"

Everyone, except Sicano, agreed the bridge, although more than risky, was the only practical option.

Through the binoculars, Ryder studied the trestlework of steel girders supporting the bridge and in particular the guardhouse and its proximity to the structure.

"We have two choices," he eventually said. "Either cross under the bridge through the trestlework, or wait until nightfall to cross on top and take out the guards."

"Both very chancy; the second even more so," said Shiron.

"If those guards see us before we get close enough we'll be sitting targets," Sicano said, looking intensely at Ryder, sharp features blunted by shaggy black beard.

Another thought struck Ryder, "Maybe we don't need to all cross together." He paused to think clearly, "Maybe me, you, Sergeant," he glanced at Shiron, "and you," turning to Kellar, "can cross through the trestlework when dark, take out the guards, then the rest of you can cross on the top." He waited expectantly for a response, but silence prevailed.

Then, "Tricky, attempting the steelwork," said Shiron.

"There is another way," offered Sicano. "We could wait for a convoy going south and take out the last vehicle on the bend down there," he pointed to where the road curved at almost 90 degrees around the outcrop below.

"Could work if the convoy was well spread," said Hellmann.

"If successful we could stay with the convoy until safe to ditch, maybe thirty to forty miles further south-east – travelling fast and in relative comfort," Sicano pressed.

Good option, thought Ryder. "Worth a try, but if nothing comes before nightfall we cross on the girders and take out the guards." He hoped a convoy would come along soon. That settled, the group slipped down to the roadside and waited in the cover of a ditch below the level of the tarsealed surface.

The day drew on with not a sign of any vehicle until eventually the shadows grew long and finally dusk fell.

Ryder raised binoculars and focused on the bridge guardhouse for the last time in the fading light. From his position in the ditch he could see one guard standing stamping his feet by the barrier and another through the glass-fronted structure. He then ran the glasses over what he could see of the bridge structure itself, and shuddered at the thought of clambering through the myriad of angled girders in the dark some 100 feet above the narrow river that ran at the bottom. In another half hour he would have to make the attempt.

The minutes ticked by and full darkness fell.

"Okay, the bridge it is," he said finally.

"Wait another fifteen minutes," said Sicano.

"We're going now," Ryder growled, tired of the cold ditch and not wanting to hang around any longer. "It'll take time to get through that maze of girders. If the opportunity comes in the form of a truck and you think you can take it then be my guest. If you get by the guards, wait for us somewhere along the road on the other side. We'll find you." He paused, waiting for a response, none came so he continued, "If you're still here when we get to the other side, watch for my signal, I'll walk to the barrier and wave then you cross the bridge as quickly as you can." He turned to Shiron and Kellar, "Take only pistol and knife, we need to be light shifting through that structure." Then to the rest, "Take our packs."

With that he led the Israeli and the American crawling along the ditch until they reached the steel stanchions supporting the main trusses at the beginning of the bridge. Swinging up on to the bottom chord of the outside truss that clear-spanned to the other side, terminating next to the guardhouse, the three men edged their way gingerly along the steelwork using the bracing between the main uprights and cross-struts to maintain balance and avoid plunging to the rocks below. A cold wind whistled through the steelwork. Ryder felt its bite, but he dared not relax his grip. With fingers numb he grimly felt his way forward along the narrow, slippery metal.

Suddenly, halfway across, a gasp; Ryder turned in time to see Shiron, several steps behind, fall, fling out his arms and wrap them around a metal strut that angled out to the centre of the bridge. In sheer desperation he hung there; eyes full of fear. Kellar, a few feet back, tried to reach him, slipped himself and he too almost fell in the process.

Ryder edged back, reached the T-shaped strut, and with one arm anchored around a cross-brace leant outward as far as he could and grasped the Israeli's nearest wrist with an iron-like grip. He pulled Shiron slowly down the strut towards the base of the main truss until he was able to hoist the Israeli, with some difficulty, back upright again on the bottom chord. Shiron held on to the metalwork for a moment, controlling his fear before the three continued on.

Ryder reached the other side fired up with adrenaline and ready to take out the guards. Having not heard the rumble of vehicles on the structure whilst clambering through the bridge girders, he assumed the others would now be moving up ready to cross on foot.

He emerged from the steelwork maze leading the other two and clambered up the short rock incline until all three lay on a ledge just below the level of the guardhouse. Ryder could see a soldier by the barrier, AK slung over his shoulder, and the head and shoulders of another inside the guardhouse itself. He signalled for Kellar to deal with the guard at the barrier whilst he and Shiron would take the other.

In the darkness, with the sound of wind gusting around the buildings nearby, Ryder and the Israeli left the ledge shortly after Kellar, covered the few yards' separation from the guardhouse and crept stealthily towards the rear entrance. Kellar, in the meantime, had headed for the barrier, concealing himself behind the bridge parapet only a few feet away from the guard but out of sight of the other. He would wait for Ryder to make the first move.

At the door, Ryder knocked with knife handle and placed his back hard up against the side wall. Shiron did the same opposite.

A shout from inside, the sound of boots on a timber floor and the door opened. A large, heavy-set man poked his head out on a long neck but before he could utter a word, Ryder, with one powerful sweep upwards, sunk the knife deep into the guard's throat severing the trachea and larynx, stifling any sound, before withdrawing it swiftly as he fell. Shiron caught him, lowered the twitching body to the ground, rolled it to the edge of the gorge and pushed it over.

Kellar watched the guard in the hut move out of sight and guessed Ryder was about to make his move. The other guard by the lowered barrier, back to parapet, stamped his feet to combat the cold. The American silently waited for several seconds with knife gripped firmly in his right hand, then leapt, placing left hand firmly over the guard's mouth before plunging the 8-inch steel blade under the man's shoulder and upwards deep into his heart. The soldier died instantly and without a sound. Dragging the body the short distance to the edge of the gorge, he tipped it over.

Ryder and Shiron joined Kellar at the barrier. Ryder signalled to the others concealed in the ditch on the far side of the bridge. They emerged one by one and began to hurriedly cross, arriving minutes later at the barrier. Snow flurries swirled as the group made their way silently towards the main building. Light emanated through small, high-level windows and the strains of Arab music could be heard over the gusting wind. Ryder, closely watching the entrance door and feeling very vulnerable at this point, hoped like hell no one inside would choose this moment to step out. As they passed without mishap and reached the two army trucks he had an idea and called the group into the lee of the nearest vehicle out of sight of the buildings. He spoke to Kellar, "Sergeant, jump in and tell me if you can handle it."

The American opened the cab door and climbed in. Seconds later he came back out and said, "No problem – even has key in the ignition."

Ryder nodded, thankful for small mercies. "Here's what we do, Sergeant," he looked intently at Kellar, "take the wheel; the rest of us will push this fucker and you let it roll." He pointed towards the relatively steep incline of the road running away from the bridge. "Once you're well down and out of earshot, start the engine and we'll clamber aboard." He paused looking at each of the group in turn for any comment; none came. "Okay, let's do it."

Kellar got back into the cab and released the handbrake whilst the rest quietly got behind the Iranian 2.5 ton Neynava army truck and began to push. Slowly, the vehicle edged silently forward, gathering speed, and rolled from where it was parked out on to the road. Shortly, enough speed was gained to enable it to continue unaided.

A hundred yards further on Kellar applied the brakes and waited for the others to catch up. Once they all had, Ryder joined the American in the cab and the rest clambered into the rear, settling amongst several timber crates. Kellar brought the diesel to life, slipped the vehicle into gear and pulled away. They had crossed the bridge without cost, but Ryder knew it would not be long before the dead guards would be missed together with the truck. He hoped it would take the remaining guards a little time to work out what had exactly happened, at least enough for the group to put as many miles as possible between themselves and the bridge. Now safely away, the tension eased and he could look forward to travelling the next thirty miles or so in relative comfort, free of the wind and the numbing, biting cold.

14

It was pitch black and sleet fell when Kellar drove the truck off the winding road and into dense scrub. The journey from the bridge had been thankfully free of incident and now, fifty miles further on with tank all but empty, it was time to abandon. The American stopped well away from the road and, together with Ryder, clambered into the rear, where all agreed to stay until dawn. During the journey the crates had been opened to find tinned food, mountain fatigues and, above all, a small cache of weapons and ammunition, including some Semtex with detonators, which they gratefully distributed.

Dawn soon broke to an overcast day and they reluctantly abandoned the warmth of the truck to head single file into the scrub. Ryder, the last to leave, took a final glance at the rear and was about to clamber over the tailboard when his eye caught an object which looked like a piece of folded cloth poking out between one of the boxes and the metal side. Curious, he removed the thin white fabric, unfolded it and was surprised to see wording in Farsi. He read the scribble which briefly described their destination, the reason for going and the names of everyone in the group, but no clue as to the author. Ryder was totally stunned by the discovery, he could hardly believe it: a traitor in their midst? Everything now had been placed in serious jeopardy and everyone, except for that person – or persons – was now threatened by capture; or worse still, death before they ever found the objective. Should he tell?

What effect would this have? It could be any one of them, but surely not an American or one of the Israelis? The thought unnerved him even more. He decided to say nothing for the time being and hoped to try and flush out the culprit. From now on though, he would keep his own council and remain especially vigilant. Pocketing the piece of cloth, he left the truck and quickly caught up with the others, mind in turmoil.

The ground undulated dramatically with a definite slant towards the west, making it difficult to maintain a south-easterly direction. To the left, the central range rose dark and majestic, silhouetted against a pale early-morning sky; a bitter wind cut deep on the exposed ridges and the plateaus they traversed. The column, led by Shiron with Ryder bringing up the rear, kept close together and moved as quickly as legs and the terrain would allow. The punishing pace was maintained throughout the morning and well into the afternoon, moving relentlessly through sparse, rolling foothills with hardly any cover other than a few stands of trees and occasional thick scrub. Brady's flesh wound had improved considerably with the lichen treatment and he now just about managed to keep up fully unaided. To Ryder, though, he was one tough bugger and still needed to be kept an eye on as well as the others. If they did find the objective, despite the traitor, every gun would count.

Shortly before the sun dipped in the west, Shiron stopped and pointed to movement in the valley below. Ryder followed the outstretched arm and saw a file of black dots against the snow, almost a half-mile distant, moving along the valley floor towards them.

"Patrol?" shot Sicano.

"Mountain troops for sure," Ryder snapped. "Okay, MOVE," he ordered, putting himself in the lead and Shiron at the rear. He headed away from the patrol, keeping up a fast pace until darkness had fully descended before deciding it was safe to camp for the night in dense scrub. A fire was not lit and they spoke little, grateful to rest weary bodies, chew on raw meat and get as much rest as they could before daylight arrived. The watch was agreed. Ryder's turn would be the last so he found a spot where everyone could be seen, including those on watch. Eventually, tiredness overcame him and he reluctantly nodded off into a light, fitful sleep.

The night passed without event. At first light the group, in single file, headed out south-east led by Shiron with Ryder in the rear to watch the others, glad to be once more on the move. They kept close together, meandering through the rocky outcrops on the thinly wooded ridge before descending again into yet another valley. The Iranians kept up the pace, although now and then, Afari was offered a hand by Ryder when negotiating the outcrops which she promptly refused.

They had covered no more than a mile when suddenly, as the grey light of dawn began to filter through low cloud, a shot rang out, followed shortly by several more; bullets spurting up the ground about them.

Tariq coughed, staggered forward and fell face down into the dirt, a gaping hole at the back of his head.

Everyone scrambled desperately for cover, returning fire randomly as more bullets ricocheted off the surrounding rocks and trees.

Shiron worked his way back until beside Ryder. With field glasses, Ryder quickly scanned the slopes above, both to locate the attackers and also to make sure he knew where each of the others were in case the traitor thought it was a good opportunity to take a few out.

"How many?" the Israeli asked, eyes darting from rock to rock scattered between the clumps of trees.

"Several. Probably the patrol we saw," he replied, sweeping the slope and seeing a soldier with a radio transmitter on his back suddenly move behind a rock 100 yards to his left. Letting glasses fall, Ryder swung his rifle into a firing position and lined up the rock, waiting for the man to reappear.

Seconds later he did. Ryder squeezed the trigger; the soldier spun and staggered a few paces before crumbling face down onto the open ground.

Shiron then frantically sprayed the huddled heap.

"He's dead! He's dead!" Ryder shouted above the staccato of fire, pushing down the muzzle of the Israeli's gun. "Don't waste ammo!"

Shiron stopped and turned, eyes burning into Ryder. "Making sure that transmitter's fucked. Don't want anybody giving our position away, now do we?"

The way he said that, Ryder wondered if the Israeli knew about the traitor.

All around, the others were returning fire in short, sharp bursts each time they saw movement amongst the scrub and rock above, the sound reverberating loudly down the valley.

They held their position with some difficulty as the patrol tried to outflank them. Ryder ordered an immediate withdrawal to counter the move and the group, firing blindly, scrambled for new cover, at the same time keeping the patrol at bay.

A cry of pain and another Iranian soldier pitched forward.

A burst of fire from Kellar dropped two more. They now had the advantage and Ryder ordered them to spread out and attack.

Shortly, two more died, staggering out from their rocky cover and rolling down the slope before the last soldier surrounded, finally surrendered and stepped out from behind a boulder, hands on head, stumbling forward.

Hellmann dragged him into the centre of the group.

"You searching for us?" shot Shiron in Farsi, staring hard at the man as they enclosed around him.

The soldier stood silently, eyes darting, one man to another, from hardened features. *Definitely Special Forces,* thought Ryder.

"How did they know we were here?" questioned Sicano, turning to the other Americans.

The two Israelis glanced at one another.

Ryder wanted to say: 'the traitor amongst us,' but decided against. He looked for a possible sign, but there was none. "After the bridge they probably put two and two together," he answered.

Shiron put his question again to the soldier, but he remained silent.

"Yeah, but that doesn't explain how they tracked us so fucking accurately. We could've been anywhere in these goddamn hills," said Kellar, looking a little bewildered.

"It seems to me they know what direction we're heading," said Sicano.

"Strange, the way they've kept on our tail," added Brady.

Again Ryder wanted to tell; it was on the tip of his tongue, but he resisted.

The soldier was questioned again – no reply.

"Whatta we do with him?" Kellar shot, voicing the thoughts of the others.

Fehed stepped forward. "Awad was my friend. I will make him talk," he said, and he stuck the barrel of his automatic hard under the soldier's chin.

Fear seared across the soldier's face, eyes pleading. He dropped his arms and blurted out that he did not know, admitting orders were to seek and destroy, but only the patrol leader knew the target.

Bullshit, thought Ryder; they would all have known who they were out to kill. Standard procedure for SF operatives, no matter what country, otherwise only shambles would occur at the time of executing, especially if something happened to the leader.

"Who do you think he was looking for?" shot Sicano.

Features contorted with fear, the soldier cried, "Kurdish insurgents – terrorists!"

"You lie!" Fehed jerked the muzzle harder into the man's throat.

The soldier grunted with pain, looking frantically at Fehed.

Ryder was certain whoever wrote that message had probably left more along the route. This patrol was more than likely the result. Others could be out there right now, tracking. He glanced at the rest. "We'll get nothing out of him."

Everyone agreed.

Shiron questioned the soldier once more, waited, and when he received no reply he turned to Ryder. "Kill him and let's get the fuck away."

The man had to die, but Ryder would have preferred this not to happen under the present circumstances. However, they could not take him prisoner, or leave him behind to give intelligence. Reluctantly he looked at Fehed and nodded.

The soldier continued to plead for his life, knowing he was about to die.

Fehed, without hesitation, pulled the trigger, sending a single 7.62mm bullet into the soldier's throat and up through the skull, blowing most of it away at the back of his head. The man crumbled to the snow, the sound of the shot reverberating through the valley and on through the surrounding hills.

They buried Tariq quickly, and as best they could, removed maps, ammunition and anything else of use from the dead soldiers and left the now useless transmitter shot up by Shiron, much to Ryder's disappointment, before hurriedly making their way along the valley heading south-east. That patrol, and the prospect of others, made Ryder become even more concerned now about the traitor in their midst.

15

Ryder kept his focus at the rear of the single file led by Shiron, as they toiled under a clear azure sky through hilly terrain scattered with stands of trees and tussock some 3,000 feet above sea level. At one point they saw, away in the distance, a narrow black ribbon of road snaking across the white patchy landscape. A few vehicles could be seen but no humans were encountered; they gave the road a wide berth. By late afternoon they came to a large lake on their left between sloping mountains running steeply down to its surface. Ryder's view ahead was blocked by rugged mountainside but to his right he could see a river on a plateau below in the distance.

"Lake Karun," said Afari, walking just in front him. "Reservoir, held back by the Shahid Abbaspour Dam in the narrow gorge on the other side of that." She pointed to the rising ground ahead.

Fuck! Another bloody major obstacle; country's full of rivers, dams and gorges, he thought.

"Need to take a look," he growled and made his way down the slope, followed by the others, to where he could get a view of the dam.

After a short scouring of the sparsely vegetated and rocky landscape, Ryder found a suitable vantage point giving a full view of the dam and its surrounds. From here, concealed in the shade of a boulder outcrop, he focused his glasses on the massive, curved concrete bowl-shaped structure and then the buildings and roadways surrounding below. Vehicles moved on roads sprinkled with a light dusting of snow and people could be seen mingling around the various buildings. On the far side of the dam, three huge concrete spillways plunged some 600 feet down at an angle of 60 degrees to the river, which curved away to the right, with buildings sparsely located on either bank. Further down the river, away in the distance, he could make out two narrow bridges spanning the slow-moving green strip of water. Sweeping glasses towards the narrow crest of the dam he studied the road on top, perhaps 20 feet in width, running the entire length of the curve. At a circular junction-point two-thirds of the way across, the road veered off at a right angle to span the spillways before ending at a concrete wall against the mountain slope on the other side. He swung the glasses back along the top to the side they were on but could not see where it ended due to the slope of mountain blocking his view. The imposing structure rose and connected halfway up the sharply angled mountain and he wondered how access to the dam crest was achieved. Then it dawned – *must be a tunnel!* He turned and focused the glasses on the road behind and below his position. And there it was: a hole in the rock – almost a horizontal slit – where he'd thought the road had petered out. When scanned earlier, this section of mountainside had then been in shadow; now he could clearly see the road disappearing under an overhang which could only mean one thing: a tunnel entrance. Although he was unable to observe an opening in the blind spot on the dam side because of the bulk of the mountain blocking his view, he was more than certain one would be there.

"A tunnel connects to the dam crest from that road down there," he said, more to himself than to the others. Then turning to Saad, the nearest, and handing him the glasses, he pointed to the bridges in the far distance. "Are there any other closer crossings?"

The Iranian quickly scanned and passed the glasses back. "No," then he nodded towards the lake. "That reservoir is one of a series of lakes that form part of the Karun River; no bridges, unless you want to go back well to the north-east."

"Back how far?"

"Thirty – maybe forty miles."

"That'll take us well out of our way," said Shiron, disappointment in his voice. "We must stay in a south-easterly direction."

Ryder ignored him and pointed west beyond the sprawling workshops and power grids on the plain below, "And that way?"

"The nearest crossing is the Karun Number Three Dam, about fifty miles, and close to Masjed Soleiman."

"Masjed Soleiman?" Hellmann asked.

This time Afari answered, "Big town, population around 250,000."

"You sure there is no way to avoid this river and continue south?"

"Not unless you want to backtrack north and cross the Zagros at its highest or go 150 miles west to the Iraqi border," Fehed replied.

After a few moments, "Looks like we'll be taking one of those bridges then," said Ryder, looking towards the river.

"That'll mean having to thread our way through those buildings and people down there to get to the nearest," voiced Sicano. "Look how far away that is; it'll take hours and present enormous risks."

"Nowhere near as risky as the dam," countered Ryder. "What else can anyone suggest?"

Silence except for the wind whistling across the mountain slope.

"Cross on top of the dam; it'll be quicker," offered Kellar.

"And far more dangerous," Ryder shot.

Brady, scanning the dam and the facilities beyond, lowered his glasses and asked Ryder, the two Israelis and the other two Americans to join him out of earshot of the three Iranians. When a short distance away from the cluster of boulders he came out straight with what he had to say. "We came here to blow a dam, why not this one?"

Ryder was taken aback, "With respect, Sergeant—"

"Hey," the American cut in. "Let's not get too formal here; call me Jed."

"Okay, *Jed,* we don't have anywhere near enough punch to take out this dam and you well know it. What little we do have I assumed would be used on this so-called missile base we're sacrificing so fucking much to find."

"Hang fire a minute, Frank. I wasn't referring to the dam itself, but to that power-grid enclosure." He pointed to the other side of the dam. "With what we have at least we can knock out a few pylons and maybe a transformer or two."

"Jed's right," Kellar backed.

Ryder raised his glasses and took a long look, running lenses over a fenced tangle of steel pylons, cables and a number of large transformers just beyond a cluster of single-storey buildings situated above the top level of the spillways. A road, parallel to the power-grid enclosure, was partly cut into the mountainside and terminated alongside the buildings against a concrete parapet wall. The road looked to be about 15 feet higher than the road which spanned the spillways butting into the other side of the parapet.

"If we do enough damage to disrupt the region's power supply, even for a short time," pressed Brady, "that for me would, at least, be some compensation for failing the original mission."

"Yeah, I agree," added Sicano.

Ryder let the glasses drop. He was in two minds. What the American voiced was true but the risks involved crossing the dam and placing charges in the grid enclosure were extremely high; would they be so bold if they knew one of the group was a traitor? Less risk to take the long way to the nearest bridge. But, then again, if they managed to succeed they could at least justify what they had suffered so far would not have been all in vain. He turned to the Israelis. "What about you?"

"If we locate a base we'll need the Semtex; we should take a bridge," said Shiron, resolutely.

"It's almost a third of a mile across the top of that dam," Hellmann added. "Even if we get to the other side without discovery, how the fuck are we going to scale that sheer concrete wall with the gear? No, I'm with Yari; take a bridge."

Ryder guessed getting onto the dam itself direct from where they now hid would be a task in itself and scaling the steep slope down to the crest without ropes was out of the question. That left only the tunnel – a veritable trap. He came to a decision, not sure if it was the influence of the Americans, or perhaps subconsciously wanting the traitor to show his hand; even compensation, maybe, for what he regarded as a wild-goose chase attempting to locate a missile base, but – if the truth be known – he was trained to sabotage and kill. It was ingrained. "We'll cross the dam and take out a piece of that grid."

Shiron made to protest, but before he could, Ryder fired, "I know. I know what you're going to say," holding up a hand, his previous thoughts about not wanting to cross the dam now definitely gone. "To go the bridge way could take over a day to skirt the complex, if not more. We could be over the dam and on the other side in less than thirty minutes, including through the tunnel, at the same time giving the bastards a bloody nose."

"Yeah, but at least we have more chance of staying alive going the long way," Shiron countered.

Ryder was not going to back down; his voice hardened. "The choice has been made. If you want us to help find your base, then this is the way we go. Take it or leave it."

"We'll leave it," Shiron shot back.

"Fine with me," Ryder replied, a little surprised, knowing without the Israelis no way could they locate a base.

"Wait!" It was Hellmann. "How you going to scale that wall?" he said, in an attempt to diffuse the situation.

Shiron fixed him sharply. "Hold it, Corporal."

Hellmann did, and began to shift uneasily.

The question told Ryder that the corporal was in favour of the dam. Maybe he had been a bit hasty putting the Israeli sergeant on the spot. He decided to give it another go. "Look, you're Sayeret Mat'kal, and Unit 269 at that," he said in a conciliatory tone. "This is an opportunity for you to get even, if not for yourselves, then for Israel. Think about it: there may not be a missile base and what we're doing could well be all for nothing; at least inflicting some damage to the power grid could compensate in a small way."

The Israelis glanced at one another as if something was on their minds they could not say.

After a prolonged silence Shiron spoke, "How much Semtex do we have?"

Ryder looked at Kellar.

"Enough to knock out a trani or two with some left over to maybe put a little dent in a missile base should we find one."

"Okay, we will join you," Shiron said abruptly and stared hard at Ryder. "I trust, Frank, we won't be making a habit of sidetracking our mission again?"

He nodded, but it really was out of his hands. He wondered what was going on in the thoughts of the person who hid the note; would he, or she, somehow make an attempt to foil what they had in mind now or later?

"To answer your question about the wall, Corporal," said Ryder, "we'll use the sergeant here," he eyed Kellar and the American gave a weak grin. "He'll hoist you on to his shoulders then push you up so you can grab the parapet and clamber over; the others will follow, helped by you once you're at the top. We're only talking of about 15 feet."

"What about him?" Shiron glanced at Brady. "Roping up that wall with shoulder like it is, won't be easy."

"Don't worry about me, Sergeant; it's healing good," Brady came back, fixing the Israeli with a cold stare. "Climbing that wall is nuthin' compared to what we all might have to face if we find that base you're looking for."

"And the gear?" pressed Shiron.

133

"We'll pass it up once you're at the top then finally pull 'Bear' up himself," Ryder answered.

"Could be cameras in the tunnel," Shiron wouldn't let go.

"If there is then we'll take 'em out," Ryder countered.

"What happens if we're blown on the dam or, for that matter, in the tunnel?" pushed the Israeli sergeant.

"Then we're all fucked, is the short answer," Ryder replied sharply, annoyed at the Israeli's stubbornness. "But, remember, we've been up against worse: the lake, the bridge, not to mention the quake which started all this." He raised his glasses to look at the crest. "There's nobody on the dam now and in fact, I've seen nobody, not even a vehicle, all the time looking."

"That goes for me, too," offered Brady.

"We'll go in darkness, keep to the deeper shadows. With a little luck we should make it," said Ryder, hoping he would be right.

They returned to the boulder, told the others what they intended and waited for nightfall. In the meantime, Kellar made up several explosive charges in preparation for quick placement, carefully stowing them in a backpack. Ryder reached over. "I'll take two of those," he said to the American. "To place at the tunnel entrance as insurance."

★ ★ ★

In the fast-fading light, Ryder and the others made their way, single file down to the tunnel entrance on the mountainside facing away from the dam. The night sky was clear, displaying a plethora of stars accompanied by a half-moon. Lights twinkled at the base of the dam and in the buildings spread out on the plain below. He had kept a constant watch for the remainder of the daylight hours and saw no movement whatsoever on the dam itself. Although he could not see what was in the blind spot where it met the mountain down to his left, he could make out several floodlights on poles spaced evenly across what he could see of the crest, and this concerned him. As darkness grew, however, the floodlights remained off. Instead, three red beacon lights came on, spaced along the rim on the reservoir side, leaving the entire dam top in shadow; much to his relief.

The eight men and Afari reached the road and cautiously approached the tunnel. Ryder told Shiron to lead and he went to the rear to keep an eye on the others. From what he could make out, he guessed the tunnel to be some 18 feet high at the apex and 36 feet wide at the base in the form of a ragged half-circle, hewn out of solid rock in a crude fashion. The rugged appearance looked menacing in the dimming light. The file entered the tunnel and kept close to the uneven walls. A string of loosely-looped naked light-bulbs ran down the centre, well apart, casting a gloomy light over the jagged black and brown surfaces. Ryder looked for cameras but could see none, at least around the entrance, and hoped this indicated that none were inside. Removing the two Semtex charges from his backpack, he concealed them in a crevice each side of the opening, set the detonator timers for two hours, and trusted the resulting blast would not only collapse the entrance itself, but would also bring down enough rock to block it completely. Satisfied he'd placed the explosives where they would do the most damage Ryder made his way quickly down the tunnel and shortly caught up the others.

When they were almost two-thirds along the tunnel an engine starting shattered the silence and headlight beams flooded the space ahead, residue spilling to where they stood frozen, the source hidden by the curve of the tunnel.

Everyone scrambled into wall crevices for cover. Ryder pulled Afari in with him and both had to press hard up against one another to keep within the shadows and avoid the wash of light.

"What the fuck's that?" shot Kellar, from the crevice beside them.

Ryder's mind raced; no vehicles had been on the dam when he last looked shortly before leaving the hide. If any had entered the tunnel since, they would have noticed them descending the mountainside. Was there a guard point at the end, in the blind spot, where the dam met the tunnel? He cursed himself for having overlooked that possibility.

"Sounds like a diesel, and coming this way," he shot back, pulling Afari closer into the narrow crevice as the vehicle rumbled towards them, headlamps now much stronger. He prayed they were all well concealed by the shadows cast.

Shortly, a small Jeep-like vehicle came into view. Ryder glimpsed a uniformed man at the wheel as it swept by, driver unaware of those concealed in the tunnel wall. Both Ryder and Afari let out a sigh of relief; he could feel her breath hot on his cheek and the warmth of her body tight against his. For a fleeting moment all thought of danger evaporated, but quickly returned as he eased her and himself out from the slit in the rock.

What was at the end? Ryder took the lead from Shiron and five minutes later saw in the dim light a small guardhouse to the left with a closed bar barrier framed in the jagged archway, beyond which lay the road across the dam. From the light of a small portable TV flickering inside the guardhouse he could make out the head of a man sitting watching. He was alone.

Shiron and Brady moved to his side.

"Must be the night shift replacing the guy who passed in the Jeep," whispered the American.

"But why a guard?" asked Shiron. "Not as if anyone is likely to blow this dam without a hefty amount of high-ex. It'll take truckloads, which wouldn't get anywhere near this place."

"Probably to keep check on unauthorized personnel using it to fish the reservoir, or maybe even drag racers using the road," Brady grinned.

The American may joke, but we are not going to get across the dam with the guard there, thought Ryder.

"What now?" shot Brady, rubbing his shoulder.

"Take him out," Ryder said.

"How?" hissed Shiron.

"I'll take him; when I do, head for the road. Keep below the parapet line on the reservoir side and don't stop until you reach the other side. I'll be following close behind."

Ryder then crept away towards the guardhouse. Keeping low, he crossed the tunnel to the opposite side and edged his way slowly up behind the small, half-glazed cubicle, no more than 6 feet square. The entrance door was on the side he faced and the guard conveniently sat with back to the door, watching a football match on the portable TV. Reaching the door, he pulled it open. The guard turned, face registering alarm, as Ryder pounced, grabbed him about the throat and expertly wrenched his head to one side, breaking the man's neck. He dragged the body out of the cubicle, pulled the dead weight towards the reservoir parapet and eased it over, hoping no one would hear the splash as it entered the water some 25 feet below. When the Iranians found him he hoped they would think it was an accident.

A pale light reflected off the surface of the reservoir from the half-moon that peaked over the mountain. Ryder turned and followed the others, running crouched below the parapet line. The desolate aspect of being on the narrow top of this huge dam made him feel exposed and vulnerable, expecting floodlights to sear the roadway at any moment, compounded by the thought that they had to be well away from this place before the charges in the tunnel blew. He wondered what was the strange, loud hissing noise he could hear dominating all others, and then realised it was the sound of sand blown by the wind, hitting the massive bowl-like structure and racing up the face of the concrete at great speed.

He caught up with the others and, after what seemed an interminable time, they reached that part of the crest where the road turned almost at right angles and ran across the spillways. Here, if anywhere, they would easily be seen from the buildings on the other side should anyone be observing. Ryder prayed this would not be the case. Trailing quickly across the bridge structure close to a parapet, black void of the spillways to their right and pale waters of the reservoir to the left, they eventually reached the 15-foot-high concrete retaining wall on the other side undetected. Above them, over the parapet, lay the road that led directly to the power-grid enclosure beyond. After a short breather, Kellar hoisted Hellmann onto his shoulders. Both men steadied themselves against the wall to allow Brady to clamber up using their bodies as a ladder. The American reached the top experiencing no problem with the climb; the others followed in quick succession until only Kellar was left. Then, with Sicano dangling almost halfway down the wall, feet held by Hellmann and Shiron, he and the two Israelis pulled the big American up and over the parapet.

Ryder, relieved they had made it safely across the dam, now focused his mind on the power-grid enclosure. From where he stood in the darkness, the surroundings looked very different from those he had seen through binoculars earlier that day, making it difficult to orientate himself. Keeping to the shadows, he skirted the darkened buildings overlooking the spillway, followed in line by the others. After a short while, thankful no one seemed to be about, he instructed Shiron to take the lead and he went to the rear. The Israeli headed them along the edge of a tarsealed road which would lead to the grid enclosure.

It was not long before the humming sound of electrical current coursing through overhead cables could be clearly heard. Lights twinkled to the right on the plain below, and up ahead, Ryder could just see the black outline of heavy transformers with a maze of skeletal metal pylons scattered above. Moving as fast as they dared over the powdery snow dotting the landscape they eventually came to a wire-mesh fence enclosing the power-grid area. Here they concealed themselves in a shallow ditch between the road and the wire-mesh fence topped with three strands of barbed wire.

"Cutters would be handy right now," said Shiron, tugging at the wire.

Ryder looked closely at where the wire went past the front of the nearest concrete post. "Mesh is secured to the post by clips and nails. No problem, we'll tear it out, and bingo, we're in." He pulled out his knife and began to chip away at the post clip.

Several minutes later the mesh came loose and was lifted sufficiently for a man to crawl under.

"Sergeant, this was your idea," Ryder said to Brady. "If you're up to it, you got the honour."

The American moved towards the gap. "Shoulder's okay; pass the charges."

"Jed, you sure you wanna do this?" Kellar asked. Then, without waiting for a reply, "The pack's heavy. Don't aggravate that shoulder, at least until it's healed more. I prepared the charges; better I place."

For a second or two, Ryder wondered if the American's offer was from genuine concern for the sergeant, or did he have an ulterior motive – like not arming the charges and leaving a message at the same time. He let it pass.

"Thanks, Bear, I appreciate that. You're right; I should take it easy for a little longer. You take it."

With that, Brady moved to one side, making way for Kellar.

"Distribute the best you can, where you think the most damage will be done. Set timers for one hour," said Ryder to the American as he slipped under the wire and ran low towards the transformers. He wanted these charges to go off around about the same time as those he placed at the tunnel entrance.

Shortly after Kellar vanished into the blackness the sound of approaching vehicles suddenly came on the wind emanating from somewhere further down the mountain. Ryder's attention immediately focused towards the road. Moments later he saw wavering beams of light reflecting off the mountainside before they became two sets of headlamps cresting the road and heading towards them. As the vehicles came closer he steeled himself for action. Was the ditch deep enough? If discovered, would this position be defendable?

Moments later the two vehicles swept by only feet away, headlights rimming the ditch, with civilian drivers and two passengers in each, much to his relief. The cars stopped not far up the road; doors slammed, laughter, and all the occupants vanished into the buildings which overlooked the spillways. Ryder hoped there would be no more before Kellar returned and they were well away.

The wind whistled along the ditch as Ryder huddled silently with the others, shielding himself from the cold. It seemed the American had been away hours before he finally returned but in fact, when Ryder checked his watch, it had been less than fifteen minutes. Kellar gave the thumbs-up sign and grabbed his belongings.

"Okay, let's get the fuck outta here," Ryder urged, relieved to get away. "We don't want to be around when this lot goes up."

One by one they filed out of the ditch and headed down the darkened road with only the stars and moon to light the way. Following the road as it wound its way down to the river plain, they entered bush and scrub off to the side, when headlamps of more vehicles could be seen heading upwards. The slope was steeper than expected and dangerous to negotiate in the dark, but Ryder knew they could not stop or slow down, and began to worry they might not be far enough away when the charges blew. If the Iranians determined someone had sabotaged the dam and a search was made of the surrounding terrain come daylight, using dogs, the chances of being found would definitely be high. Spreading out, leaving enough space between to catch anyone should they slip, Ryder and the group made good progress down the mountainside until they arrived at a dried-up river bed. Here, speed was doubled now they could move over the dusty, flat surface, despite the slight upward gradient.

Around an hour after leaving the power-grid enclosure, low booming sounds from behind suddenly broke the stillness, followed by a series of erratic blue flashes on the horizon that briefly seared the night sky like bolts of lightning. No one uttered a word; just stood and stared. Ryder guessed that all, with the exception of one, would be experiencing some form of satisfaction, at least in part; the Americans: small consolation for missing out on the somewhat larger mission they had first set out to achieve; the Israelis: for their earlier failure; and the Iranians: for what the regime had done to them and their families. For Ryder it was the satisfaction of knowing that, at least in some small way, he had exacted revenge for what the Iranians had done to him in that godforsaken prison.

When the show ended, he checked his compass, turned and quickly headed up the valley, more buoyant now of finding a base. The rest followed.

16

Light snow began to fall as Ryder and his party moved out of the valley and negotiated the steeply rising ground covered in tussock and scrub. The wind was bitterly cold and there was hardly enough cover from its biting effect. They had trudged with only short stops throughout the night, and by mid-afternoon, under a clearing sky revealing high peaks, Ryder once again checked their position using GPS, establishing they were well into the western Zagros by some 350 miles from where they had started and around 400 miles from the objective. On that basis, he reckoned they should reach the mountain within twenty to thirty days at the present rate, but acknowledged they had yet to cross the highest and most difficult part of the range.

Not long after they had traversed a narrow plateau the group came upon human tracks in the thin, patchy snow.

"Hunters?" questioned Sicano.

"Another patrol, more like," snapped Ryder.

"They look fresh… maybe two-three hours old," said Shiron.

Brady bent down. "The sides are as hard as the bases. My guess: several hours," he said.

Suddenly, Corporal Hellmann pointed urgently towards a shallow gully on their right and placed finger to lips. They all looked and saw a small deer grazing on tussock.

Hellmann quickly raised rifle and lined up the animal.

"Hold it, Corporal," Brady snapped, placing his hand firmly on the barrel. "We can't risk it if these are fresh; another patrol could be close by."

The Israeli looked at his sergeant then at Ryder. "We need food – fresh meat. We must risk it."

The Israeli was right; the risk had to be taken. Ryder cast a look of disagreement at the American. "I'll make that call," he shot, then to Hellmann, "Kill it."

The corporal lined up again, squeezed the trigger, and dropped the unfortunate animal.

The report echoed loudly, accompanying Saad and Fehed as they ran to retrieve the carcass. Shortly after, with the animal slung on Saad's shoulders, the group moved as fast as they could away from the spot.

Twilight fell when they made camp in a small hollow surrounded by scrub, well concealed and protected from the wind. It had been a long day and now they desperately needed warmth, cooked food and a good rest. Despite the risk, a fire was lit and soon each gorged themselves on venison. They sat watching the flames dance merrily in the darkness, illuminating the hollow and the drawn, bearded faces. Bellies full, they began to relax in the cold stillness of the night.

Ryder sat silently watching the flames flicker and dance, occasionally eyeing each of the others in turn, finding it difficult to accept one of them as a traitor. He pieced together the events since the escape to pinpoint anything that might give a clue, but drew a blank. From his point of view the most disturbing factor – if the three remaining Iranians were to be excluded – was: what kind of bitterness would drive one of the Americans, or Israelis for that matter, to betray his country? What possible motive could they have to shift allegiance? He studied Fehed, Saad and Afari squatting quietly on the other side of the flames; had they known the true objective they would have been prime suspects. Whoever wrote that note knew the objective; and only the Americans and Israelis had that information. The note had been written in Farsi; the

Israelis and the Americans were fluent. He decided to probe – see what happened.

"Funny how we've been tracked all this way. Take the lake; it was as if our position was known even then. Who do you think they were anyway – Iraqis, Iranians, terrorists?"

"Iraqi – Iranian border guards," Brady replied. "Does it matter?"

"The two gunboats that gave chase were almost on us before we pulled away from the jetty. Someone warned them," Ryder pressed.

"My money is on Iraqis," said Sicano. "As far as them knowing where we were going, the firefight held them back long enough to radio out we were running for the boats."

"Maybe, but I get the feeling our path is being anticipated; as if someone's… " He stopped short.

The two Israelis shot a glance at each other.

"You saying, Frank, we have a traitor here?" Sicano asked.

"No. I'm saying: it seems a little strange – too much of a coincidence maybe," he replied, trying to stay casual. He decided he'd probed enough for the time being, hoping a seed had been sown that might just deter the culprit from taking further chances and make the others more aware of what each were doing. He changed the subject, focusing on Shiron, "How long you been with Special Forces?"

"Four years."

"Sayeret Mat'kal?"

He nodded, intense brown eyes fixing Ryder in the firelight; cheek scar still prominent through the growing beard.

"Tough outfit." *The Israeli has done well to last that length of time,* Ryder thought.

"You're British Special Air Service; what you doing with American Green Berets?"

"Advisor," he left it at that and moved on, "You orthodox or unorthodox?"

"Neither, I'm Christian – Catholic." From the way he said that, sharp features seemingly softening, Ryder guessed Shiron might be devout, making him think about his own lack of faith, having lost it from a very early age in the mean streets of Brixton. "We may all need to believe to get through this one."

"More likely lady luck," murmured Brady.

"You religious, Frank?" asked Shiron.

Ryder shrugged, "Never tuned in to the bigotry and hypocrisy. Millions starve, the Pope preaches but never do we see any of that vast wealth he controls to ease the pain and suffering. All those different religions squabbling amongst themselves believing their way is the right way, turns me off."

"Humanity needs to believe in something," the Israeli countered, "otherwise there's no point to all this. Believing is hoping!"

"I'll go with that," Brady added. "Believing, though, has to be above all that bible fable crap."

"I take it you're the same as Frank, Sergeant?" said Shiron, turning to Kellar.

"No… I'm Catholic like you, only I leave the practising to the priests."

The Israeli then looked at Sicano, "What about you?"

"Agnostic… it's all bullshit to me. More wars and killing are carried out in the name of religion than anything else as far as I'm concerned."

"Never a believer?" pressed Shiron.

"Never gave a shit one way or the other; too busy making a life."

It looked to Ryder that maybe he'd opened a religious can of worms by giving the Israeli a platform.

Shiron then turned and looked over the fire at the Iranians. "What about you three – Muslim?"

Afari said nothing, just nodded, hands spread to the flames. She looked worn out.

Saad, small frame hunched forward towards the fire replied quietly, "Buddhist."

"Buddhism – unusual for an Iranian."

He nodded. "Reason I was first imprisoned; my beliefs were not understood. They saw me as a danger to the regime. I became a so-called terrorist soon after. I am of the Mahayana sect. It teaches that salvation is possible for everyone and that suffering is inseparable from existence." He paused and stared into the flames. "The cause of suffering is desire, and suppression of desire can be obtained through discipline. Perfect peace and bliss is our reward."

"Suppression of desire where I hail from would be regarded as suffering to the extreme," said Kellar, grinning.

"And where would that be, Sergeant?" asked Hellmann, speaking for the first time, brooding features glistening in the flames.

"Baltimore, Virginia."

"Hey, small world," the Israeli shot back, smiling broadly at the American. "I've a niece in Highlandtown, married name, Laid. You know her?"

"Can't say I do, but with a name like that though, who'd forget?" Kellar replied, still with a grin on his face.

"For a pacifist, you've handled yourself well," Shiron said to Saad.

"Don't be misled. I have spent months in the hills, and even more in the stinking prisons. I'm hardened to pain and degradation; my beliefs make suffering a pleasure."

The Israeli turned to Fehed, "Why were you in that hell-hole?"

The Iranian poked at the flames with a stick. "I was a pilot in the armed forces, flew helicopters for SF until falsely accused of associating with the MEK," he looked away into the darkness. Moments later, he spoke with vehemence, "I was arrested; government henchmen killed my wife and child. I want revenge." Fehed slammed the stick into the fire, sparks rose and he spat into the flames.

"How long were you in?" Sicano asked.

"I don't know, maybe three or four weeks. Before that I was in

146

a military prison for several months. They got nothing from me; probably why I was transferred to that shit-hole."

"And in there?" pressed Sicano.

"Tried to break me, but the methods they used… " he trailed off and put head into his hands. "It was only a matter of time before I would tell them anything they wanted to hear just to stop the pain."

Ryder winced at the thought of what he had probably suffered.

"Why did you stay with us, instead of making for Turkey?" Shiron asked.

"The Turks would have handed me back for the sake of good relations. You are our best chance of obtaining asylum in the west when we reach the Gulf States."

Shiron glanced at Ryder, murmured something about if they ever got there, and turned to Afari, but she was fast asleep.

Ryder decided to up the ante, looking at the Americans, he didn't mince his words. "It bothers me how that psycho knew about the dams; he would've only known from one of us. I didn't break. Did any of you?"

The three glanced incredulously at each other. Kellar gave him an angry look. "What the fuck you saying, Ryder: that one of us is a traitor?"

"We wouldn't do that? You must be crazy," shot Sicano.

Then Brady, "Even if it did happen, how the fuck does it affect what we're doing now – unless you reckon one of us has been turned and is getting messages out somehow."

The two Israelis threw each other a troubled glance; the Iranian men looked on, bewildered.

He wanted to tell them about the note but something urged him to hold back, at least for now. "Might explain why we seem to be constantly tracked; that it's not just coincidence."

"Frank, they found us – the plane, remember?" said Sicano. "So they know we're heading south somewhere. Don't need to be a genius to figure out possible routes through these mountains and send patrols out accordingly."

Kellar, now a little calmer said, "Well, for what it's worth, I didn't."

"Me neither," Sicano followed.

Both then looked at Brady.

"Don't the fuck look at me," he shot back angrily, "no way did I tell'em."

One of you did, so that puts each of you in the frame, Ryder thought, but he could not exclude the Israelis or the others, although the Iranians would be the last on his list. He needed tangible evidence before he could place blame.

The mood now was pretty sombre, and silence descended. Ryder's probing had left him no nearer to discovering who the traitor might be. If he was to find out, he would need to hit on another way, and soon.

After a short while staring into the flames they eventually agreed the watch and turned in. The fire was doused as Ryder and Brady positioned themselves on the edge of the hollow taking the first watch, knowing they must remain alert for at least the next two hours. Both men stared silently through the light, swirling snow into the darkness, immersed in their own thoughts, hoping the night would pass without event. It kept bothering Ryder how many more notes might have been left for pursuers to find. He was still pondering this question, and more, when eventually Shiron and Hellmann took over the watch.

17

Ryder awoke abruptly in the cold grey light of dawn and immediately sensed danger. Instinctively he rolled then froze the moment he felt the icy end of a rifle barrel pressed against his temple. Fear gripped as he looked up at the crouching, grim-faced soldier holding an AK47. A massive surge of adrenaline followed and the fear quickly turned into defence mode. He sensed the others were in a similar position. From the corner of his eye he could see Sicano and Kellar, both face down at the side of the hollow in an unconscious state.

Sicano groaned, turned over, and held the back of his head, followed a little later by Kellar, blood flowing from a gash on the forehead. Both men were roughly prodded up amidst confused shouting. The rest, too, were forced at gunpoint to their feet and all were herded into line, hands on heads, whilst two of the six-man patrol systematically searched each one, relieving them of all weapons.

Ryder's mind raced, eyes everywhere for possible escape routes, but it seemed there was no way out of this one; they had paid heavily for the fire earlier and the venison fare.

The hollow was searched and all equipment stacked on the edge. Ryder watched in despair, shocked at the swiftness and stealth by which they had been overcome. *Well and truly fucked now.*

Afari cowered as two of the patrol holding her leered, one with the muzzle of his rifle nudging suggestively at her crotch.

The leader, a short, powerfully built man in dirty-white alpine fatigues with small, darting eyes, walked down the line studying each man closely, before turning and yelling orders. He looked tired, and from the appearance of the patrol, they had been away from base some time. Two of the patrol quickly emptied the contents of the group's packs, filled two with all the captured weapons and hoisted them onto their backs. He barked again. Ryder and the others were then roughly roped together, pushed out of the hollow and marched down into the valley, led by the officer, with two of the patrol on each flank and one bringing up the rear. Haze shrouded the valley as they made their way slowly through the scattered trees and scrub heading north-west, the dark, brooding mass of the Zagros filling the horizon to the north and east. The sun climbed higher, slowly dispersing the haze, until the whole valley and hills surrounding came into focus. After what seemed like endless hours the tethered captives eventually arrived at three circular huts nestled at the base of a tussock-covered knoll guarding the end of the valley.

The officer leading disappeared into the nearest hut and returned shortly to herd the captives inside where they were penned with goats at the rear, still roped together. He then ordered the soldier carrying a transmitter to contact base for a helicopter to airlift them out.

The atmosphere inside the hut was smoky and fetid. The leader sat in the centre with the small group of Luris while the soldiers spread themselves around the circular space. Two women prepared food over an open fire and shortly bowls of gruel were handed to the leader and his men. The captives went without.

One of the soldiers nearest the pen quickly emptied his bowl, stood up and went over for more. Ryder, squatting next to the low wicker enclosure, looking for the chance to escape, attempted to loosen his bonds. He eyed the soldier's rifle propped against the wall only a few feet beyond the enclosure. The rope binding his hands in front would not fully give despite his efforts. However, he gauged they were spaced far enough apart to just about fire the rifle if only he could get hold of it. It was now or never. Without hesitating, he leapt the barrier and lunged for the automatic, but was cruelly pulled up short by the taut rope joining him to Sicano.

The sudden movement jolted the others into action immediately as they realised what was happening and all lunged forward too, only to be brought down in a heap when Sicano, Hellmann and Kellar became entangled before any could jump the barrier.

In those few desperate moments, the Iranian officer sprung to his feet, quickly drew pistol, and in one swift movement, shot Brady dead as he tried to get over the barrier and dive to yank the gun away. He then swung and levelled his weapon at the others sprawled helplessly amongst the bleating goats until finally his men regained control, beating the captives back into the pen with the butts of their rifles. Trampled under the hoofs of the panicking goats, Ryder did his best to defend against the blows, devastated that his bid to escape had failed and that Sergeant Brady had paid the price with his life. Had he not attempted to go for the rifle the American would still be alive.

18

It was late afternoon the following day when the sound of an approaching helicopter roused the captives from their apathy. Immediately, they were ordered from the pen and herded outside. A red sun hung low in the sky and a strong wind whipped coldly down the valley. Ryder watched dispassionately, resigned to the situation, wishing now he had not embarked on this crazy venture; and to make it worse, knowing whoever the traitor was had won out. The grey helicopter descended like a huge insect to the thin carpet of white; powerful motors blotting out all other sounds and billowing clouds of snow high into the air.

The big Russian-built Mi-17 landed, the motors powered-down and remained ticking over as four armed men in white alpine fatigues sprang from the side and hurried towards the huddled group. A brief discussion between the patrol leader and one of the men and the captives were quickly manhandled towards the craft. Brady's body was to be left, strongly objected to by the other two Americans, but they were ignored and for their trouble, beaten again. Ten minutes later, when all eight were on board, plus the ten soldiers and equipment, the pilot powered-up the motors and the helicopter soared back into the sky.

Ryder and the others held on grimly to overhead straps, watched closely by the soldiers positioned in the fuselage front and rear. Conditions were cramped and of the twenty people on board, only the pilot and co-pilot had room to themselves. Turbulence was bad in the mountain currents. In one particularly violent lurch, Ryder swung hard against a soldier who tried to steady himself, missed the metal fuselage rib altogether and bounced back, hitting Ryder squarely in the chest. He winced at the impact, raised hand instinctively to avoid a repeat and suddenly felt a grenade firmly within his grasp. Ryder did not hesitate; pulling the grenade from the clip, he pushed the soldier aside, removed the pin and held the grenade aloft for everyone to see, yelling at the same time for attention above the roar of the motors.

Horror registered on the faces of the soldiers when they fully realised what was happening.

Sergeant Shiron reacted first. Grabbing a rifle from the nearest man, he leapt to the flight deck and, in front of the dumbfounded pilots, smashed the radio equipment with the butt. Seconds later he yelled at the co-pilot to go to the rear and then placed the rifle muzzle against the pilot's throat.

The helicopter bucked wildly, Ryder rolled with the lurch, one hand firmly gripping the overhead strap, the other clutching the grenade. He shouted orders at the others to strip the soldiers of weapons and anything else of use and keep them covered.

On the flight deck, Shiron, now in the empty co-pilot seat, surveyed the instruments. From his basic training in military helicopters he could see it was equipped with the latest enhanced navigational and infrared radar systems of the type used in the IF Super Frelons, and fuel gauges registered the tanks were almost full.

With the Iranians disarmed and guns trained on them, the captives were in full control of the rear. Ryder ordered Kellar to open the hatch so he could now get rid of the grenade. Edging his way towards the opening, recoiling as the icy blast hit him full on, he threw the grenade out as hard as he could to see it explode seconds later somewhere harmlessly below. He then joined Shiron on the flight deck, followed by Sicano.

"Do we have enough fuel to get us to the Gulf?" the American shouted at the pilot when he got there.

The pilot remained silent. Shiron replied instead, telling him the tanks were almost full, therefore theoretically they could. The Israeli looked desperately at Ryder.

"Do we have enough to take us to the objective?" he asked.

The Israeli nodded. "She's also rigged for night flying."

"Over these mountains?" shot Sicano, surprise on his face. "You fucking crazy?"

Ryder, adrenaline pumping, came to a decision. "We're going to finish the job."

The Israeli beamed.

"Shit, Frank! We'll be lucky to get over those fucking peaks!" Sicano shouted, losing it. "If the grenade explosion failed to be monitored, you bet MIGs will be up anyways once its established radio contact is lost and the blip on the radar is us. They'll shoot us right out of the fucking sky."

"Maybe, but we're on our way," Ryder shouted back through the roar, turning to the pilot and asking how far away they were from base. "Forty-five minutes," he replied, adding that fighters would have already scrambled.

Ryder ordered the pilot to turn off the navigational lights then scanned the rapidly darkening horizon streaked in red and magenta through the almost vertical glass screen of the cockpit.

"How far to the peaks?" asked Sicano, a little calmer, staring intently out through the screen.

"Forty, maybe fifty miles on this course," Shiron came back. "At this altitude, airspeed can be no more than a hundred. A little less than thirty minutes would see us in the high range."

"If MIGs are on the way we can kiss State-side goodbye for sure," the American replied, voice shaking.

"We've a chance, hugging the ground. It would be far too risky for them to attack us now in failing light. Once amongst those peaks they would definitely have to break away," said Shiron, trying to reassure Sicano and give Ryder some confidence in his decision.

Ryder knew enough to understand they would be taking a

tremendous risk flying the helicopter through mountain terrain in darkness, especially at high altitude where the weather could be so severe and unpredictable, but as far as he was concerned, he'd given his word to the Israelis; there was no turning back.

"Safer to dump the chopper; those mountains at night would be asking to meet our Maker," pressed the American.

"Sure… sure it's dangerous – extremely dangerous," Ryder shouted, "but only a little more so than crossing the hard way. We're not equipped to tackle the terrain on foot. This chopper provides the answer. It's rigged for night flying and it's bloody quicker than walking."

Sicano turned to the pilot, still under the muzzle of Shiron's automatic, and asked him if he had night-flying experience in the range; the look on the pilot's face said it all.

"This guy's scared shitless!" fired the American. "We can't risk everything on his fucking judgement."

"I'll do the flying," said Shiron, a little hesitantly, then a bit more forcibly, "This bird is much like a 321G Super Frelon, and I've had night experience. We've a fifty-fifty chance of making it. Luck's been good to us so far, so let's push it some more. I can do it."

Ryder was not so sure. The Israeli somehow did not give him the necessary confidence. In the meantime, the helicopter continued to rush towards the high peaks. "What training you had?"

"I've never flown one of these, but I'm familiar with the Mi-17's capabilities though: speed, range, ceiling max, powered by two Isotov TV2-117A Turbo shaft engines. I did basics in Frelons – similar."

"Basics!" shot Sicano, almost losing it again, turning to Ryder, "We can't let him take us through these mountains, Frank; he'll kill us all!" The Iranian helicopter pilot looked desperately at the American.

Ryder knew he was right; maybe they should ditch and go on foot after all. Then he had a thought and shouted back down into the fuselage, "Send Fehed up here, *now!*"

Shortly, the Iranian's thin, gangly body squeezed onto the cockpit deck, forcing Sicano to move partway into the fuselage area.

"You said you'd flown helis for Special Forces?" Ryder asked, then, "You flown one of these at night?"

The Iranian's brown eyes fixed him intensely over his prominent nose then turned away and scanned the controls. Seconds later he glanced up and nodded.

"Good. You take over," shot Ryder, feeling relief before turning to Shiron and pointing at the pilot. "Take him to the rear." After they left, Fehed quickly strapped himself into the vacated seat and took immediate control, confirming the helicopter's range, altitude and fuel status. Ryder strapped himself into the co-pilot's seat and told the Iranian immediately to change course south-east.

Suddenly Ryder shouted, "Here they come – two o'clock!"

Sicano, together with Fehed, looked up and saw through the screen two black objects approaching fast from the east, "Holy shit! We ain't got a show!" the American cried.

Two MIG fighters swept low from left to right across the helicopter's path, separated and banked steeply away, wings glittering red in the evening sky before sweeping around in a tight turn and coming back at them from the rear.

Ryder felt and saw the aircraft thunder past and felt every fibre of his body contract waiting for the dreadful moment when cannon impacted. But it never came. The two fighters, almost level on either side, flew up into the southern sky.

Shortly, once again the jets with landing lights full on and wheels down, swooped, not so close this time, but close enough to force Fehed to take the helicopter even lower. Minutes later they climbed steeply away and out of sight to the rear.

"They're not shooting; they're not fucking shooting!" shouted Sicano, incredulously. "We were right on line and they goddamn let us go for the second time!"

"They want us down in one piece," said Ryder, craning forward to see where the next approach would be from.

"Whadda we do now?" yelled Sicano. "They'll knock shit out of us for sure next time!"

"We'll go right down; let them think we intend to land," he turned to Fehed, fighting to keep control of the helicopter. "Keep her at full throttle, as close to the ground as we dare. Another ten minutes and we'll be into the high range."

"We have to lose weight!" the Iranian shouted. "Once in those mountains, every pound will count."

Ryder could feel the heli was busting a gut. "Go down! Go down! We'll dump the Iranians."

"Frank! Those soldiers are keeping us from being blown out of the fucking sky!" Sicano pressed.

The two jet fighters swept by again much lower, but well above the Mi-17.

Fehed levelled off at 200 feet and gave full throttle.

"They won't come much lower!" he shouted, "If they do… " he trailed off.

Ryder looked at the bewildering array of instruments glowing green in the dim light of the cockpit, in particular at the infrared ground-following radar and GPS systems, as they rapidly approached the high range at 100 mph. He then turned and shouted back to the others to retain guns, ammunition, food, clothes and anything else useful and dump the rest, including the Iranians.

Shortly, all was ready. Fehed descended holding the helicopter steady just above the ground. Twice the jets swooped over as low as they dared; no doubt assuming the Mi-17 was about to land.

"Jettison!" shouted Ryder. "As soon as the last—" he stopped short and stared transfixed through the cockpit screen, "My God: choppers!"

The prisoners were bundled towards the now-opened hatch where everyone immediately saw two helicopters approaching from the right, silhouetted against the orange blaze of the western sky with white conical searchlights piercing the darkness ahead.

Ryder felt desperation as the two black insect-like shapes raced towards them, knowing there was nothing he could do but rely on Fehed, praying he was good enough at the controls to avoid getting them all blown out of the sky, not only by these oncoming choppers but by the MIGs that menaced them from above.

"Let's go! Let's go!" yelled Ryder, eager to soar away, watching the Iranian controlling the collective pitch lever with one eye and the other on what was happening behind in the fuselage.

Sicano rushed from the deck into the fuselage and, with the others, herded the Iranian troops out of the hatch. Seconds later, when the last man fell to the ground several feet below, he shouted at Ryder to take her away and at the same time threw surplus equipment out as the helicopter rapidly rose.

The Mi-17 surged upwards considerably more buoyant now. Fehed handled the craft skilfully and, before the oncoming helicopters could block their southerly path, managed to gain a good head start.

From the hatchway, Sicano, Kellar and the others watched the rear helicopter break off and descend to the men bunched on the ground, but hurriedly slammed it shut as the first helicopter began to strafe the side with machine-gun fire.

The two jets came at them again very low and from the west. Within seconds they opened fire sending streams of cannon and tracer across the Mi-17's path, so close the shells almost removed paint from the nose.

They all watched the jets climb steeply away to the left, bank and line up for yet another run. From what Ryder could see through the screen he figured they would get one more before the helicopter reached the protection of the peaks.

Fehed flew the Mi-17 dangerously close to the ground and headed towards a large wedge-shaped ravine barely visible in the fading light. Focusing on the infrared terrain scanner issuing data on height relative to type and bearing of ground formation below, he went at maximum speed towards the gap now only three miles ahead.

The two jets approached again, straight at them from the right, higher than the previous run, and opened fire sending cannon all around. The barrage was terrifying, forcing him to reduce airspeed and height dramatically to almost ground level. To Ryder, strapped in beside the Iranian, every ounce of Fehed's experience and skill was now in play to keep the helicopter in the air; all their lives were now most certainly in his hands.

As soon as the jets swept overhead he increased altitude and sped towards the gap. The Mi-17 responded easily, manoeuvring erratically both horizontally and vertically over the fast-rising ground, as Fehed tried desperately to confuse the jets and shake off the pursuing helicopter.

Both MIGs banked steeply and turned in an incredibly tight circle, no doubt aware this would be their last run, and began the approach from the left, parallel to the rising range.

Fehed desperately tried to increase speed, but at this altitude the most he could get was 100 mph. Ryder prayed they would make the gap in time. It was all or nothing now.

"Jesus! Those mother-fuckers are gonna take us this time!" cried Sicano, back on the cockpit deck, half looking at the mass of rock ahead and half at the oncoming fighters.

Fehed pushed the cyclic lever, sending the Mi-17 headlong into the mouth of the ravine as four AT-2 'Stinger' missiles swept by and exploded into the hillside both sides.

"That was close – too fucking close!" Sicano shouted.

Ryder looked back desperately to see if the other helicopter had followed them in.

"We made it! We made it!" Sicano came again; this time the tone screaming jubilance.

"Not yet," replied Ryder, "that chopper's still on our tail, and gaining fast."

Fehed opened the throttle. The helicopter careered up the broadening ravine, staying in the centre, one step ahead of the other machine and making sure the angle between them remained tight to hinder the gunner. Ryder prayed they were not carrying missiles. In a little more than a minute they soared into the inky blackness of a narrow valley beyond. Desperately, Fehed fought to keep control against severe turbulence and gusting winds, and at the same time pilot the helicopter between shadowy walls of sheer rock showing dangerously close on the screens. No matter how much he tried to lose the other craft, it stuck like glue, strafing every time the opportunity arose. The pursuing pilot knew his stuff, and slowly, but surely, began to gain.

Suddenly, shells penetrated the rear fuselage, whining murderously off the metalwork, sending everyone diving for the deck. Hellmann gave an agonised cry as one nicked his shoulder, and another came from Kellar as a shell seared across the back of his hand.

Fehed gave more throttle, the machine lurched faster, increasing the distance between itsself and the following helicopter, but only temporarily. Two minutes later they were being strafed again.

"There're gaining!" Sicano voiced over the roaring engines. "If the tanks get hit we're dead meat!"

The windows of the cockpit were filled with the blur of mountain blackness and jagged peaks, purple edged against a vast backdrop of bright stars in an indigo sky to the south and east. The Iranian fought hard to keep the Mi-17 under control, eyes flashing between screens, altimeter and airspeed indicator. Watching, Ryder's adrenaline soared at the desperate situation they were in. The twin conical headlights of the pursuing helicopter closed fast, despite the frantic efforts to keep ahead, and Ryder felt so helpless knowing there was nothing he could do; his life now depended entirely upon the skill of the Iranian next to him.

Fehed flung the machine sideways and down to the right, opening throttle full out.

The sudden move caught the following pilot unawares and the helicopter swept over and was now in front, momentarily unable to use its guns.

Immediately, Fehed, in a reflex reaction, released all four AT-2 'Stinger' missiles, at the same time activating the machine gun in the nose.

The missiles missed, but shells raked the rear fuselage. He tried desperately to hold the position, but the skill of the Iranian pilot was too good and he soon swept back onto their tail.

The two helicopters narrowly cleared a ridge, with only feet to spare, and rode the strong current of air on the other side, carrying them higher, before releasing its grip, dropping them down again into a narrow valley below; peaks soaring either side.

The screens and radar indicated almost sheer rock walls both sides of the corridor and a mass of rock five miles ahead where the valley came abruptly to an end. The radar also indicated a small central gap in the mass. The data defined the gap to be only 300 yards wide and less than half a mile long, slightly curving in a solid wall of rock towering thousands of feet, but most definitely leading to open space beyond.

Fehed shouted he intended to go for the gap – it was their only chance.

"You'll kill us all!" Sicano cried.

"No choice!" he yelled back, sending the helicopter arcing towards the gap.

"We'll never make it! One gust of wind! We'll never make it!" Sicano's voice was full of fear and panic.

Face taut with concentration, Ryder watched the Iranian throttle back and line up the gap. In several seconds he and the others would find out just how good a pilot Fehed was.

Ryder prepared to die as he watched the gap hurtle towards them. Would the other helicopter follow them in? It flashed through his mind that the traitor, whoever he was, must be doing the same. There would be no redemption now for any of them.

Ryder watched Fehed hold the machine steady, not once taking his eyes away from the screens, focusing intently on the image of the gap, measuring distance, speed and angle of the approach.

Seconds later the Mi-17 entered centre-on like an express train into a tunnel, and hurtled at over 100 mph along its path, barely yards from the massive sheer walls. Inside this nightmarish hell of noise and blackness, Fehed struggled frantically to keep the machine on course, and Ryder hung on for dear life.

Suddenly, almost out the other side, a tremendous explosion rocked the helicopter and blew it clear into the valley beyond. For one awful moment, Ryder thought the end had come; then with overwhelming relief, realised they had made it and it was the other helicopter that had failed.

Tensions eased and adrenaline levels fell, but the ordeal was not over yet; getting through the range still had to be achieved. Ryder determined they were in the centre and still on a south-easterly course. Should they be able to maintain this course it would take them to within a hundred miles of the objective on the south-eastern side of the Zagros's western arm.

"They'll be waiting for us on the eastern side with MIGs," said Sicano, visibly shaken but now in a much calmer state, "And probably with choppers to flush us out."

"Without AWACS they can't track us," replied Ryder. "If we keep low we'll have them guessing. No reason to suspect we're heading anywhere else other than to the Gulf. It's logical from their point of view. Why would we want to penetrate deeper into Iran? I doubt we'll meet opposition heading south-east. We'll take this baby all the way until she runs out of juice." He was jubilant they had made it.

In the following two-and-a-half hours, the helicopter plummeted, yawed and pitched at crazy angles through the darkness, sending men and equipment sprawling. Fehed fought hard to guide the aircraft between the peaks, riding the savage currents and turbulence which, every minute, threatened to plunge all into obscurity. Countless times Ryder watched snow-covered rocky ground rush at them through the windows, and waited, heart in mouth for that awful moment of impact, then to watch it rush away again, so helpless, so vulnerable to the whim of fate that nausea struck every time. When it finally ended he was so emotionally drained it took a little time to accept that he was still alive. Never with the regiment, the Increment or the unit had he endured such a long, hair-raising experience out of his control. They had survived, thanks to the piloting skills of the Iranian.

In the rear, relief showed clearly now that they were not being thrown around so much. Afari, in particular, it being her first time in a helicopter, was traumatised by the experience. Her body ached and she could not wait to get back on the ground. Of the others, only Saad had escaped small injuries from ricocheting bullets and the crazy antics of the aircraft.

The helicopter eventually landed with a heavy jolt in a desolate valley, tanks empty. Fehed, Ryder and Sicano staggered from the cockpit. Kellar pulled open the side hatch and one by one the battered and bruised group fell to the ground, mentally and physically drained. Fehed threw up and collapsed. Afari staggered about, trying to regain her balance, before she too collapsed. They had all experienced a harrowing flight, travelling some 300 miles in less than four hours through rugged mountains and had miraculously survived. Ryder was definitely glad to be back on terra firma.

The wind began to bite. Ryder gathered himself and, after a short rest to collect their feet, ordered all to quickly unload equipment, share out clothes, rations, guns and ammunition, including what additional explosives had been taken from the SF soldiers. He told the group the objective would remain; he did not elaborate. The three Iranians still believed they were heading for the Gulf. Using new maps taken from the helicopter and the GPS, they established their position to be on the eastern edge of the valley plain between the two main fingers of the southern Zagros range, midway between the towns of Marvast and Shahr-e Babak. After Shiron gave Ryder the co-ordinates for Kuh-e Mohammadabad, they established they were less than seventy-five miles from the objective, located due east. Ryder now had to face the prospect of attempting to expose the traitor in a hurry before it was reached. He guessed the Iranian authorities would search this side of the Zagros once it became evident they had not crashed or headed west. In the meantime, at least, it would give them a head start to reach the mountain they had come all this way to find.

Soon everything was ready for moving out. They hurriedly made an effort to camouflage the Mi-17 as best they could with branches and scrub before all eight struck out due east led by Ryder. Visible on the distant horizon stood Kuh-e Mohammadabad, prominent in the jagged black line, under an orange flame that formed the eastern finger of the Zagros Mountains; beyond them, the central deserts of Iran. In a few hours it would be full light, and they needed to put as much distance between themselves and the helicopter as possible.

19

Sleet turned to light rain as dawn arrived and grey clouds scudded across the sky promising more. The group, in single file, led by Ryder, snaked over the patchy, snow-covered rising ground, desert-like and covered in tussock and thinly scattered bush. They kept up a good tab speed, despite the thin air at 4,000 feet and the heavy packs, toiling on in zombie fashion brought about by lack of sleep and pushing themselves beyond the limit. Ryder's body, trained to function days without sleep, was now in a state of heightened perception transcending aching limbs and impervious to the biting cold. The Iranians, too, seemed to be handling the rigors without complaint, Afari in particular, much to his amazement. She was much tougher than she looked.

Using GPS, compass and maps, Ryder was able to determine, with some certainty, that Kuh-e Mohammadabad could be reached in less than two days. The plain stretched out before him, rising at irregular intervals towards the foothills. As he looked at the target white-capped mountain, sharply rising, clearly visible now on the horizon, a strong feeling of isolation and doubt engulfed him. Would they find a missile base, and if they did, what would happen with a traitor in their midst? The pressure to expose whoever it was grew with each hour that passed and weighed heavily, but he was determined to press on and hope the traitor would be uncovered before they reached the objective.

After hours of steady slog nightfall came and they made camp in the lee of a shallow gully amongst dense bush. As they dug in, Ryder decided against a fire and the exhausted group made do with cold rations. The earlier rain had stopped but a stiff wind blew across the plain, heralding a cold and miserable night ahead. Nobody said much; all were almost out on their feet. When finished eating, Shiron and Hellmann volunteered to take first watch and the rest finally settled down to sleep as best they could in the shelter of the bush.

Night passed quietly. Shortly before dawn, as they began to stir, Fehed leaned across to awaken Saad. "Aheee! Allah, have mercy!" he cried, recoiling back, eyes wide, staring in disbelief at his fellow Iranian.

Ryder swung round, as did the rest, and what they saw made them, too, recoil in horror.

Saad lay dead, knife plunged upwards deep into his throat with such force that the blade tip protruded through the base of his skull. Blood covered the whole front of the body.

"Jesus, fucking, Christ… what son-of-a-bitch would do a thing like that?" questioned Sicano, voice quivering.

The others gathered around, stunned by the sight then stepped back, looking accusingly at Fehed.

The Iranian moved quickly away from the body and looked askance at Ryder, blurting out he had nothing to do with this; Saad had been his friend.

"Why, for Chrissake? Why?" shot Kellar, staring intently down at the sprawled Iranian.

"I'll tell you why!" said Hellmann after several seconds, anger clearly showing.

"Corporal, say nothing!" snapped Shiron.

"They have to know now," pleaded Hellmann.

The sergeant flashed a glance of disagreement and turned away.

"What the fuck's going down here?" asked Ryder, staring intently at the two Israelis.

"Okay! I'll tell you!" Shiron shouted, turning back. Then more

166

calmly, "Something happened in the gully where the Iranian's arm was removed that seemed strange at the time, something in itself not alarming, but enough to arouse suspicion something was not quite right." He paused and glanced at those around him. "Corporal Hellmann said he thought the transmitter had possibly been tampered with, although he wasn't sure; and it wasn't the first time."

The others gasped, looking stunned again at one another, except for Ryder. It confirmed to him why the Israeli sergeant had fired so violently at the soldier carrying the transmitter in the ambush; he didn't want to chance this one being used by whoever tampered with the first.

"Tampered with?" shot Sicano.

"Used to send a signal," replied Shiron, curtly. "Corporal switched it off before turning in; when he awoke it was on, set to another frequency."

"So?" pressed Sicano.

"What the fuck – so!" spat Hellmann, eyes boring into Sicano's. "It means one of us here probably used it for some fucking reason. Listen, I was very particular about conserving the battery, always turned it off without touching the frequency."

"Hold it. Hold it," Shiron intervened. "Danny, you admitted yourself you could've made a mistake."

"I told you it happened before. I passed that off then as a mistake, but that last time in the gully made me real suspicious."

"Was that why you wanted to move out in a hurry?" Ryder questioned, fixing Shiron.

"I guess so," the Israeli replied resignedly. "Hoped we might spring the bastard and avoid aborting the mission, also avoid a potentially dangerous situation if every man became suspicious of the next." He glanced at Fehed. "That now no longer applies."

"For fuck's sake, a man lies dead there," said Kellar in a low, menacing voice, pointing to Saad, "and one of us here did it. So, who gives a shit about the trani?"

A stunned silence hung over the group for several seconds. Ryder decided it was time to tell them what he knew. "I found a note in the truck."

All turned to him in disbelief.

"A note saying what?" shot Shiron.

"Who we are, and where we were heading."

Everyone looked accusingly at the other.

"Who would've written that?" Sicano asked.

No one answered.

"Do you have it?" Kellar questioned.

"No, it was taken when we were captured. It was in Farsi."

All were fluent in Farsi.

"So they know our intentions. You should've told me earlier about this, Frank," said Shiron, a sharpness to his voice. "With the Iranians knowing the contents of that note, we could be walking into a trap if a base exists."

Ryder shrugged. "The same could be said about the trani, Sergeant." He didn't intend to explain why he held back. Everyone here, as when he found the note, was under suspicion. "It's my guess the Iranian found out who and has paid for it with his life," he finished, looking at each of them for a tell-tale sign.

Everyone stood in silence, glancing at one another and then at Fehed and the body with bewildered expressions.

"Any other revelations?" asked Ryder, finally, glancing at each of the group.

"No. How about you, Corporal?" voiced Shiron.

"No," answered Hellmann, sullenly.

"As you said, Frank: the Iranian found out 'who'," replied Kellar. Then, after a short pause, "Now we know why we've been so closely tracked; God knows how often the transmitter was used, or how many messages might have been left."

"It has to be one of them," shot Shiron, glancing angrily at Fehed and Afari. "To believe otherwise is too hard to accept."

They all nervously glanced at one another again.

"I'll get it out of the little shit," spat Hellmann, making a move towards Fehed.

Ryder quickly looked at Shiron expecting him to intervene, but the sergeant said nothing.

If you're not stepping in, I will. Ryder moved swiftly, standing in front of Fehed, pointing his automatic at Hellmann's throat.

"Back off, Corporal."

Hellmann reluctantly moved back.

Shiron remained silent too, looking intently at Ryder.

"He did not do this!" Afari intervened, "He is innocent; he would not kill his friend."

With the exception of Ryder and Fehed, all eyes turned to her.

"So it's you then," said Sicano, looking as if he was about to grab her but she swiftly drew pistol and pointed it straight at his head. "I wouldn't if I were you," she said menacingly.

"Okay, let's establish a few facts before anyone starts accusing," Ryder said, calming things down a little. "Who's missing a blade?"

They looked and all had a knife sheathed. The killer had used Saad's own.

Ryder eyed each man closely; none had blood on hands or clothes.

"Did anyone see or hear anything unusual during the night?"

Kellar answered, "At the beginning of my watch, a mist was down and I couldn't see more than a few yards, I thought I heard a thud and a cough, but dismissed it."

Afari then said she heard a scraping noise, but the others said they heard nothing.

Everything was now out in the open; the trust needed to accomplish the mission had completely evaporated. Which one of these men could kill so violently and why?

Ryder faced a dilemma: should they abandon the mission or carry on? He would let the others decide. "With what's happened, do we continue? From now on each of us will be watching his back – not good for what we have in mind. Trust is paramount; you know that." He looked at the Israelis.

"This will not stop us completing the mission… I say shoot him so we don't have to watch our backs and let's get on with what we came here to do," said Shiron firmly, glancing at Hellmann who nodded in agreement. "What about you, Frank?" he questioned.

Ryder had come this far and was not about to give up either now they were in sight of the objective. "I'm with you," he shot back then looked at the two Americans for their response.

Both threw glances at one another before Sicano spoke, "Maybe we should abort under the circumstances, Frank, and go for the Gulf." A long pause, "But if you guys are prepared to take the risk, then so are we. Count us in, but we want that shit," he glanced at Fehed, "properly secured and guarded. You agree with that, Bear?"

Kellar nodded.

"That man you call a 'shit' saved our asses flying that helicopter, or had you forgotten?" Ryder angrily replied. "But if it makes you feel better we'll do it. Once we've eyeballed the mountain then we'll decide what to do with him."

The Americans looked a little sheepish but seemed satisfied at getting what they wanted.

Ryder wanted it that way too, for the time being anyway, to let the Americans and Israelis focus anger on the Iranian, taking the attention away from themselves and hopefully encouraging the real killer to drop his guard and make a mistake that might expose him. He was convinced Fehed was not the killer, or Afari for that matter. The Iranian looked as if he hadn't the strength – although he did handle that helicopter without showing a great deal of fatigue – and no way could she deliver a blow like that. Whoever killed Saad was an expert and strong to have made such a thrust at that angle; he would not have known what hit him. They would be playing a very dangerous game now until the killer was exposed. He wondered if all this was worth the 'Queen's shilling'; a cigarette now would certainly ease the stress he felt at this moment. Mouth real dry; he took a swig of water from his flask instead; a sick, anxious feeling tugging at his gut.

Ryder looked over to Afari and saw shock and horror on her

features no doubt wondering, after what had happened, who she could trust. He couldn't blame her; of the five Iranians starting out only two were left. Who would be next? She looked vulnerable and seemed to be struggling within, but suddenly rallied, stared at him and asked quietly, more as a statement than a question, "We were never going to the Gulf in the first place, were we?"

Everyone focused on Ryder.

"No, we were not." It was time she and Fehed heard the truth. "See that big mountain over there," he pointed to the range dominating the horizon. "We're going to check it out then we'll head for the Gulf."

Afari looked at Fehed who could only stare back, stunned, "For what reason?" she questioned, sharply.

He nodded towards the two Israelis. "They believe it might house a base intending to launch missiles at Israel; if so, they want to try and disable it somehow, with our help."

Ryder could almost see Afari's mind gauging the significance of what she had just heard. He guessed this might present an unexpected opportunity to gain revenge big-time on the regime that killed her parents, despite the uncertainty of everything that Saad's death now presented.

Moments later she turned and looked at him straight in the eye and said, voice tense and full of emotion, "I will join you and so will Fehed; he is a brave man."

He was relieved; they would need all the firepower available if a base did exist. But the question of Fehed remained in the air.

"Okay, it's your choice," he shot back. "So, we stay with the plan and take the Iranian with us. I want him kept secure, and you, Sergeant," he looked at Kellar, "will be responsible to ensure he remains that way." He glanced around the circle of taut, bewildered faces, dwelling on the two Americans, then the two Israelis and thought, *one of you four is a killer,* before barking, "Bury the man and let's move out."

20

At the centre of the wide valley plain the file of six silent men and one woman, led by Shiron with Ryder bringing up the rear, reached the edge of a saline marsh criss-crossed by narrow streams. The streams, as far as Ryder could tell, were less than knee-deep and easy to negotiate. But the openness of the whole area, stretching for several miles, would leave them highly exposed, especially as there were clear signs of human habitation in the form of small huts and dirt tracks scattered over the marsh. After scanning the flats with his glasses, Ryder decided it was far too risky to cross in daylight and ordered the group to rest until darkness arrived. Finding a shallow gully, lined with rock and bush which gave an unobstructed view for miles around between vegetation on the rim, they kept together within sight of one another and bedded down to get some sleep. Sicano and Kellar took the first watch.

A few hours later, on his watch with Afari late in the afternoon, Ryder turned to the Iranian. She looked tired and worn out. He felt a pang of concern, if not guilt, at what they were expecting of her; the brutal death of Saad may have been the last straw, shattering her resolve, making her regret the decision to join them. Maybe he could talk her into getting away whilst she still had the chance. He said in a low, soft voice, "If a base exists it'll be tough – if not suicidal – attempting to get inside and disable. You prepared to risk that?"

She gave him a wary, piercing look but did not answer, ignoring him and glancing away, her cocked pistol held firmly in one hand, finger on the trigger.

"You don't have to do this," he pressed, knowing full well the kind of dangers they would face if they had to enter that mountain, especially with a killer in tow. "None of us would feel bad if you were to leave now and make for the Gulf."

She swung back and hissed, "Fehed would," her wide, defiant eyes boring into him, "you think I can just skulk away because the going gets tough after all I and Fehed have been through? I will not leave him. He did not kill Saad; they were good friends… no, I could not leave him; we will take our revenge together, or die in the attempt." She stared hard at him and then spat, "Do not speak to me of this again."

He was taken aback by the sharp rebuke; little doubt she was determined as ever to see it through. It was time to tell her what he thought. "If it's any consolation I do not believe your friend is the killer either – or you for that matter."

She turned fully towards him, an expression of surprise etched on her features. "And why is that?" she whispered with a thin smile.

"Because Fehed and you wouldn't have known the objective prior to today; the note I found proves it. Anyhow, what possible motive could you have for doing it? You all had good reasons to destroy the regime, not yourselves. Besides, that knife thrust would've taken a great deal of strength to execute. No disrespect, but you both don't look capable."

"You suspect anyone?" she asked, voice tense, taking furtive glances over at the others out of earshot several yards away.

He struggled to believe it could be one of the Americans, even one of the Israelis, but it had to be one of them and if forced to choose, Shiron or Hellman would be the first in line, but he replied, "No. What about you?"

He could see by the sudden change in her body language and expression she was considering that he might be the killer. "I do not know. All I know is that we," she glanced over to where Fehed lay, "did not do this." She paused, looking him straight in the eye, "You are British; why were you in an Iranian prison? You said you are SAS, has that something to do with it?" she probed, obviously trying to eliminate him from suspicion.

"Ex SAS."

"If you are a civilian; why do you lead? And what are you doing here in my country?"

"Good questions." She deserved to know the truth but it could not be told. "To your first question: been here before, understand a bit about the culture, and I do have a military background. And, as you know, the others wanted it that way." He paused for a reaction, but none came, so he continued, "To your second: I suppose 'working holiday' would cover it; selling engine parts when arrested, not sure why." He'd kept it short and uncomplicated but could tell she was not convinced, eyeing him with some uncertainty. He wanted to convince her. "If you suspect me; forget it, trust me, I'm on your side. I have no reason to even be here, or the Americans, we are passengers. Fate threw us into this situation just like you. What possible motive could I have for killing your countryman like that? The Israelis apparently always had this mountain as their objective; we joined them to help find what they were looking for. Maybe they have something to hide?" Weak, he agreed, but that was all he could think of.

She seemed to relax a little, uncocked the pistol but kept it firmly within her grip. Energy seemed to drain from her and the conversation ended. Suddenly, she pointed towards the horizon. Ryder followed her gaze, raised binoculars, and saw in the distance plumes of dust in the direction of the mountains they had left twenty-four hours earlier.

"What could it be?" she shot.

"By the size of the plume, I'd guess trucks – and heading our way."

"How far?"

"Five – six miles… four vehicles." Ryder let the glasses drop and

174

pulled out a map. "No roads shown; must be a dirt track." Raising binoculars again he scanned the surrounding ground. "There's a broad track on the other side of that stream; it fords the stream and runs right past our position." Seconds later, "Shit; it's the one they're on."

Afari looked through her glasses, confirming Ryder's fears, then back again to the plume. "Much closer now; we need to find cover," she said urgently.

Ryder called to the others telling them to gather equipment and conceal themselves as best they could. The gully gave scant cover but all quickly found a bush big enough to scramble under hard against the six-foot-high, sharply rising bank on the track side, hopefully giving maximum concealment from above.

The growl of diesel engines increased together with the sound of wheels splashing across shallow water and then the shuddering of the ground, before the growl engulfed everything as the first truck sped past only yards away.

Then, the hiss of air brakes; the screech of tortured metal and the convoy abruptly came to a halt, the third truck stopping alongside where they hid. The throb of idling engines filled the air.

Ryder's adrenaline surged.

The next thing: slamming of doors, tailboards dropping and boots hitting the ground. He prayed dogs were not on board.

Ryder released his pistol safety-catch, gripped the handle ready and listened to the banter of many soldiers moving towards the edge of the gully. If he was about to die he would take as many with him as possible. He waited, expecting discovery at any moment. Then, suddenly, streams of urine hit the bush, percolating down through the dense foliage, trickling over his back; he waited for shit but it never came. Banter and diesels drowned out everything else. The flow of urine gradually stopped. The soldiers drifted back to the trucks and clambered in. Doors slammed, diesels revved and the convoy got underway, to Ryder's relief.

When the vehicles were well away they emerged from hiding and shook themselves down, cursing. None, thankfully, had suffered much of a drenching from the thirty or so men relieving themselves over the edge of the gully. Luckily the fatigues they wore were waterproof and the urine had run off.

"Thank Christ they only pissed on us; could've been worse," said Kellar, checking his rifle. "Any closer and we'd be goners. Could almost taste what they had for fucking breakfast – you hear what they were banging on about?"

"Something about a place called Abbasabad," Sicano replied.

The two Israelis exchanged glances.

Shiron spoke, "It's a village on the west flank of the mountain we're checking out. Small army garrison supposed to be stationed there. If a missile base exists, the land around could be patrolled. I guess the garrison is most likely used for that."

If the Israeli was right that could make the search much more difficult and risky. Ryder hoped the Israeli was wrong.

"It'll be a lot bigger once those trucks arrive – if that's the destination," Kellar voiced, and then, as if as an afterthought, "At least, in some ways, it's a sign we may not be wasting our time after all," he finished, forcing a grin.

Sicano looked at the Israelis, "If those trucks are going to that town, it tells me they know we're coming."

"You mean the note Frank found?" shot Shiron.

"Yeah, and whatever else; reinforcements like that crawling everywhere would make it virtually impossible to penetrate any base we may find in that mountain." Sicano threw sharp glances at the others and spat, "More so, with a killer loose."

"He's right, Frank," backed Kellar. "Maybe we should abort?"

Ryder had to admit he was having serious doubts himself after the Iranian's murder and now the practicalities of getting into a base should they find one with a killer still loose; the Americans did have a point. He turned to Shiron and asked in a curt voice, "Do you agree with that, Sergeant?"

The Israeli didn't hesitate, replying coldly, "We didn't come this far to back out now."

"You, Corporal?" he asked of Hellmann.

"I'm with the Sergeant."

In some ways Ryder was glad the Israelis wanted to press on, and after a few moments' consideration said, "Okay, we stay with the plan."

Relief was clearly visible on the faces of the two Israelis. The two Americans just stared at Ryder whilst Afari and Fehed huddled together and looked blankly at the departing convoy.

Cleaning themselves up the best they could they moved on down the gully away from the stink and settled in to await the twilight. When it eventually arrived, they struck out into the marsh and focussed on the yellow-tipped peaks of Kuh-e Mohammadabad and its twin, Kuh-e Alasahun dominating the skyline. A waning moon would light their path when darkness finally fell.

Ryder stayed at the rear of the file, keeping a close eye on those in front. Fehed, roped to Sergeant Kellar, carried his backpack with hands tied. Afari did everything she could to help him over the uneven ground and through the shallow streams. A bitter wind blew across the plain from the north giving concern that the wind chill factor may rise to a dangerous level, despite the good protection given by the fatigues and sturdy fur-lined boots. Ryder, however, worried that crossing the streams in the depths of winter would drain resistance. He could feel a numbness creeping into his body already.

The few streams encountered were easily negotiated, but the last before leaving the marsh was quite wide and relatively deep, and could not be crossed without getting seriously wet. Ryder ordered Fehed to be secured to a tree stump whilst he and the two Israelis searched the bank to the right for raft material, or perhaps even a boat. Sicano, Kellar and Afari were ordered to do the same in the opposite direction. Out of earshot of the others Ryder had warned her to keep ever on guard and watch both Americans carefully.

A comparatively short distance later, Ryder came upon a domed hut close to the water's edge. In front was moored a small timber boat with oars. A wisp of smoke spiralled up from the top of the hut. In the silence of dusk it was unlikely they would be able to take the boat without making some noise, but he decided to try anyway, thankful for the absence of dogs.

The three crept to the water edge. Hellmann and Shiron carefully slipped into the boat whilst Ryder undid the rope on the bank.

Suddenly, the flap on the hut flew open and a man jumped out pointing a rifle directly at Ryder, shouting to leave his boat or he would shoot.

Ryder heard the hammer on the rifle click back, swung up his own to fire, when a sudden blur of movement came from the boat. The man instantly dropped the rifle, gurgling and clutching desperately at a knife imbedded deep into his throat. Hellmann calmly stepped out of the boat and, without looking at Ryder, strode passed him and over to where the dying man lay. He kicked the rifle aside, removed the knife and wiped it clean before resheathing.

The whole incident had taken less than a few seconds. The Israeli corporal had hit the target at a distance of more than 15 feet in semi-darkness. Ryder was impressed; the corporal had probably saved his life. Was he the killer?

Without anyone saying a word, Hellmann got back into the boat, followed by Ryder and they rowed back in silence to where Fehed was tied.

When Sicano and the others returned not long after, the group crossed the stream taking two trips. Once all on the other side Kellar pushed the boat back into midstream and, in single file led by Ryder, struck out into what remained of the saline marsh.

The ground began to rise dramatically once they reached the foothills of the secondary range. Much closer now, less than twenty miles distant, Kuh-e Mohammadabad rose high with its ragged, uneven outline silhouetted against a clear dawn sky. Ryder referred to the GPS and maps regularly now to ensure the peak ahead, to the left of its twin, was the one they had come to check out. He led them on over sparsely vegetated and patchy snow-covered ground, making sure to keep to the protection of gullies and shallow ravines, until full daylight finally arrived. That night they had covered more than fifteen miles and were now almost at the objective, exhausted and chilled to the bone. Choosing a sheltered depression, well camouflaged by scrub on a low, rocky mound overlooking the rapidly rising foothills of Kuh-e Mohammadabad, they made camp. Tomorrow the group would begin to reconnoitre the mountain. They settled down, keeping to themselves, eyeing one another with suspicion. Ryder made sure he could see them all and kept alert. It troubled him the way Hellman had thrown that knife with such accuracy and power back in the marsh. He would not get much sleep in the coming days, although he had the ability through constant practise to rest his mind and body whilst appearing to be awake. More than ever now, he had to be ready to spring into action the moment it was necessary.

21

Ryder raised binoculars and scanned the empty road below, then beyond to the steep, rising tussock and scrub-covered ground which filtered into the jagged, rocky surfaces of Kuh-e Mohammadabad less than five miles away. For as far as the eye could see the mountain range spread along the horizon, the twin peaks of Kuh-e Mohammadabad to the left, 11,800 feet high, and Kuh-e Alasahun to the right, 11,200 feet high, twenty-five miles apart, looming large and majestic like sentinels in the clear morning air. He ran the binoculars slowly over the barren, snow-covered left-hand peak and down the craggy features of the mountain's western face, attempting to pinpoint anything that might give a clue to a base, but from this distance he saw nothing. A tarseal road, running almost on an east-west axis, bisected the valley and ran on up into the range away to the left on the western side of Kuh-e Mohammadabad. As it snaked through the lower hills, furrowed snow and darkened slush on the surface indicated the road was used recently by vehicles. Patchy snow covered the slopes, becoming widespread higher up. A strong wind blew sheets of powdery snow off the peaks and buffeted the foothills below. He let the glasses drop with a sense of foreboding; searching to determine if this mountain housed a missile base was not going to be easy.

Using the GPS and co-ordinates given to him by Shiron, Ryder once more verified the bleak mountain mass to his left was in fact the objective. He turned to Sicano, also surveying the mountain through binoculars.

"See anything unusual?"

"Nothing; you sure this is the mountain?"

"Certain." He handed Sicano the GPS, together with map.

A minute or two later the American looked up and said, "Yeah, I agree." He then raised glasses to look again at the mountain and muttered, "Sure hope we ain't come all this way for nothin."

Ryder turned to Shiron. "Does this area match the briefing data?"

The Israeli nodded, "Checks out with aerial shots, including the road."

"According to this map, the road runs east to Abbasabad about seven miles into the range near the base of the mountain."

"The silo outlets would probably be on the western side," Shiron said, glancing towards the peak. "Our experts covered every inch of the aerials, found nothing unusual – rock, scrub, snow, that's all. We were to check overhangs and all tracks on the western side. If nothing was found at the lower levels we were to move upwards."

Ryder focused the glasses back on the mountain and then down to the road, following until it disappeared into the hills before turning to Sicano.

"You and Clint scout the south-eastern flank; look for tracks and anything else that might be suspicious… You two," he glanced at the Israelis, "will come with me to cover the western flank."

"And him?" Kellar asked, glancing at Fehed.

"He comes with us." He turned to Afari. "You stay here and keep an eye on the road. I want to know what comes and goes."

She nodded.

To Ryder, she seemed suddenly to have lost the lethargy displayed over the past few days; he hoped so. Maybe the closeness of the mountain and the possibility of some action had something to do with it. Anyway, he had more to think about now they were

181

separating into two groups. Would the killer see this as an opportunity to take out another? Keeping the Americans and the Israelis apart might reduce this possibility; although having the Israelis as part of his team was possibly placing himself at more risk.

He continued, "This will be base, get back here in three days max. Watch for patrols, bury your shit and leave nothing to give away our presence. Do as you've been trained. You're looking for anything that could be a penetration point into the mountain: silo head, vent stacks, anything not natural." He paused and looked at each man, "Any questions?"

Silence.

"Okay, move out."

Under a mostly clear dawn sky streaked with wisps of orange and white cirrus clouds, the Americans left the ridge and made their way down towards the road and into the scrub beyond, keeping to what little cover there was and avoiding patches of snow to avoid leaving an obvious trail. Ryder held back until they were out of sight then said to Shiron, "Untie him."

The two Israelis glanced at each other, stunned; Hellmann's brooding eyes boring into Ryder. Both just stood there tensely until Shiron broke the silence, "You can't do that; you want to end up like the other Iranian? Why put us at unnecessary risk?"

He wasn't going to waste time explaining; obviously they had yet to work out that Fehed could not possibly be the killer.

"Do as I say," Ryder ordered, eyes boring into them both.

The two did not move.

"Do as I say!" he hissed, eyes shifting to the corporal in case he went for the knife. For one moment he wondered if he should confront the Israelis openly right now accusing them of killing Saad, but on reflection decided now would not be a good time; he would wait until he had backup from the others.

Moments later Shiron shrugged, stepped forward and untied the Iranian.

"Give him a rifle and ammo."

Again an exchange of glances; this time of real alarm.

"Do it!" Ryder spat menacingly.

This time Hellmann did what was ordered.

Then for the sake of the two Israelis, Ryder said to the Iranian, "You make one wrong move and I, or these two, will kill you – understood?"

Fehed nodded.

With that they left the ridge and moved down the slope towards the mountain. To ease the tension, Ryder told Fehed to lead so he could be seen by all whilst he remained at the rear of the file as they began their search in earnest across the steeply rising terrain.

By late afternoon Ryder had covered several miles of the lower mountain without incident. Thick clouds had descended making it difficult, if not impossible, to see the upper slopes. At one point he focused his glasses on a large and lengthy overhang, but cloud blanked out his vision of what looked to be an oddly flat piece of vertical black rock positioned immediately under the overhang for almost its entire length. After a few minutes trying to determine if it was man-made, he gave up; he would take a closer look on the way back – weather permitting. Down to the left as night fell, Ryder could make out the road and, beyond that, lights twinkling away in the distance, which he assumed was Abbasabad. Soon they would need to find suitable shelter. The thought of spending darkness in a dugout did not exactly appeal. At this altitude, constant alert for patrols and searching the mountainside sapped strength and the ability to remain focused. He feared the gruelling existence of the past weeks was beginning to take its toll on him more than expected. No doubt the others would be feeling it too, including the traitor, which gave him some degree of solace.

Eventually, Ryder called a halt and they rested amongst rocks sheltered from the wind. Huddled together silently, chewing meagre rations and listening to the wind whistling across the slopes, they made themselves as comfortable as the cramped conditions would allow. Ryder agreed to take the first watch leaving the

Israelis, keeping a close eye on the Iranian, to take the remaining until dawn. He resolved to stay awake for as long possible.

Dawn arrived. Ryder had catnapped throughout the night. After chewing some more meat, the group, cold and stiff, left the boulders and recommenced the search. Now well into the western flank of the mountain, low cloud made it difficult to see much above them, or very far ahead, but slowly they made progress, scouring every yard of the rock and tussock surfaces. By early afternoon the clouds began to lift. The wind that had so far plagued them, eased and they made better headway. Hawks screeched overhead, searching for prey.

Cresting a ridge, Ryder looked out across a narrow valley towards a broad spur, some 500 yards distant. Shiron said the spur looked like the one he had seen on the aerial shots but couldn't be sure. He suggested they should stake-out where the spur met the mountain. Ryder agreed and they headed down the slope towards the long, scrub-covered finger of land.

On reaching the crest the four men could see the surface had been skimmed exposing rock to form a track capable of taking heavy loads. At first glance it could easily be judged natural, but on closer inspection the work of machinery was obvious. Despite boulders and rubble disguising its meandering path, there could be little doubt this track was subject to regular use. This fact energised the two Israelis who now took the lead following the track.

They headed up the spur on the leeward side, keeping to the edge just below the level of the ridge, using what cover they could. Finally arriving where the spur and track met sheer rock, Ryder observed nothing unusual but it seemed illogical for the track to end abruptly like this. From a concealed position well away, he scanned the rock face with his binoculars; if an entrance did exist it would surely be under camera surveillance, or heat imaging. However, no equipment could be detected, but he decided it too risky to make a close-up inspection, resolving to dig-in and wait to see if anything happened before they had to leave the next day.

The night was long, cold and uneventful. No matter how comfortable they tried to make themselves in the narrow, cramped conditions of the individual dugouts none succeeded. When the dawn arrived to the screeching of hawks above, Ryder decided to wait until full daylight before heading back to the base. When a pale sun partly hidden by cloud illuminated the spur without change in respect of the rock face and anyone using the track, he gave the order to move out.

On the way back the overhang observed the previous day was still shrouded in low cloud but Ryder's attention was quickly drawn away at the sound of barking dogs. Focusing binoculars down the mountainside he could see a patrol of several men, in single file, some distance down the slope, making their way slowly between the shrub and boulders. The file, accompanied by a pair of fierce looking Alsatians straining at leads, was thankfully heading in the opposite direction. They hid amongst the tussock and Ryder watched the patrol through his scope until they soon disappeared out of sight; a timely reminder they were not alone in this hostile wilderness and should remain ever vigilant if they were to survive.

As light began to fade on the third day, Ryder arrived back on the ridge with the others, exhausted and hungry, followed shortly by the Americans.

After eating a scant meal cooked by Afari over a small fire, Ryder questioned the Americans. "I guess you found nothing?"

Both nodded then Sicano said, "Pretty rugged ground up that eastern side, nothing but rock, scrub and goat trails… nothing that would remotely suggest access, air-vents, comms or the movement of heavy vehicles; the weather was shitty too. We'll try higher tomorrow."

"No different with us," said Ryder, "although we did locate what could be described as a rough track capable of taking vehicles. Strange thing is it came to an abrupt end hard against a sheer rock face."

"Concealed entrance, maybe," offered Kellar.

"Didn't attempt to go close in case of surveillance eyes, but from what we could see through the bins it looked natural, no firm linear lines that would suggest sliders."

"Encounter patrols?" Sicano asked, turning to Shiron.

Both the Israelis had said nothing since returning but had kept a close eye on Fehed, now tied up again outside the circle. Ryder had ordered it to avoid trouble at this stage with the Americans. "Yeah, one, but well away," the Israeli growled.

"Did you?" Ryder asked the Americans.

"No, only wind, sleet and hawks," Kellar replied.

"Suggests nothing to be found on that side then," Ryder paused to gather his thoughts. "Okay, this is what we do. In the light of the negative result on the eastern side, we'll now cover the spur on the west. We've sufficient rations to last almost a fortnight, if used sparingly it will allow several days of continuous surveillance before the need to make south for the Gulf. It won't be productive for all of us to spend the time holed up together on that exposed spur, it's cramped and extremely uncomfortable, so I suggest me and you two," he looked across at Shiron and Hellmann, "and you too," at the Iranian, "will take the first four days, and you—"

"You taking the Iranian?" cut in Sicano.

"I am," he replied firmly. "I want to keep a close eye on him. You have a problem with that?" What he really meant to say was: 'I'm not leaving him with you.'

The American shrugged, "Have it your way."

Ryder was glad he backed off; things might have turned nasty otherwise. "Okay, you and Bear can take the remaining surveillance time. Meanwhile Afari, and those not on the spur, will monitor traffic on the road below." He glanced around the circle, "Again, anyone have a problem with that?" He had but wasn't going to say. Leaving the two Americans alone on the ridge with Afari was a real risk if one of them was the traitor; the culprit could well kill the other two and take off to Abbasabad.

No response. He looked over at Afari who had just finished

feeding the bound Fehed, "Much traffic while we were absent?"

"Several vehicles, mostly sedans and private trucks; some individuals with donkeys but no military as far as I could tell; that's it," she replied.

Ryder would have expected some military vehicles on the road if a base did exist; but then why that patrol, and why the garrison in Abbasabad? One contradicted the other, strengthening his opinion that they had come all this way for nothing. Silence prevailed after that and fatigue took over; the watch was agreed and finally they all turned in.

The following morning as pre-dawn light began to percolate above the peak, Ryder and his party prepared to leave. The four then made their way down to the road and melted into the semi-darkness beyond. They made good progress, but about four miles out from the spur faint voices were heard on the wind ahead; all dived for a crevasse in a nearby rock outcrop. Waiting tensely in silence with Ryder scanning the terrain through a gap, he suddenly saw a soldier crest the ridge ahead followed by another, then another with dog on a leash.

Shit. "Patrol, coming our way with a fucking dog," he spat at the others, huddled below. "Sure to sniff us out."

"How many and how far away?" shot Shiron.

"Three… about seventy yards."

"Take'em now," Shiron urged.

"We shoot, it'll echo for miles and we'll have the whole fucking garrison down on us," Hellmann quickly responded.

"What else do you suggest then, Corporal – give ourselves up?" Shiron shot back,

Ryder knew that to eliminate this patrol would end any further searching for a base and they all would be lucky to escape to the Gulf alive, but he had no choice. Moving out from the crevasse he went up around the rocks on the blind side, followed by the others. He prayed they were upwind; if not, the dog would, any second, catch their scent.

The patrol was now less than thirty yards away.

Leaning against the outcrop to steady their aim, the four raised AK47s, released safety-catches and lined up the targets; Ryder the dog; the others, a man apiece.

Ryder was about to squeeze the trigger when the patrol suddenly stopped in its tracks. The leader turned and said something to those behind before raising his binoculars and scanning the lower slopes; something had caught his eye.

With gunsight trained on the dog's head, Ryder waited tensely.

Moments later he grew curious, put the rifle aside and raised binoculars to look down the slope in the same direction. On the road bisecting the valley, well away in the distance, the lenses found a large military truck with a flashing blue light. Milling about the vehicle were a number of armed men; *fuck, reinforcements.* But he need not have worried. The leader put away his binoculars and the three-man patrol turned and began to descend the slope, every step taking them further away. He breathed a sigh of relief.

"That was close," said Shiron, forcing a thin smile. "Looks like a timely end to their shift; another few seconds and they would've been dead."

"Yeah," muttered Ryder. "So would we if a firefight had happened with that lot down there." He nodded towards the twenty or so men spreading away from the truck and from where they hid.

When the patrol eventually disappeared out of sight, the four left the outcrop, Ryder focused more now on what lay ahead instead of upwards at the mountain. However, he did make a point of looking again at the unusual rock formation under the long overhang, but cloud, once more, prevented him from seeing it. With Fehed leading and himself in the rear they eventually arrived at the spur early in the afternoon without a hitch.

They settled in the dugouts just below the level of the ridge with an unobstructed view of the rock face where it joined the spur. This would be home for the next four days and Ryder hoped the weather would be kind. Making himself as comfortable as possible in the bleak conditions, he began to carefully scan the sheer rock wall.

Time passed and the four, cramped in the confining earth depressions, experienced bitter winds and occasional drizzle with only hawks screeching above for company. Without the waterproof clothing taken from the helicopter, they would hardly have survived the gruelling conditions. Nourished only by dried meat and water, they maintained energy by remaining constantly in the dugouts, silently vigilant, moving only when required to perform bodily functions.

On the afternoon of the fourth day the cloudy conditions lifted bringing much needed sunlight and a little warmth. The track had been under constant surveillance with nothing to show; one more day and the rations would be gone. Tomorrow the two Americans would take over. Ryder felt frustrated, knowing instinctively the mountain had something to yield and wanting answers.

Dusk came and they prepared for yet another cold and miserable night. Ryder would take the first watch, the Israelis the second and third and finally Fehed until dawn. Time passed slowly and he fought to stay awake, counting stars in the clear indigo sky and worrying how to flush out the killer. Of the four men he suspected, Hellmann, in the dugout next to him, had aroused his suspicions the most, only because he was strong, handled a knife well and did have easy access to the transmitter before it was destroyed. The story about the battery running out, he thought, had been a little weak. But then again, why would he have mentioned to his sergeant that it had been tampered with in the first place? He also had a growing suspicion of Sicano for reasons he could not quite put his finger on, but the American's aggressiveness and attitude had been niggling away at him since the helicopter episode. What possible motive either of these two men could have to commit murder and leave notes for their pursuers baffled him. He would have to confront them soon.

Suddenly, well into his watch and almost nodding off, Ryder heard a familiar sound on the wind and looked down the spur. It came again, and then he knew – diesels!

Adrenaline surged, cold and discomfort forgotten. He roused the others, who also heard the growl of engines, and then, several hundred yards down the spur, all four saw three sets of hooded headlamps crest the rise. Within minutes, three army trucks, silhouetted against the darkening sky, hooded headlamps illuminating the one in front, roared by and pulled up in front of the rock face. The length and shape of the cargos left little doubt they were carrying missiles. The trucks waited, engines idling, until a low, powerful hiss of hydraulics, followed by a deep rumbling sound, and a twenty-foot square section of the rock face retreated inwards several feet before it began to slide to one side.

Ryder watched transfixed as the vehicles moved into the mountain, engines reverberating loudly once inside the cavernous entrance. Within minutes the huge vehicles disappeared into the blackened hole and the rock face slid back into a seamlessly closed position A feeling of exhilaration, mixed with fear and trepidation, ran through him; a base did exist, it had not been a wild-goose chase after all. The Israelis had been right, too, and could hardly contain their jubilation; all the suffering to get here had now been fully justified. When what they had just witnessed finally sunk in, Ryder and the others hurriedly removed all signs of their presence as best they could, left the dugouts and slunk away into the darkness.

22

Sicano turned away from the fire, looked directly at Ryder and said in an urgent voice, "Why risk going in? Now it's established a base exists, let's get the hell outta here and tell the generals; let them blast the shit outta the place." He paused for emphasis, "To go in would be suicide… too risky, Frank, with no stats, no intel – nothing!"

Ryder remained silent.

"Why come all this way to do nothing?" questioned Shiron, voice tinged with anger. "We've come too far to back out now."

"C'mon Sergeant," snapped Sicano. "Get real. We've established a base exists so why the fuck put ourselves at more risk?"

"Our orders were to disable," pressed the Israeli. "Besides, there's no guarantee we'll get back to tell any generals."

"We've no idea what's inside – layout, personnel, security. It's craz—"

"Hold it! Hold it!" Ryder intervened. "I'll decide what goes down here."

"We'll go without you," countered Shiron, looking daggers at the American; Hellmann at his side nodding in agreement.

"I said hold it, Sergeant!" Ryder shouted, eyes levelled menacingly at the Israeli.

"But—"

"Cut it, I said," he snapped again then turning to Sicano and Kellar, "We knew what we were putting down here. You wanted this to get rid of the 'failure', the 'guilt' – remember?" His features hardened. "This is a hostile secret base – missile base. The Israelis have orders to disable if proven. Well, it's proven. I command and I'm ordering we follow through."

Silence except for the sound of wind buffeting the hideaway.

The two Israelis appeared visibly relieved. Ryder, too, but he didn't show it.

"Thank you, Frank," said Shiron.

"Don't thank me. This is our business, it's what we do. We're professionals and we didn't come all this way for a holiday."

"Frank, going in blind is a helluva risky business," said Kellar. "Doing it knowing—"

"Someone here is a killer," Ryder finished for him.

"Yeah…well, you have to trust the man next to you; you know that, or you'll be looking over your shoulder every fucking minute," the American pressed, eyes shifting around the huddled group.

Another prolonged silence.

Kellar was right; it was against all the rules. Ryder stared into the flames then replied quietly, glancing intently at each man. "No choice unless that person wants to own up."

All, except Ryder and Afari, looked hard at the bound Iranian.

"Kill him!" spat Hellmann.

"No!" shot Ryder. "This man saved our butts flying that heli. If he'd wanted, he could've killed us all."

"And himself; that's why he didn't," Hellmann countered.

Although the Iranian understood little English, fear clearly registered.

Ryder was surprised the Americans and Israelis had yet to work out that it was highly unlikely the Iranian was the killer. Or maybe they had, but didn't want to accept that it could be one of them. One was attempting to deflect attention from himself; the question: who?

"Why take the risk?" Sicano pressed again. "He's not even trained for the kinda heat we can expect."

Ryder reached a decision. "We'll leave him here, bound. If we get back, then we shoot him. If we don't, he'll die anyway. Agreed?"

Silence as they thought about it, then the Israelis nodded in agreement.

Ryder looked at the two Americans. "You in?"

Both men glanced at one another then nodded.

"Okay, that's settled. Now, how do we get inside that mountain?"

"Vent shafts maybe," offered Shiron.

"We've spent more than several days scouring that mountain and found nothing," Sicano voiced.

"What about taking a closer look at that unusual rock formation?" suggested Shiron.

"A possibility," Ryder replied. "Could be an outlet of some kind, but its high up, difficult to reach, we'd need ropes. Besides, once up there, how would we get through?"

"Blast our way?" pressed Shiron.

"And broadcast our presence? Not an option, Sergeant. What else do we have?"

"The main entrance," said Kellar. "Wait until it opens to let vehicles through, then slip in."

"We'll never get near the entrance without detection. They'll have cameras and heat imaging for sure. I would advise against," said Sicano, looking determinedly at Ryder.

"Maybe not," said Hellmann, supporting Kellar.

"He's right," replied Shiron, on Sicano's side. "Without external guards, there has to be."

"There is another option," offered Ryder. "Hijack a truck."

"How could we be sure it was heading for the base?" Sicano asked.

Afari chipped in, "Three convoys have passed since you left. That means out of the three, only the one you saw went to the base."

Ryder turned to Sicano, "Unless you want to go back up that

mountain and search for another way in, it seems to me it's our only chance." He placed a log on the fire. "The only way in as I see it, would be attached to a convoy like the one we saw. To cut away a single truck would definitely create suspicion and to go up the spur in a single vehicle would most likely rouse suspicion. Any vehicle destined for the base would be pre-scheduled anyway." He paused and looked at each of the others in turn. "The whole deal is going to depend on a large slice of luck, but for the moment let's work on a basic plan. At dawn we make our way down to the road, conceal ourselves and wait. We'll take out a truck in the first convoy that comes along heading west, providing it's not carrying troops. You, Sergeant," he looked at Shiron, "will move out in front of the last truck and play dead. You and you," he pointed at Sergeant Kellar and Corporal Hellmann, "will check inside," then to Sicano, "Sergeant, you and me will take the cab occupants. Afari, keep an eye on him," he nodded at Fehed. "If all goes well; pray the convoy is heading to the base."

"What can we expect inside the mountain?" Kellar asked.

Ryder looked at Shiron to answer that.

"Our experts said we could expect a Western-style subterranean structure," the sergeant replied, poking at the flames. "It could possibly be a two or three level structure entered at the highest level with control, storage and missile firing operations on the lowest. There would probably be a large entry chamber with a tunnel to penetrate well into the mountain; the chamber and tunnel would be big enough to take heavy vehicles and equipment, at least we know from what we saw, that's true. Security would be strong."

"What about personnel?"

"Probably a hundred or more; fifty per cent would be security."

"And firing chambers?"

The Israeli quickly answered, "Unlikely to be conventional silos; mobile gantries, more likely in one or more chambers."

"What size?"

"Enough to take a six-cluster; experts reckon Shahab-4 missiles

194

could be used. That indicates the firing tubes could be in excess of 40 feet in length."

"What would the tubes be made of?" Kellar asked.

"Tubes and gantries in steel; tubes lined with non-combustibles."

"We'd need some grunt to knock them out," said the American to Ryder.

"What we have will do, as long as the charges are well placed."

"How does the whole thing work?" Kellar pressed.

"Tubes would be loaded using overhead cranes, and elevated towards an outlet slot in the mountainside – that unusual surface under the overhang could be an outlet – the slot covers would slide open to fresh air, the missiles would be primed and then fired from the control centre. To disrupt this we would need to place charges around the base of the gantry supports. When they blow, the tube frame will collapse."

"Assuming we even reach the chambers," said Sicano.

"Naturally," agreed Shiron.

"If not, we place them wherever we can," Ryder said firmly.

"How accessible would the chambers be?" asked Kellar.

"Maybe through tunnels from a control centre; chambers would be remote in case of accidents."

A moment's silence, then, "Anything else we need to know, Sergeant?" Ryder asked.

"No, that's about it," replied the Israeli.

"Okay, here's the scenario," said Ryder. "Assuming we hijack a truck heading for the base, we con our way in, you and me that is," he glanced at Sicano. "The rest of you will remain hidden in the back until inside and safe to get out. Depending on what we find we then make our way down to the lowest level, if there is one, otherwise we search the level we're on. Once in the firing chambers, we place the charges anywhere that'll do the most damage, and then get out fast. If two chambers exist, we separate. Oscar and you, Bear, including you," he glanced at Afari, "will deal

195

with one, and you two," he turned to the Israelis, "will come with me to the other. If we get out safely, we regroup here. Questions?"

"Loose game plan, Frank," said Sicano. "Not what they taught at Campbell."

"Best we have," Ryder countered, fully aware of the risks. Now the whole thing had become a reality he could not help but feel concern tinged with fear at what they were contemplating, but pushed it aside.

They continued to talk well into darkness, covering details of the operation, overhauling weapons, checking and storing ammunition and grenades in backpacks together with rations and other items considered essential. Last of all, and most importantly, they carefully prepared charges using what little Semtex they had, taped together with Russian-made detonators and timers to form lethal explosive packs capable of doing serious damage if correctly placed.

Finally, preparations were complete ready to move out at first light. The success or failure of the whole operation now depended entirely upon what they found inside the mountain, the determination of each man, and what the killer intended. Ryder made up his mind to confront Hellman, and if necessary, Sicano before they left.

23

Dawn broke under a leaden sky, thankfully without rain. Ryder stirred after little sleep, silently suffering the cold and discomfort. Not much was said as he and the others gathered equipment, chewed on dried meat, and prepared to leave the ridge. When all were ready, Ryder decided he could not delay confronting Hellmann any longer; no way was he about to go into that mountain with a killer loose.

"Corporal Hellmann."

The Israeli stopped what he was doing and turned to face Ryder as he approached.

"Why did you—?"

"Hold it right there," a voice suddenly shot out of the semi-darkness with such menace it made Ryder and the others turn to where it came from.

A beam of light blinded the group.

"For fuck's sake; turn that off!" Ryder shouted. "You crazy? A patrol could home in."

"That's the idea, Frank."

Sicano! He'd singled out the wrong man.

All reached for rifles.

"I wouldn't do that if I were you," said the American, firing a few rounds into the ground making them all jump back, the sound reverberating loudly through the valley.

"Believe me, it would be a pleasure to blow you away, but you'll be more valuable to my colleagues. I will, however, if I have to – be warned." Sicano then fired more rounds into the air.

"You motherfucker... you son-of-a-bitch," Kellar snarled, looking completely stunned. "How the fuck can you do this? What the hell's in all this for you?"

"Nothing you would understand. But for the record: there was no way I could let you get into that base."

Desperation gripped Ryder; he hoped patrols were not nearby. So he had been wrong about Hellmann; one problem had gone away at least, but a much bigger one had taken its place. It must not end like this, not now, not after all they had been through. He had to find a way to disarm Sicano; keeping him talking for now was all he could do. "Why are you doing this?" he asked, still trying to come to terms with what was happening. "Who're your masters?"

"Shut the fuck up, Brit. Keep outta this," he spat back.

A long silence as the American sergeant seemed to consider the question.

"On second thoughts I'll answer your question, Brit – it will amuse me while we wait." He let off another burst and when the noise died he continued, "Just to make sure my people have no difficulty in locating us."

"So, in the pay of the Iranians," Kellar said, voice more under control.

"You got it, and have been for some time; one of a number in your Armed Forces. We all do our bit, some shoot people in your military bases, others like me feed out information that might be considered useful to my country."

"Did you betray Overflow?" he pressed coldly.

Sicano hesitated, "No, but if we hadn't been in lock-down from the get-go, I would've."

"You shit, you can't take us all," shot Kellar.

"Bear, rest assured, I can and I will if you continue to provoke me."

"Why did you suffer in that shit-hole of a prison?" the American barked. "Why not tell your friends then about the dams?"

"Would've thought that obvious," Sicano came back. "Until there was proof I wasn't the enemy, any explanations would fall on deaf ears. Same reason I'm not going into that mountain; they'll shoot first and ask questions later; same reason I kept quiet at other opportunities like at the bridge, the dam and when we stumbled on the patrol. In that shit-hole of a place as you call it, I told them just enough to establish my bona fides which were verified. The interrogating officer was not far enough up the chain to know my full cover. Anyhow, to your first question: I didn't. To your second: I did. How d'yer think they knew about the dams?"

"Why the killing spree the day we left when they already knew everything from you?" growled Ryder.

"As I told you, I didn't tell them everything, and as the psycho said, he couldn't wait any longer. He wanted total confessions and wanted all the glory of breaking you completely. Your confessions televised around the world; and he would've gotten it."

"Fucking traitor!" shouted Kellar, moving towards Sicano.

"I wouldn't if I were you, Sergeant," he snarled, firing a few rounds into the ground at Kellar's feet.

The American stumbled back. "You motherfucker!" Kellar hissed. "Why put you in the truck?" he fired, looking as if he was about to launch himself again at Sicano.

"It had to look, to you and the rest of the world, that I was still one of the team. You'd eventually confess at the new camp and I would've too. Once we were exchanged, which was the plan, I'd carry on as before. The landslide changed all that and when the Israelis told us about the possible missile base, saying they were going on alone to find it, I wanted to go just in case one existed and the Israelis survived to tell. Now we've proved it you cannot be allowed to tell anyone, or destroy it."

"Why wait till now?" asked Ryder, bitterness to his voice.

"Never thought we'd get this far. I left messages, used the

transmitter, but it seems you were too good at keeping one step ahead."

"So, we can expect a welcoming committee?"

"More than likely," the sergeant replied with a malevolent smile. "You saw those trucks full of troops heading for here; probably part of the reception, but you won't get to meet it now though."

"Assuming the messages were found," countered Ryder.

"No matter; for you it's now all over."

"As well as the Iranian, you caused Jed's death, too," said Kellar, hatred clear in his voice.

"Yeah, kept the rope just tight enough so the Brit couldn't reach the rifle… as for the Iranian, he'd gotten too inquisitive; wanted to know why I was searching the packs."

"And why were you?" shot Ryder, ready to spring at the American.

"Needed something to write on – get another message out. The stupid fuck thought I was stealing food, so I shut him down."

"Why didn't you take out Bear when you were alone with him up on the mountain and again here with Afari over the last few days?"

"Yeah, I thought about it but decided against. Finding a base was unlikely from where I stood despite all that shit about troops and the garrison. Why jeopardise my cover when we'd soon be on our way to the Gulf? Wrongly it seems now, but at the time I thought if I'd turned myself in telling them I was on their side – an Iranian spy," he chuckled, "who would have believed me in this remote fucking place; more likely I'd been shot before my bona fides could be verified. Now that still might be the case." He paused a moment or two, as if reflecting, then, swinging the rifle in an arc at the feet of the stunned group he said, "Another thing, it would not have helped my cover when exchanged as planned if I was the only one to have survived all this; someone back in the States might just have soon gotten suspicious. Anyhow all this doesn't matter now. Fuck America!"

Ryder caught Hellmann's eye and guessed what the corporal was thinking. The Israeli's hand moved almost imperceptibly down towards knife strapped to thigh. He had to keep Sicano talking.

"What made you change sides?" he asked coldly.

"Money… what else?"

"You did it for money!" shouted Kellar. "You betrayed your country for fucking money!"

Sicano looked menacingly at Kellar. "What the fuck do I care about America."

"They gave you a career you could've been proud of," he shot back.

"That's your opinion."

"You told us your mother is American, father, Turkish," said Kellar. Then suddenly, it dawned, "Your father's Iranian; you're a fucking sleeper – a spook!"

Sicano did not answer straight away, just stared emptily at Kellar then spat, "You call it what you like; I don't give a shit. You fucking Americans killed my father on an oil rig in the Persian Gulf. What would you know about the pain and suffering after losing him and watching my mother suffer so bitterly; revenge is sweet and what I'm doing now is even sweeter. My countrymen will now take over to deal with you as they see fit. One thing's for sure: you'll not see the land of your birth again." He quickly glanced at Afari and Fehed, "That excludes you two, of course, but your days will be numbered, too."

Corporal Hellmann's hand was now at his thigh, only inches away from the sheathed knife.

Ryder had to risk getting Sicano's full attention. It was now or never.

He lunged sideways for rifle. At that same moment, Afari dived for hers, momentarily confusing Sicano with the two bodies, a blur flying in opposite directions. The American fired at Afari first, she screamed, then he swung and fired at Ryder sending a bullet whizzing past his ear. But before he could fire off another, Ryder had rolled and, in one swift movement, grabbed up the rifle, turned and shot the sergeant cleanly through the head milli-seconds before Hellmann's knife sunk deep into the American's heart.

Ryder sprang quickly to Sicano's convulsing body and kicked the rifle away, then ran to where Afari lay holding her neck.

"You okay?"

She nodded and he gently removed her hand, relieved to see the bullet had not penetrated the skin but left a raw-looking welt; she was lucky to still be alive. Had she not distracted the American when she did he doubted he would have reached the rifle alive.

"It's a surface wound. You'll be fine… that move was perfectly timed. I owe you."

She gave him a weak smile and he returned to the American.

Sicano coughed once, blood flowed from his mouth and vacant eyes stared blankly into space. The convulsions stopped and he lay still.

"Is he dead?" hissed Shiron.

"All but," Hellmann replied, as Sicano took his last gasp and the Israeli pulled out the knife with a single jerk to wipe it clean on the American's shirt.

Fehed and Afari looked coldly down at the dead body; Saad had been avenged.

Ryder was now anxious to get away. "Let's move; we've got a truck to catch." He glanced at Kellar. "Take the body. We'll dump it away from here. You," he looked at Hellmann, "untie the Iranian and give him a rifle and pack." As Ryder turned away, Hellmann asked, "What were you going to ask earlier, Frank?"

"Forget it; it was nothing." He dared not think what the consequences would have been had he accused the wrong man. If the American had held off just a little longer from making his move it might well have been a whole different story. However, his immediate concern now was to avoid patrols coming this way alerted by the gunfire.

Without wasting another moment the five unkempt, bearded men and Afari fled the ridge and headed swiftly down the slope towards the road; Ryder, relieved the traitor problem had gone away and that he could now fully focus on the highly dangerous task that lay ahead.

PART THREE

Retribution

24

Keeping up a gruelling pace eastwards after escaping the knoll ridge, it was early afternoon before Ryder decided to wait concealed in a ditch that ran parallel and below the level of the tarsealed road connecting the towns of Kahbar and Javazm. Strong, gusting winds under an oppressive sky buffeted the group as they huddled together. The stretch of road to the right was relatively straight for a fairly long way and to the left disappeared around a sharp bend that led into a ravine; an ideal place to wait and hijack a vehicle. Sparse traffic passed and Ryder worried that it might be difficult to remain unseen should anyone come by on foot.

Sicano's body had been dumped well away from the knoll and no patrols had been encountered, although activity could vaguely be seen through binoculars back on the knoll away in the distance. He worried that security would be intensified after what happened and should they find the body. If road blocks are set up on the way to the base, thoroughly searching all vehicles, all chance of succeeding with the mission would certainly end. Ryder went over the plan again. He looked at the Israelis. "You two, position yourselves down the road at least twenty or thirty yards over there," he pointed along the straight stretch of road, "and signal if the last truck is carrying troops. Give the 'clear' signal as soon as you can. We'll abort if carrying troops or if the trucks are too closely bunched and await the next."

"Preceding trucks should tell," said Shiron.

"Agreed, but the last could be carrying supplies." Ryder turned to the Iranian, "Fehed, you move closer to the bend and wait. If we get the clear, and as soon as the second to last truck disappears around the bend, you halt the last. I don't care how you do it, but don't fail. Me and Bear will take out those in the cab. We'll use knives." He turned to Afari, "You wait for the all-clear then jump into the back with the others." After a short pause he ended, "The side road turn-off towards Abbasabad I calculate is less than ten miles from here and Kahbar more than fifteen miles further on. If we take a truck let's hope it's heading for the former."

They spent the next several hours mostly in silence, listening, before the growl of diesel engines came on the wind from the right – the direction of Javazm. Scrambling to road level Ryder saw through binoculars in the fading light a convoy of six trucks approaching less than a mile away, headlamps ablaze. He scanned the line of dark-green vehicles.

Shiron did the same, telling Ryder they looked like supply trucks. He ordered the Israelis and Fehed to take up positions.

The convoy drew nearer until, with a deafening roar, the first of the big trucks rumbled past, followed by the rest at some 50-yard intervals.

Ryder waited, adrenaline pumping, counting the vehicles as they passed.

Shiron signalled the last was not carrying troops.

When the fifth eventually disappeared around the bend, Ryder signalled Fehed to make his move.

The Iranian sprang from the ditch and ran towards the sixth truck in its path, arms waving.

The driver slammed on brakes; a hiss of compressed air and the truck began to skid across the surface before coming to a screeching halt only feet away from where Fehed had thrown himself to the ground.

Ryder, with Kellar close behind, dashed across the tarseal and vaulted onto the running board on the driver's side, wrenched open the cabin door and pulled the startled man out. As he fell to the road, Ryder stabbed him through the heart before dragging the body to the ditch and throwing it in. Kellar did the same with the co-driver on the other side.

Running back to the truck, Ryder clambered up into the driver's seat and slammed the vehicle into gear as Kellar scrambled in beside him. Through the rear window of the cabin he could just make out the two Israelis with Afari and Fehed hoisting themselves and equipment over the tailboard. He pressed down hard on the accelerator; the idling engine roared into life and gathered speed towards the bend. Crunching through the gears, he swung the vehicle around the bend into the ravine and soon caught up with the rest of the unsuspecting convoy; the whole process had taken less than a minute. At the speed they were travelling, he estimated they would reach the turn-off to Abbasabad in less than fifteen minutes.

In the rear, Shiron, Hellmann and Fehed forced open several timber crates to reveal machine parts, blankets and, surprisingly, army uniforms and rope. The uniforms would help get them into the base and the rope may well come in handy once inside. Hurriedly they discarded smelly fatigues, including Afari, not caring about modesty. Uniforms were passed through the cabin window to Ryder and Kellar, who awkwardly helped each other to change and still keep up with the convoy whilst sharing the steering and accelerator. The crates were then resealed and stacked to form a cavity behind the cabin big enough for the four in the back to conceal themselves in the narrow gap.

The convoy took the turn-off to Abbasabad, much to Ryder's relief, and eventually, after a bumpy ride on a long, winding road, entered the village as full darkness descended. Ryder drove down a dimly lit main street before coming to a small central square surrounded by single-storey dwellings. Here he became concerned by the number of troops milling around, fuelling fears that a reception committee would be at the base. If a garrison compound was the convoy's destination they would have to abandon the vehicle before reaching it; once inside they would be trapped.

The convoy passed through the square and approached what looked like a military compound enclosed with a high barbed-wire fence and double-gated entrance leading off from the road they were on. By this time Ryder was worried; any thought of abandoning the truck now, with the presence of so many troops along the roadside, had gone. Ahead he watched fearfully as headlamps of the leading truck swung left towards the compound entrance followed by the second then the third – anxiety levels doubled.

The fourth and fifth trucks in front began to slow. He decelerated, changed gear and glanced quickly at Kellar. "Hold on Bear; we take off at those gates," then he yelled at the others in the rear to prepare for action.

Suddenly, the fourth truck increased speed, passed the entrance, followed by the fifth, and before Ryder could fully appreciate what had happened, they swept by too. Hope surged; could the trucks now be heading for the base?

"Holy shit!" exclaimed Kellar, amidst shouts of jubilation from the rear.

Ryder grinned, "Now for the big one."

25

From the truck cabin, Ryder watched, steeling himself, as the rock surface slid open and the leading vehicle entered the mountain. Seconds later, he engaged gear and followed into a cavernous chamber, adrenaline pumping. The lead vehicle stopped at a checkpoint

After a tense wait, weapon primed and ready across his knee, Ryder's turn eventually came.

Three security guards approached; one asked for the cargo manifest whilst the other two went to the rear.

Fuck! Searching the trucks. His heart sunk; there was no escape now if the others were found.

Fumbling in the open compartment in front of the steering wheel, Ryder pulled out a bundle of papers and handed them over, praying they were what the guard wanted.

The man looked at the sheets, nodded, kept one and handed the rest back. Relieved, Ryder eased his finger off the trigger of the machine pistol and let out a silent breath.

The two guards at the rear lowered the tailboard, clambered in and began to check the crates. Ryder, outwardly calm, smiled down at the guard beside the cabin; if the two in the back discovered the others he would blast away and to hell with the consequences.

Seconds passed. He heard crates noisily moved around and jemmied open; if those concealing the four were checked, all would be over; his finger tightened on the trigger. He listened, pulse racing, to the guards cursing, sniffing at the air and commenting on the pungent smell; agreeing it was foul before both decided they had seen enough. Clambering out, the two men thudded back down to the ground, replaced the tailboard, and made their way to the front. Ryder watched the two join the other. The one who had checked the manifest took one last look at him, before he turned away and headed for the front of the convoy. He glanced sideways at Kellar and grinned, hardly able to believe their luck. The leading truck began to move; he engaged gear and followed towards a tunnel entrance at the rear of the chamber.

Shortly the convoy emerged from the short tunnel into another well lit, cavernous space. Following the lead truck to the left, Ryder backed into a dock alongside the other vehicles. He cut the engine and watched as the crew of the truck alongside jumped down from the cabin and headed for a door in the wall adjacent to the dock. The remaining crew lingered in front of the first truck but, thankfully, soon dispersed.

Eventually he and Kellar clambered down from the cabin. Ryder made for the back whilst Kellar lifted the bonnet and busied himself with the engine. Technicians and armed security personnel were everywhere about the dock area, but paid no attention to the trucks. In the back the others remained concealed until Ryder entered. He and the others then emptied the larger crates and began to fill them again with weapons, ammunition vests and explosives in packs, including coils of the nylon rope, but kept knives concealed within uniforms.

"Go check the dock and chamber. See what kind of reception we can expect," Ryder whispered to Shiron as he continued to load the four crates.

The Israeli slipped away.

Not long after, he returned with Kellar in tow. He whispered, "Looks as if storage is on this side; admin and personnel quarters on the other. Place full of soldiers... definite sense of urgency;

everyone seems to be pumping… I saw two lifts, at the end of the dock. Staircases both sides went downwards only, confirming a multi-levelled complex. But wait for it: I saw nuclear warheads being hoisted below; looked like multiples to me."

"Left the best till last then, I see." The American grinned at Ryder; white teeth prominent in the dim light.

Shiron, looking intently at Kellar, said with a hint of sarcasm, "Nukes; I'm not surprised. The Iranians are not supposed to have that kind of capability according to you Americans and to most of the Western world."

Kellar ignored the remark. "What could they put them on?"

"Shahab-4s," snapped Shiron.

Suddenly, the rear canvas flap parted and a soldier peered in; everyone froze.

Hellmann, the closest, was the first to react, striking the startled man hard on the head with the butt of his rifle before dragging him swiftly over the tailboard and expertly breaking his neck. Ryder hurriedly searched the dead man's pockets, removed wallet and a security card – *might come in handy* – and told Kellar to put the body in one of the empty crates. Once this was done they prepared to leave. Ryder hoped it would be some time before the truck crew and the guard would be missed. He hoped too, that Afari would pass for a young fresh-faced guard in her ill-fitting uniform with hair tied up under a slightly oversized cap.

Ryder decided they would take one of the lifts direct to the lowest level. Checking to make sure all was clear, he and Shiron lowered the tailboard onto the raised dock and boldly strode through the milling personnel to the back wall lined with timber boxes and machinery parts. Here they took two flatbed carriers, returning minutes later. Trying not to look suspicious, Ryder, running high on adrenaline, placed the four crates filled with gear onto the carriers, helped by the other five, and headed for the lifts at the far end of the dock.

Inside the large lift, Shiron slammed shut the lattice metal gates and Ryder hit the button for the lowest level – level three. With a jolt, the lift began to slowly descend.

At level two the lift stopped to reveal through the latticework a group of technicians and several security personnel. Ryder gripped the handle of his concealed knife and prepared to use it. The group entered, ignoring him and the others, shut the lattice gate and continued to talk animatedly amongst themselves. The chatter confirmed Shahab-4 missiles would soon be released carrying multiple nuclear warheads. Ryder glanced urgently at the others; although their expressions remained passive he guessed they were as equally shocked as himself.

The lift arrived at level three. The personnel hurried out and disappeared down the corridor. Ryder and the others followed, pushing the carriers along the wide, busy corridor and into another lined with numerous doors and screens; the whine of machinery much louder now. He scanned for CCTV cameras and was surprised to see none; that helped, knowing they couldn't be tracked. Technicians criss-crossed the corridor but took little notice of the group manhandling the two carriers. At the end Ryder entered into yet another corridor, this time short and narrow. Here only two pairs of doors broke its grey concrete walls, one pair at the far end and the other halfway down on the right. The pair halfway was padlocked and the international symbol for explosives was displayed clearly on the metal surface. More explosives were needed; after sabotaging the dam power grid, Ryder had worried that what they had left would not be enough for the task intended. Without hesitation he instructed Afari and Fehed to remain outside whilst he, Kellar and the two Israelis broke into the magazine. Ryder picked the padlock, swung back the door and the four entered pushing a carrier. Fehed slid the padlock back into place and both he and Afari then tried to look as if they had a reason to be there inspecting the wheels of the remaining carrier.

The magazine was well stocked. *Definitely go up with a bang,* thought Ryder; an opportunity too good to pass. Cases of Semtex

214

and detonators were quickly located amongst the stacks of weapons and ammunition. Hurriedly, several makeshift charges were put together with four placed in a crate on the carrier for later and the rest in strategic positions around the magazine; timers were set.

"No need to continue on, Frank," said Kellar, back with the others at the carrier. "We should get outta here *now*. Once this pile blows the whole fucking mountain will likely go with it."

For a few seconds no one spoke, the hum of the air conditioning filling the silence.

"If the silos remain intact they can still be used," shot Shiron, looking pleadingly at Ryder. "We're here now; let's finish it."

Kellar stared at Ryder, wiping sweat from his forehead, "What's the point risking more?" Look at this stuff," he swung his arm at the stacks of weapons, "when it blows, it'll sure take the guts outta here."

Ryder faced the American. He knew it was crazy not to get out; all his senses screamed to bolt, but something inside urged him to continue.

Shiron looked coldly at the American then at Ryder, "We'll go alone if necessary."

This was no time for a confrontation. *What the fuck is wrong with the American; has he suddenly lost his courage?* Ryder turned to him, "You want out, then go for it; we're carrying on." He was not going to even attempt to argue with Kellar. With this place about to go up in only a few hours he wanted to find the silos, place charges and get out as fast as possible. He turned away from the American and, pushing the carrier, made for the entrance.

"Wait!" shot Kellar, stepping in front of the carrier. "Okay, okay I'm with you, count me in. Sorry, Frank; wasn't thinking straight. Better we all die together, huh," he said, half grinning.

Ryder gave him an icy look, "Forget it, Sergeant." He then told them to grab spare magazines for the AKs and stuff them into the crates. Once this was done they headed for the door.

★ ★ ★

Meanwhile, outside in the corridor, Fehed and Afari were doing their best to appear occupied in fixing the carrier wheels; she on her knees and he bent holding the front axle. Suddenly, the door at the end through which they had entered burst open and two armed personnel approached. Both stiffened.

The two men reached the carrier.

"What are you doing?" asked one.

"Wheel stuck – won't turn," Fehed replied, grimacing as he held up the front axial.

The Iranian looked at the wheel then at him suspiciously. He swung to Afari, lingering on her, "Why are you here in this part of the complex? The stores are back that way," he pointed to the doors they had come through.

Fehed answered quickly in an authoritative voice, still holding up the axial, "We are new here; took the wrong corridor, as soon as we get this wheel fixed, we'll be on our way."

The two men stared at the crates. The less inquisitive one urged his companion to hurry or they would be late for the shift, but the other man ignored him and said, "IDs please, and open the crates," not taking his eyes away from her.

Afari shot a telling glance at Fehed and reached into her pocket. Fehed knew instinctively what she had conveyed, let the carrier drop and he too went for his pocket.

At that moment the padlock on the doors rattled; both guards were immediately distracted.

In that split second Afari and Fehed drew knives and before the soldiers had a chance to react leapt and plunged the blades into their necks.

The two men fell choking to the floor clutching at throats, blood beginning to ooze between their fingers.

Fehed swiftly moved to the door, disengaged the padlock and let Ryder and the others out.

"Shit, what happened?" Ryder shot, taking in the chaotic scene, then, "Hurry, get them into the magazine."

The bodies were quickly dragged in by the two Israelis as Fehed quickly explained.

Moments later Shiron and Hellmann returned.

"I was wrong, you know how to use a blade," Ryder said to Afari.

She looked at him, defiance in her eyes, but said nothing.

Hurrying down the corridor towards the doors at the end, Ryder felt the adrenaline surge guessing they were close to the heart. Through those doors, he hoped, would be the silos. They were electronically operated, Ryder fished out the security card taken from the dead guard earlier, swiped it through the keypad and, to his relief, they parted.

Entering a huge, brightly lit cavern, he saw beyond rows of metal racking, sleek, white missiles on cradles surrounded by gangs of technicians labouring at benches. Mingling with the technicians were armed guards. At the far left-hand side of the cavern a tunnel entrance was clearly visible. To the right of this opening, flatbed transporters on tracks stood coupled to a small locomotive. Ryder hoped it was the tunnel leading to a firing chamber.

He led them past the racking and the cradled missiles shining under halogen lights, pushing the carriers boldly between the benches and machinery. No one paid much attention until just short of the tunnel entrance where they were challenged by a guard. Ryder put a hand inside his jacket and gripped the handle of his knife. If the man asked for IDs he'd have no choice but to kill him and hope for the best.

He moved closer to the guard as the others manoeuvred the carriers to just inside the tunnel entrance. The American and the two Israelis then joined Ryder, attempting to screen him from the rest of the cavern, knowing what he would have to do if the guard raised the alarm.

"Your purpose for entering the tunnel?" the man asked, resting his arm on the barrel of a machine pistol slung from his shoulder.

Ryder scrambled for an answer and blurted, "Equipment for the firing chamber."

The guard looked at him suspiciously and then at the crates on the carriers. "Then those should be loaded onto a flatbed," he said, pointing to the locomotive.

Ryder took a chance, "A launch is due soon; the equipment is needed now and cannot wait for the engine to be made ready."

The guard looked at him again with more suspicion. "Show me ID."

No choice now. Ryder reached inside his jacket, hand feeling for knife.

Suddenly, the cavern erupted with the deafening wail of sirens. The guard immediately diverted attention to the sound and moved quickly away shouting to take up emergency stations. Ryder threw a glance at the others; this was it, no going back now.

In the confusion, Ryder rushed into the tunnel with the others close behind. Hurriedly he, Kellar and the two Israelis broke open the crates as they ran whilst Fehed and Afari pushed the carriers. Removing weapons, ammunition vests and packs holding ropes and the charges, the carriers were abandoned and all raced down the tracks. It did not take the guard who had challenged them long to realise Ryder and those with him had vanished into the tunnel. Immediately he raised the alarm and gave chase.

Ryder ran alongside the tracks, keeping close to the curving tunnel wall. Up ahead, around a bend some thirty yards away, several armed guards suddenly came into view. He threw himself hard against the ribbed structure and opened up at the oncoming men, killing all in one prolonged burst before they realised what was happening. He turned to look back. Kellar, the Israelis, Fehed and Afari, AK-47s bucking violently, emptied magazine after magazine into an oncoming phalanx of soldiers. Ryder's courage almost gave way to desperation at the sight of so many. The noise was deafening. He knew if the silos were not at the end of the tunnel they were all dead, but if they were, time would be needed to lay and set the charges. Without hesitating, Ryder bellowed at Kellar, Hellmann and Fehed to fight a holding action whilst he, Shiron and Afari made for the end. Slamming in a fresh magazine he raced along the tracks, ignoring bullets ricocheting off the structure.

With Shiron and Afari closely trailing, he followed the bending tunnel for almost 100 yards, arriving at the entrance to a large rectangular chamber hewn out of solid rock – the firing chamber. Relief mixed with fear engulfed him as he saw a metal gantry framework supported on tracks, carrying twelve metal firing tubes in two banks of six. In front of the gantry for almost its entire length, were two massive sliding doors hung on the longer rock wall of the chamber now in an open position 30 feet or so above the floor. He could see a star-studded sky beneath a wide external overhanging rock formation. This overhang, probably the one he was prevented from seeing due to low cloud, obviously protected the opening from aerial view. The firing tubes were angled to allow the missiles to emerge from the mountain through the gap on a 35 degree trajectory westward. Ryder entered and hurriedly scanned the gantry and banks of grey tubes. Fortunately, no one else was about and it looked to him as if everything was prepared for a launch.

Wailing sirens and staccato gunfire filled the tunnel and the chamber. Ryder quickly removed ropes from packs and handed them to Shiron, telling him to make three scaling lines up to the opening. The Israeli hurriedly searched for something he could use for grappling hooks. Then, helped by Afari, Ryder removed charges from the packs and raced towards the tubes. Here, both frantically searched the framework before placing charges in relatively obvious positions and more well hidden in the latticework of the gantry supports. With a superhuman effort, he clambered to the top of the 40-foot-high gantry support and placed two more charges, lowered with rope, down inside the tubular void to rest on a bracing ledge just above the nose of the missile inside. These charges would be difficult to locate and retrieve without cutting through the steel casing. With timers set prior to climbing the gantry he let the ropes fall into the tubes.

Shiron found three metal bars and bent them as best he could into crude hooks before securing to ropes. He then expertly swung and threw the bars up to the gap and, after only two tries, managed to maintain a firm hold. Tugging until he was satisfied all three were well secured he retrieved his rifle and, joining with Ryder and Afari, raced back into the tunnel.

Kellar, Hellmann and Fehed, now less than fifteen yards from the chamber entrance, had managed to keep the Iranians at bay, but only just. When Ryder and the others arrived the Iranian advance was halted by their added firepower.

Fehed was hit in the arm and leg, but still returned stinging fire. Kellar and Hellmann kept the Iranians pinned down with accurate and persistent firing, but ammunition was running short. Ryder could see the situation had now become desperate; they had to get out fast, but he knew as soon as they made a run for the ropes, the Iranians would be upon them. Shiron and Afari shared out remaining ammunition and began lobbing grenades, the explosions deafening in the tunnel confines.

Hellmann suddenly cried out, clutched desperately at a gaping hole in his chest and crumbled to the track. Shiron jumped to help him but Ryder caught the Israeli and dragged him back. Hellmann was dead before he'd hit the ground.

Fehed's magazine emptied. Frantically, he groped for another and as he did a hail of bullets sent him crashing to the ground, life-blood gushing from the swathe of holes from neck to groin.

Kellar leapt to Fehed's assistance and he too took a bullet through the shoulder, throwing him heavily onto the dead Iranian.

Ryder, Shiron and Afari continued to return rapid fire; Afari equally as ferociously as the men, no doubt aware this would be the last opportunity to exact revenge. Ryder knew too, it would only be a matter of minutes before they all died in this tunnel.

From around the bend, a carriage pushed by a locomotive came into view. On the flat-bed, guards fired from behind a large metal shield, fully protected from whatever the remaining members of the group could throw at them. *This is it; this is how it's going to end,* thought Ryder as he lobbed a grenade onto the track, hoping to derail the oncoming train.

He had no choice now. Ordering the others to retreat into the chamber he and Shiron helped Kellar between them, still returning fire, the American taking another hit as they ran.

At the entrance Ryder saw with horror the sliding doors to the outside beginning to close. No way would Kellar be able to scramble up the rope in time, and he knew it.

They continued to return rapid fire. Ryder would not leave the American and ordered Shiron and Afari to get out whilst they still could. Both hesitated, then, reluctantly, turned and ran for the ropes.

Over the noise, and still firing, Kellar shouted at Ryder, "*Go! I'll hold long enough for you to get out – Go!*"

He glanced at Kellar's wound; he'd taken a big hit in his lower chest; a large hole oozed blood which also began to trickle from the corner of his mouth. It was fatal; the American did not have long to live.

He and Kellar, together with Shiron and Afari, now on the opening ledge above, kept up continuous fire towards the chamber entrance.

Suddenly, the American's big frame jolted back and rolled lifelessly to the floor; a bullet had blown off the top of his head.

Time to get the fuck outta here! Ryder's inner voice screamed. Having used the last clip, he looked desperately up at the huge, rumbling doors which had now almost closed. Removing pins

221

from two remaining grenades, he hurled them through the entrance into the tunnel and darted for the nearest rope.

The grenades exploded loudly and he felt the shock wave hit as Shiron swiftly hauled him up the 30-foot-high wall to the opening, while Afari continued to spray the chamber entrance. Reaching the ledge in seconds he followed her through the narrow gap just as the doors finally closed. Before they did, Ryder, amidst the hail of bullets pinging off the metal, glanced back and saw Iranian soldiers flood the chamber and attack the American's body.

Outside in the cold night, wind whipping the rocky surfaces, the three survivors, using ropes Shiron had hauled up, began a hurried descent down the sheer mountain face to the tussock-covered slopes 40 feet below. Clambering down safely, Ryder quickly made his way, followed by Shiron and Afari, across the lower slopes of Kuh-e Mohammadabad, heading south, glad to be alive and eager to get away as far as he could before daylight. Below in the distance, to the right, he could see vehicle headlamps leaving the garrison at Abbasabad, some heading northwards to the base entrance and others along a road that ran south-west towards them. The vehicles stopped at regular intervals, no doubt disgorging troops. Soon, Ryder guessed, the whole area would be swarming with patrols.

When the three were well down the valley, hiding amongst the rocky outcrops, backtracking and skirting exposed ground to avoid the patrols, a sudden roar filled the air. Looking back, Ryder saw one missile, then another, exhausts illuminating the darkness, streak high into the night sky. He looked at the others in desperation and horror; were they destined for Israel? Then, seconds later, came a series of explosions; a tongue of red licked out from below the rock overhang then a huge explosion from deep within seemed to rock the mountain. Desperate to get away, Ryder turned and headed as fast as he could south for the Persian Gulf, Shiron and Afari close behind. There was nothing more he could do now but hope that the base was permanently disabled, and that the unleashed missiles would not be the start of a Third World War.

26

High on the Negev Plateau the Israeli Air Force's remote anti-missile Battery No. 3, nestled below the eastern ridge of a low mountain range, was clearly visible in the moonlight bathing the bare, rocky terrain. Strategically positioned on the ridge could be seen the banks of structures housing the Arrow-2 Anti-Tactical Ballistic Missiles (ATBMs) and Patriot PAC3SAMs which operated as part of Israel's highly sophisticated Ofeq-4 satellite surveillance system. Battery No. 3 formed the southernmost part of the defence shield to protect the Jewish State. Three other batteries, including the Iron Dome anti-missile system, covered Jerusalem, Tel Aviv and Haifa to the north.

Inside the control bunker a young duty commander sat staring at the banks of computers with one eye on the clock. In five minutes it would be midnight and his watch would be over. He scanned the row of wall screens above the line of computers and operatives monitoring the tracking and control systems; Green Pine fire-control system, Citron Tree fire-control radar and the Hazelnut launch-control all hooked into the Ofeq-4 satellite network. The satellites in low east-west orbit, using high-resolution cameras, together with infrared sensors, gave Israel real-time coverage of the whole of the Middle East, in particular Syria and the western borders of Iran. On detection of missile heat signatures at launch, the data would be immediately fed direct to every one of the defence batteries which evaluated direction of inbound missiles and probable point of impact. Linked computers in automatic mode would then determine which battery would be able to give maximum protection and optimum launch pattern to intercept sixty to seventy miles out from the battery position. Each Arrow-2 battery comprised four missile launchers with six tubes each, and three SAM missile launch vehicles. Normally the battery would be equipped with at least fifty missiles, but due to a shortage, Battery No. 3 had less than thirty-five operational Arrows and SAMs at present.

The commanding officer was about to remove his headset when suddenly a red light on one of the computer consuls began to flash and the operator's voice came urgently through the earpiece.

"Two unidentified tracks: Sector four, fifteen miles south of Al Basrah. Inbound!"

The officer hurriedly replaced the headset, adrenaline surging. *Was this for real?*

The computers automatically gave each missile a three-digit number.

"Go to Alert-Four," shot the officer, trying to remain calm.

The alarm went off conveying to the thirty personnel in the control centre that hostile missiles were heading towards Israel.

"Launch footprint?"

"Negative."

"Impact zone?"

"Negative."

"SCUDs? MRBMs?"

"Negative."

"Advise immediately when ballistic and impact zone data available," snapped the officer, wondering why the computers were taking so long to process the information and why there were no launch signatures before picking up the tracks.

"Why the fuck is it taking so long?" he yelled down the mouthpiece.

The operator clicked again on the appropriate icon. This time up popped two circles over a map of Israel with wording flowing across the bottom of the screen.

"Launch footprint still negative," called the operator.

How can that be? puzzled the officer; all of Iraq and western Iran was supposed to be covered. However, he could not concern himself with that now. He had to know what he was up against and the exact points of impact.

"Coming through now," said the operator calmly, "Shahab-4's with multiple warheads. Impact zones: Jerusalem and Tel Aviv."

The officer had been through this many times before in exercises, but now it was the real thing; he felt fear.

The voice of the operator, showing no emotion, continued: "M001, Jerusalem; M002, Tel Aviv. Ninety-five percent certain points of impact," he finished, watching the circles on the monitor slowly reducing around these centres.

A gasp ran through the bunker as soon as the information came on the wall displays.

The officer fought hard to contain his panic. The Arrow-2s, he knew, could intercept incoming missile warheads at ranges between five to thirty miles and at altitudes of up to thirty miles, but the PAC-3s were more effective against SCUDs and not Shahabs, which had a closing velocity that limited the Patriots' defence coverage to a much narrower window around the launchers, he therefore could only use them as a last resort. He also knew the Arrows had limited capability against the Shahabs due to serious intercept problems. Travelling in excess of Mach 5 the incoming missiles would impact in less than ten minutes.

He would need permission to engage from Command Centre in Tel Aviv. Reaching for the direct line, he dialled and in less than one minute was given permission to assist the battery in Jerusalem. The remaining incoming missiles would be dealt with by batteries in Tel Aviv.

"Optimum launch window – three minutes," called the operator, "request to auto-engage missile zero-zero-one."

The officer was well aware of the Rules of Engagement when it came to the missile/anti-missile game. Israel could not afford to waste missiles; supplies were limited, forcing battery commanders to wait always until optimum launch point had passed to be certain of the incoming missiles destinations. However, this was his first real experience and his nerves began to crack.

"Confirmed, you are clear to engage. Use Bank One, four Arrows," he replied firmly.

With multiple warheads on the incoming missiles there could be as many as seven deployed on the missile his battery was after. He therefore decided to take no chances, convinced that overkill was better than being sorry later.

"Roger, clear to engage," replied the operator, repeating the missile designations before clicking on the firing icon. "Units launched."

A roar, clearly audible in the bunker, a tremor and four Arrow-2 ATBMs left Bank One casings and soared up into the night sky, accelerating to Mach 4 eastwards towards the incoming missiles.

All eyes now turned to the wall screens showing the Arrows and Shahab trajectories converge.

Seconds later the radar system picked up the tracks of three ATBMs from the battery covering Jerusalem as they too headed for the inbound missiles.

Suddenly, a number of trajectories sprung from the white dots as the hostile missiles released electronic countermeasure suites to confuse and use up the Israeli interceptors. The screen turned to momentary confusion as all Arrows exploded but the Shahab trajectories continued.

"Release Bank Two, *now!*" the duty commander screamed. Another roar and tremor and four more Arrows raced towards the Shahabs, but once again, after the screen confusion, the inbound missiles kept coming.

"Fuck! Fuck! Fuck! Use Bank Three – all four Arrows," yelled the duty commander to his subordinates. The instruction to launch was given, but this time, instead of the normal roar and tremor, there was an explosion upside.

"What the fuck was that?" he howled, clear panic now in his voice.

"Malfunction in Bank Three, sir," the immediate response, "it can't be used – too dangerous. Presently only one detonator has malfunctioned. If the Arrows explode we'll all be in deep shit." Although the battery was protected for this sort of event, an Arrow exploding in close proximity is not the sort of experience the duty commander needed right now.

"Get the last bank ready!" he yelled. Within a single minute the Shahabs were going to win the battle and proceed to their targets.

Seconds later, "Bank Four ready to fire," came through the headpiece. The duty commander gave the signal to launch. An audible roar filled the air as everyone involved hung in silence and anticipation. Four Arrows were fired and streaked out to meet the Shahabs. One Shahab was destroyed but the other kept up its relentless course.

"One down but the other still alive!" he yelled.

Everyone prayed in silence. The remaining three missiles hunted their target. The first one detonated but failed its mission; the second hit the target but didn't explode. Everyone waited, not wanting to breathe as the third moved in. It hit the target, erasing the Shahab's trajectory from the screens.

The bunker erupted, everyone ecstatically yelling, jumping up from their chairs and bouncing around the room hugging each other.

"We got them! We got them!" shouted the jubilant duty commander; an ocean of relief washing over him.

The screens were now completely empty and no further missiles had been detected. The duty commander slumped back in his seat, relieved that his battery, and the battery covering Jerusalem, had, for the time being, eliminated the danger, but for how long?

★ ★ ★

In the aftermath of the missile attack, the prime minister, Ariel Barak, his minister of defence, Binyamin Marok and his recently elected foreign secretary, Benjamin Mitsa, sat solemnly with a handful of senior military advisors in the secure basement conference room in the office of the prime minister for the State of Israel.

"Has there been much damage?" asked Barak, strain etching his strong, craggy features.

A middle-aged army general replied, "None, Prime Minister. The intercept took place over a remote part of the Negev."

"What happened to the follow-up?" pressed Barak.

The general shrugged. "Why there was no second wave remains a mystery."

"Thank God we were spared that," said Mitsa, running a stubby hand over shiny bald pate, brooding eyes fixed firmly on the PM. Diminutive and dapper in a dark pinstripe suit, white shirt and a red tie, he stood out from the casually dressed PM and the rest in dark-green battledress or unadorned blue navy and air force uniforms.

"Anyone injured?" asked Marok, hawk-like features taut under a mop of greying hair.

"No," replied the general. "The remoteness of the area ensured that, which will also keep the incident out of the public eye, at least for now."

"Should we go on full alert?" questioned Marok.

"No!" snapped Barak. "We must keep this whole episode low key – away from the public – otherwise panic will result. Make it known to all those involved that what has happened is fully classified. Is that clear?"

Everyone nodded.

"Have we determined the origin?" Marok asked.

Another advisor, this time a younger man dressed in air force colonel uniform, replied: "The missiles were Shahab-4s. We don't yet know what they were carrying but nuclear heads has been mentioned. No launch footprint was established. The warheads are being retrieved."

"Nuclear. Why am I not surprised?" said Barak, sarcastically. "They're not supposed to have the capability – the targets?"

"The tracking pointed to Jerusalem and Tel Aviv. Our surveillance SATs picked them up over Al Basrah which suggests the launch was from somewhere within south-western Iran. A signature is usual before tracking. However, it's accepted we and the Americans do have blind areas in the southern Zagros Mountains."

Barak and Marok glanced at one another each knowing what the other was thinking. Kuh-e Mohammadabad: only a few months ago, Mossad's spy networks in Tehran had reported the possibility of a missile base in the southern Zagros Mountains. Had the Special Forces unit they sent in to find out if one did exist made it, perhaps this attack may not have occurred. The fate of the men after the plane crash was still unknown to them.

"Could the missiles have been launched from mobiles?" asked Marok.

"No, the Shahab needs a fixed pad."

"Where would Iran obtain nuclear warheads?" Barak questioned.

"China, Russia, North Korea would supply anyone prepared to pay. Delivery to the buyer would be the only problem," replied Marok. "America continues to pussy-foot around believing the Iranians have some way to go before having their own, but our people think they may have already. After this, who would doubt it?"

"Colonel, we can count ourselves very lucky there wasn't a second wave," said Mitsa. "What are your thoughts on this?"

"Unusual, to say the least; I would have expected one by now."

"I agree," replied Marok. "Do we retaliate before another attack? We have the right. Our sovereignty has been violated."

"Exactly what the US president said to me less than an hour ago with one voice, and with the other: we must show restraint and await events. The president offered to send immediately their MOAB missiles, and the appropriate people to fit them onto our planes, if we show restraint. MOAB missiles will definitely enhance our systems a hundred-fold." He was referring to America's new anti-ballistic missile defence system slung under jet fighters. This extremely mobile and efficient system allowed fighters to surge vertically upwards at great speeds and release a series of interceptor missiles to engaged inbound hostile missiles high in the atmosphere well before they reached the intended targets.

"Why were we not informed earlier of this attack?" shot Barak bitterly. "What the fuck are our intelligence services doing in the precincts of our belligerent neighbours, and in the rest of the Arab world? Had those missiles found the targets, the State of Israel would not exist. Do you understand me? Not exist! Where was Mossad? I am sick and tired of fending off Islamic Jihad, Hamas and Hizbollah, now we face the open hostility of lawful governments bent on our destruction. When will it ever end?"

No one spoke, waiting for the prime minister to regain a little composure.

"How soon can they set up this defence system?" Mitsa eventually asked.

"Within forty-eight hours, and have them fully operational seventy-two hours after that," replied Barak, calmer. "Now that we know Iran has nuclear capability, the desire to become a regional nuclear power will become a reality. It will upset the balance for sure. We are the strongest at the present time; our Arab neighbours know it, and it must stay that way."

"The Shahab-4 could hit targets in central and southern Europe. On that basis I believe we should put pressure on the international community to stop this menace. A nuclear holocaust in this region would quickly spread to others and no doubt eventual oblivion for us all," stated the minister of defence.

Silence as they waited for the prime minister to reply.

"Let's hope this constitutes a reality check for our American friends. Perhaps now they will do something positive about it," he eventually said, then after a short pause, "Is *Tekumah* still in the Gulf?"

"Yes, sir," answered Major General Nemen, commander-in-chief of the Israeli Navy.

Barak was referring to one of five Dolphin-Class German-made submarines belonging to the Israeli Navy, capable of firing modified 'Popeye' long-range cruise missiles beyond 1,500kms. *Tekumah* (Hebrew for 'revival') was at present patrolling the Gulf of Oman at the entrance to the Strait of Hormuz.

"Ariel, we cannot – should not, even consider that," said a concerned Mitsa, knowing full well what Barak had in mind and voicing reason. "We'll plunge the whole of the region into a nuclear holocaust. It would be madness – suicidal."

"It would be suicidal not to," shot back Marok, knowing also what was on the PM's mind. "That attack was to test our defences. For some reason they did not follow up. But, what will happen tomorrow, the next day, next week – six months from now? They failed today… " His voice trailed off and he shrugged.

"The Cabinet will decide," said Mitsa.

"The Cabinet will do what I say," retorted Barak, coldly. "Look at us, look at our nation: so small, so vulnerable. We must teach the Arabs and the Persians we are here to stay peacefully, or otherwise. One day all will have the technology to wage war on equal terms, and then, God help us."

"We must strike now, but why *Tekumah*?" questioned Marok.

"Our silos in the Negev and elsewhere, Biny, are monitored by the Americans and God-knows who else," replied the PM in quiet, measured tones. "I want retaliation by stealth. This way we create confusion, gain time and can be ready for the inevitable – and deny all responsibility after the event. In the meantime I recommend we accept the latest missile defence systems the Americans are offering."

Mitsa began to protest, but thought better of it. He could see Barak was clearly set on this path.

"Is *Tekumah's* position Classification One?" the PM asked Nemen, almost as an afterthought.

"Yes, Prime Minister. She has been on station now for almost a week monitoring traffic in and out of the Strait."

"Good. Thank you."

A stunned silence filled the room. Barak stared at the papers on his desk then eventually looked up at Nemen. "Begin the process for a nuclear strike at Tehran and a mountain called Kuh-e Mohammadabad in the southern Zagros range. I want *Tekumah* on stand-by, 'Grand Slam' is to commence five days from now, or immediately should we be attacked again. When it is done, I want her out of the Gulf and deep in the Indian Ocean as quickly as her turbines will take her," he paused for a few seconds, then to all: "Do I make myself absolutely clear?"

"Yes, sir," came the quick reply from around the table.

Moments later Barak stood up and left the room, watched by the stunned officials now charged with the responsibility to activate Grand Slam, the long standing code name for a nuclear attack on Iran.

27

Ryder, Shiron and Afari made ground south through the valley away from the mountain. Dawn light began to touch the top of the peaks, tinging them pink, when they finally decided it was safe to rest after a gruelling non-stop twenty miles. Exhaustion and the stress of the past twelve hours had clearly taken its toll. They found a small cave and Ryder decided to rest, risking a fire for warmth, and to eat what little food remained. Once the meagre rations had gone, they settled down to ease their tortured, aching bodies until darkness came again.

Ryder studied the map. "According to this, the road below leads to Bandar Abbas, 200 miles directly south. It's the shortest route to the sea; the port is only fifty miles from Oman across the Strait of Hormuz. If we could make it to the other side, we would be safe."

"A navy vessel could still be waiting off Nay Band," said Shiron.

Ryder thought that was highly unlikely after all this time; Shiron was letting his imagination stray. "Nay Band means we have to go west over the main range, a longer and more hazardous route, with no guarantee your navy would be there."

"I agree with Frank," Afari said, "easier and quicker to go south."

Shiron gave in. "Okay, south it is. But bear in mind, the port is also Iran's main naval base on the Gulf."

"It's a risk we have to take. It will be easier there to find a vessel capable of taking us across the Strait."

With that, Ryder offered to take first watch and the others stretched to sleep.

After a full day of resting, twilight began to fall and they left the cave, quickly moving over the sparsely-covered terrain, keeping well away from the road. In the distance could be heard the throb of helicopters and single-engine airplanes flying low, following the snaking road well down into the valley. Military traffic on the road was frequent and caused Ryder some concern; it meant troops might be in the hills ahead. Darkness and the rugged nature of the valley slowed them considerably. Thankfully, the sky was overcast and the wind light, but high-altitude fatigue plagued them. Only experience and training kept the two men going and Ryder continued to be amazed at the strength and tenacity shown by Afari keeping up without complaint.

The night trek passed uneventfully and at dawn, after covering almost twenty-five miles, Ryder, tired and hungry, searched for a place to rest; they would sleep during daylight at least until clearing the valley. Soon he found a suitable gap amongst rocks big enough to accommodate all three with entrance concealed by scrub. Exhausted and almost too tired to eat, they forced themselves to chew on the last of the dried meat. Fatigue finally took hold. Ryder took first watch, Afari would take the second and Shiron, the last until nightfall.

★ ★ ★

Not long into the Israeli's watch, Ryder awoke with a start, staring down the barrel of an AK47 brandished by a tribesman gesturing sharply for him to get up; another had a gun to Afari's head; both were pushed out from the gap. Staggering into the late afternoon sunshine he saw Shiron's body sprawled by the entrance with throat cut. Seeing the Israeli almost crushed his spirit. While Ryder was roughly searched and knife removed, Afari was given a more intimate search, hands feeling all over her body. Ryder could see her humiliation and made to intervene but was sent sprawling with the butt of a rifle. He and Afari were then roughly manhandled at gunpoint down towards the road snaking through the narrow valley below. Ryder despaired; they had come so far, achieved so much and now with exhaustion fogging his brain he wanted to give up. Something deep within, however, urged him not to, not ever.

Halfway down, he heard one of the captors behind slip and curse. From the corner of his eye he caught the other, just slightly back and to one side, turn and look.

Ryder saw his chance, instantly swung the side of his hand hard against the tribesman's throat and sprang at him. As he fell, Ryder swiftly grasped the man's head in a vice-like grip and, with one violent wrench, broke his neck.

At the same time, Afari leapt at the other struggling to get to his feet.

A gun fired, Ryder heard a gasp and knew instantly Afari had been hit.

Before the tribesman could push her away, Ryder dived at the two struggling bodies.

The tribesman kicked Afari violently to one side, then Ryder, before rolling away, rifle slipping out of his grasp. He sprang to his feet, dagger in hand and lunged at Ryder; the blade missing by inches. Ryder grabbed and twisted the outstretched arm; the dagger fell and he threw him to the ground. Scooping up the knife, Ryder leapt on the back of the sprawled man, lifted his head by the hair and sliced his throat from ear to ear. Within seconds the gasping tribesman died; severed jugular spurting blood with every last pulse. *That was for Afari and the Israeli sergeant.*

He went quickly to where Afari lay, saw the bloodied patch on her right shoulder and pulled part of the jacket and the under-shirt away to expose a neat hole. He turned her over, looked at the other side and saw another hole, not so neat, where the bullet had passed right through. A flesh wound, luckily, as far as he could tell the bullet had not damaged the collarbone. Stripping away the shirt from one of the dead men, he tore it into lengths and pressed a bundle hard against both holes in an effort to stem the bleeding before wrapping the remainder around her neck and upper arm to hold everything in place. Without wasting any more time, as others could have heard the shot, he helped her gently to her feet, asked if she was able to walk, and when she nodded, led her down the valley southwards. The task to reach safety had now become much harder, but in no way was he going to give up.

28

Captain Ben Lehmann, the youthful looking, grey-haired commander of Israel's latest and most sophisticated diesel-electric submarine, *Tekumah*, looked up from the plotting table in the control centre.

"Confirm depth, speed and position," he said in a smooth, deep voice.

"Depth 250 feet, speed seven, position 26.43N, 56.23E," the immediate reply.

"Bring to periscope depth."

"Aye, sir."

Here in the command and control centre, positioned directly below the submarine's sail, stood two central plotting tables and in front the 'conn' – a raised half-circular platform with metal railing on the curved side on which two periscopes sprang. Lining the periphery bulkheads were consuls, chart stands, instruments and banks of digital screens. The whole centre was crammed into an area no larger than an average household living room.

Tekumah's Electrical Intercept (ELINT) and Communications Intercept (COMINT) were full on. The Electronic Support Measures (ESM) mast jutted just out of the water picking up signals and noise of surface traffic. Spread out behind the sleek, black craft, the towed array of sonar equipment could detect all underwater traffic within a radius of some fifty miles.

"Up periscope," ordered the captain, and stood waiting by the two grey tubes dominating the conn platform as No.1 periscope hissed into position. He reached for the foldout crossbars, then lowered and placed his forehead against the rubber eyepiece. Turning the scope for a full 360-degree view of the Strait of Hormuz above, he scanned the sensitive choke-point at the eastern end of the Persian Gulf through which twenty per cent of the world's oil supplies passed. It was dusk and the sea was calm. He studied the myriad of tankers and freighters plying the Strait; this was regular, routine work and a task he would be glad to see the end of after almost a week watching traffic in and out of the Iranian naval base at Bandar Abbas. One more week and he would thankfully head back to Israel.

He rotated the periscope towards the Iranian coastline and suddenly froze. In the murky distance he could just make out profiles of two submarines on the surface, heading across *Tekumah's* bow.

"Down periscope, come left two-seven-zero. Make your depth 200. Speed eight," he ordered.

The submarine responded.

He turned to his younger executive officer, Lieutenant Joseph Levi. "Iranian Kilos, two in line on surface."

His XO looked at him incredulously, "On the surface; two-thirds of the entire sub-operational flotilla? Do they want everyone to know they're out?"

"Obviously," the commander replied. "Captain – sonar: plot position and course. Get on the SAT immediately."

"Sonar, aye."

"Captain – sonar: Contact, faint engine lines. Relative zero-two-five, not surface machinery."

"Captain – roger. Come left two-eight-five. Resolve ambiguity."

Tekumah turned to allow sonar to confirm the bearing.

Three minutes later the faint engine signature came on the operator's screen again and the computers began to determine type, speed and range.

Seconds later, "Captain – sonar: Contact too weak to translate."

"Captain, aye."

"Captain – sonar: translation, negative."

"Captain, roger. Reduce speed to six knots. Maintain course."

"Aye, sir; reduce to six; maintain course," repeated the operator.

At a rate of knots less than seven *Tekumah* was almost undetectable to searching sonar.

"What do you make of that I wonder?" asked the commander to his XO.

"Sub on the outer limit of the ELS?"

"Possibly, on a westerly course out of Bandar?"

"We're bang in the middle of the Strait. If it had come from anywhere else we would have picked it up long before this," said the XO.

"The Iranians have three serviceable Kilos. Two we have just seen. Where's the third?"

"Still in port?" offered the XO.

"Maybe," the commander said thoughtfully. "Anyway, log the signal and get out what we have on the SAT as quickly as you can."

"Do we take a closer look at those two?" questioned the XO, voice expressing anticipation.

"Our orders are to monitor and record, and stay on station; but I think this is important enough to take a closer look. Don't you?" he grinned.

The CO returned his attention to the charts. Then a few moments later, "Left standard rudder. Course: two-six-zero. Make your depth 300 feet. Increase speed to ten knots."

"Aye, sir."

"Captain – comms: Urgent signal coming in."

"Thank you, comms. See that I get it as soon as translation completed."

Moments later, "Captain – comms: Translation completed. Code A, your eyes only."

"Bring to the conn."

Seconds later the communications officer arrived in the control centre and handed a sealed envelope to the commander.

"Thank you, comms." He turned to his XO. "You have the conn." With that he left the control centre and made for his day-cabin to decode the signal.

Once in the small area he used as an office, the captain opened the envelope, removed a single sheet and placed it on the desk. Next he opened the safe, reached for the Code Manual and began to translate the contents.

Minutes later he stared incredulously at the decoded signal:

0805FEB20TELAVIV.
FROM COMCHIEF NEMEN CENTCOMSUBIND.
TO SUBCOM TEKUMAH GULF OF OMAN.
STAND BY GRAND SLAM. REPEAT STAND BY GRAND SLAM. TARGETS TEHRAN AND MOUNTAIN IN ZAGROS RANGE CO-ORDINATES 30.34N, 54.52E. RELEASE POPEYE SLCM AT EACH TARGET FROM CO-ORDINATES 29.04N, 49.25E. EFFECTIVE ON ORDER. REPEAT EFFECTIVE ON ORDER. CONFIRM UNDERSTOOD.

Captain Lehmann left the cabin and headed grim-faced towards *Tekumah's* control centre, recent events forgotten. As he made his way, he thought of his family and the awful consequences of carrying out the order he had just received.

He entered the control centre and took the conn, "Left standard rudder. Course: two-three-zero. Make your depth 300 feet. Make your speed ten knots."

The 1925-ton Dolphin Class Type 800 submarine's diesel-electric turbines increased speed and propelled the 187-foot-long warship silently through the shallow waters of the Strait, now on a mission which could well herald the end of Israel, if not the world.

At his desk in the offices of the US National Security Agency at Fort Meade, Maryland, the navy analyst studied the latest photographs from the satellite which regularly ran a corridor pass over southern Iran. After a few minutes he looked up, pondered for a few moments, then reached for the phone and rang his divisional commander.

"Sir, Lieutenant Davis here. Can I see you? It's important, regarding Bandar Abbas." He paused listening to the voice at the other end of the line. "Thank you, sir. I'll be right up."

The young lieutenant, tall and gangly, entered Captain Alen Jackson's office, saluted and was invited to take a seat.

"Well, Lieutenant, what have you to show me?" said the stocky, grey-haired commander.

The lieutenant produced photographs from the previous day together with those taken that day and laid them out side by side on the desk.

"Two Kilos have left the base, both heading south on the surface. But where is the third?"

The commander reached for a magnifier and scanned the photographs.

"Definitely Kilos," he said eventually, "and you're right: all pens are empty. That means the whole operable flotilla is out."

"The third could still be in the covered pen."

The commander looked up, "I agree."

He studied the latest photo more closely. "No activity about the covered pen." He then studied the previous day's photo. "Something different here. The mooring stays right on the line of cover edge. It appears to have taut rope attached – but not in the latest shot." He paused, seemingly in deep thought, then, "Okay, Lieutenant, thank you, I'll take it from here."

Lieutenant Davis saluted and left the room.

One hour later the captain, together with the agency's director,

Admiral John Martin, sat in the Pentagon offices of Admiral Harry Peters, Chief of Naval Operations and Admiral Bill Johnson, Commander-in-Chief Pacific Fleet.

"What do you make of it, Harry?" asked Admiral Johnson.

"Intriguing to say the least," the chief replied. "I can only assume Iran is getting its subs out in case Israel decides on retaliation for the failed strike against them. Those missiles were undeniably Iranian Shahabs."

"Iran may well attempt another strike. Baffling why the first wasn't followed quickly by a second," said Admiral Johnson.

The others nodded.

"Unusual for the subs to stay on the surface; they know we would catch them on the overheads," said Jackson.

"Maybe that was the intention," said Admiral Martin, "but why only two Kilos?"

"Could be a diversionary tactic, allowing the third to slip away unnoticed," offered Jackson.

"For what purpose?" Admiral Martin asked.

"Your guess is as good as mine," replied Admiral Johnson.

"It wasn't that long ago the Iranians purchased several SL-1s from the Chinese. Could they have already converted a Kilo?" asked Admiral Jackson. He referred to Chinese first-generation submarine-launched ballistic missiles (SLBMs).

"Possibly, but I doubt it," replied Johnson. "They don't have the know-how."

"If they decide on a swift second strike, how can they best do that without detection?" asked Admiral Peters.

"Lobbing JL-1s from a submerged sub," offered Admiral Martin.

"Correct, but the JLs only have a range of some thousand miles; that means they can only be launched from the Mediterranean, Red Sea, or the northern half of the Persian Gulf. The Med and the Red are out, takes too long to get there; that leaves only the Gulf. To gain the attention of the watchers, and create a major diversion, why not send out Kilos in full view, heading south away from the intended action whilst, under cover of darkness, slip a missile-carrying sub unseen west into the Gulf? Interesting scenario, don't you think, gentlemen?"

The men were silent for a few moments, absorbing what Admiral Peters had said, then Admiral Johnson spoke, "Very plausible, Harry, if you are referring to a converted Kilo-class. It seems unlikely, but just in case we should inform our Israeli friends of the possibility. Do we have any subs in the Gulf?"

"*Louisiana*, *Memphis* and *Alabama*," replied Admiral Peters. "All our carrier groups are heading for the Gulf."

"Okay, warn the groups," said Admiral Johnson. "And get our subs to locate and track the Iranians. It may well be a diversion, but we need to keep an eye on them… Oh, and by the way, while you're here, and for the record, our SATS monitored low-level thermal activity bordering a major explosion in a remote part of the Zagros Mountains three days ago. The Iranians have said nothing so far and we have no record of any major industrial or military activities in that area so it remains a mystery. Unusual, but no doubt we'll get to know in due course what caused it."

With that the meeting broke up and the men dispersed.

29

Two days of relentless slog with little sleep and constantly on the alert, Ryder and Afari reached the southern end of the plain that separated the two main parallel ranges of the Zagros. The journey over the rugged territory was definitely telling on Afari and progressively she became more reliant on him to keep up. Ryder could tell she was in some pain and feared her injury might be infected even though he had placed moss on the wounds she had told him to use. The conditions made any movement agony and it was to the Iranian's credit she endured without complaint. By now they had completely exhausted all food and only a little water still remained. If they were to continue, food and water was urgently needed. The domed huts of local inhabitants became more frequent now as they crossed the undulating scrubland to the west of a major town. It was obvious Afari could not go on much longer without a prolonged rest – which was out of the question – so he decided to hijack a vehicle once they were south of the town.

They pressed on, keeping to clusters of vegetation, until full daylight arrived as the sun crested the mountain line to the east in a clear sky. Ryder, more for Afari's sake, decided to make camp in a thicket of bush.

He gently checked her shoulder; it did not look good. "Wound's holding up okay," he lied. "We'll rest here for a few hours… we need food and water; I'll see what I can scrounge from the locals."

Afari gave him a weak smile. "Be careful… tough farmers and

herders live in these parts... have a reputation for not taking too well to strangers."

He nodded, "I will, but we have to eat." Food was a priority and whatever it took to get he would do. "If I'm not back in twenty-four hours—"

"You planning to run out on me?" she cut in with another weak smile.

"I wouldn't do that," and he meant it. "We need a plan B if something happens to me. Should it, then you make for the Gulf the best you can."

Making her as comfortable as possible, leaving what little remaining water close by, he set out in search of food.

★ ★ ★

Not long after leaving the thicket, Ryder came to a lone hut. He knocked on the dwelling door and a grizzled old woman answered. Beyond her he could see two men hunched over a fire. When the woman called, they came over, each carrying a rifle. Ryder remembered all too clearly the last time he had encountered armed tribesmen and steeled himself for trouble. They looked suspiciously at him before stepping out, asking Ryder what he wanted. Trying hard to be casual, hoping the uniform would convince them he was genuine, he explained he was part of a patrol looking for two armed men on the run. Then he took the plunge and asked for food. The two men looked at one another, half smiles creasing their haggard features and invited him in. Suddenly, as he stepped over the threshold, and before Ryder had a chance to react, the larger of the two struck him so fast and with such force, it knocked him clean out.

When he came to, he struggled against tight bonds, but soon gave up and focused on his surroundings. Only one of the men and the old woman remained in the hut. The door was open; it was dark outside. How long had he been here? What of Afari? The man stood from the hearth and sauntered over to where he lay. Bending down, he told him the authorities would soon be here and he would collect the reward for capturing him. Then he asked if he was with others.

Ryder ignored the question; at least they hadn't found Afari.

The man pressed further and began to punch him.

Suddenly, Afari staggered in through the open doorway pointing rifle and screaming at the Iranian to step away. She could barely stand.

The Iranian, seeing her weakness, lunged sideways for his rifle.

Ryder kicked him hard in the chest sending him flying.

As he rolled away, Afari did not hesitate and shot him dead.

"What kept you?" Ryder joked, relieved to see her.

"Could easily have died from hunger waiting for you; it's been over twenty-four hours. Better to come looking for you than struggle to the Gulf," she replied, forcing a smile.

"How the hell did you find me – in the darkness too?"

"Luck, and following that unique ripe smell you leave behind," she joked back, wincing with pain, as she untied Ryder; the old woman wailing loudly in the background. Once free, they looked for food and took what little they could find, placing it in their backpacks before hurriedly fleeing the scene. They had to get well away; soon the other man would be returning with soldiers.

Assisted by Ryder, Afari kept up a steady pace until daylight, resting only to eat, but her efforts caused the wound to bleed heavily and she became weaker. Unless they found transport soon, he feared she may not make it to the Gulf. The two moved southwards along the slopes above a large town. Afari could now just manage unaided, but she was very weak and transport of some kind became urgent. He decided to go down into the town and steal a vehicle. Scanning the jumble of low-level buildings on the southern perimeter, his binoculars rested on a freight train in a railway siding. Two big diesel locomotives, coupled together, indicated the train might be heading south. According to the single rail line shown on the map, the tracks ended at Bandar Abbas. He tried to see the other end of the long line of wagons, but the view was blocked. This was a chance too good to miss and he decided to take it.

The two moved as fast as Afari's condition would allow, skirting the town and keeping well to cover, until they reached the siding alongside the track. Here they hid, waiting for the opportunity to board a wagon. Further down the line, military personnel were systematically searching the wagons. Although this was a worrying factor, the train being searched indicated it might well be heading south. He prayed it was.

They waited until the soldiers had passed out of sight before crossing the short open space to the nearest wagon. Ryder hurriedly hoisted Afari in through the open door of the empty wagon, then himself and the equipment. They huddled together, Ryder hoping the train's destination was Bandar Abbas some 150 miles south and would soon be on the move. Afari looked so vulnerable and a strong feeling of protectiveness shot through him. He held her close, making her as comfortable as possible on the hard wagon floor. Thankfully it was much warmer now which eased some of the discomfort.

Almost an hour passed before the two big French locomotives blew horns and began to slowly pull away, heading south much to Ryder's relief. The long line of wagons snaked out of the siding, gathering speed; he gained confidence the port was the likely destination. As the train chugged through the rugged valleys he did his best to clean up Afari's wound and give what comfort he could, holding her close and keeping her warm until she finally succumbed to sleep. Soon Ryder, himself totally exhausted, lapsed into a fitful sleep lulled by the sway of the wagon and the rhythmical sound of steel on rails.

Sometime later the train began to appreciably slow, horns blew several times, awakening the two, as the wagons rattled across tracks and into a siding where it slowly came to a halt. Hurriedly checking the map and GPS, Ryder ascertained they were in a town called Fin, fifty miles north of Bandar Abbas. Would there be a search? That fear was soon confirmed when, after only ten minutes in the siding, Ryder poked head out of the wagon and saw groups of militia making their way along the wagons, fortunately without dogs.

Where could they hide? Afari, alert now to what was happening, urged him to help her clamber up through the vent and out onto the roof. Ryder noted a trapdoor in the floor, decided against going through, although quicker. It would mean she would have to cling to the undercarriage; in her condition that was out of the question. Without another word, he hoisted Afari up onto his shoulders and pushed her through the vent, swiftly followed by the packs and rifles.

The searchers were now very close; no time to jump and lift himself up through the vent. Instead, he rushed to the floor trapdoor, opened it and slipped through. Clinging precariously to the metal framework beneath, hard up against the floorboards, he watched the legs of several Iranians pass, look into the wagon and move on. Minutes later, when he was sure it was safe, he re-entered the wagon and called quietly to Afari, who handed down the equipment before lowering herself painfully onto his shoulders and on to the boards.

Shortly, horns sounded again and the train began to pull away; Ryder certain now it was heading for Bandar Abbas. Both settled down for the remainder of the journey and he hoped there would be no more halts until they reached the port

One hour later the train rattled into the marshalling yards at Bandar Abbas; it was now dusk. Instead of waiting for the train to stop, Ryder decided it would be better to leave the wagon once it had slowed sufficiently for both to safely get clear. The wagons clattered and rolled across the numerous tracks into the sidings, slowing considerably, allowing Afari to lower herself, with his help, through the open doorway, until she felt the ground and ran alongside. He followed soon after with the equipment. They hid in the shadows of the many wagons lined up close by. Through the undercarriages and between the wagons, Ryder could just make out, in the dimming light, a wired fence which he guessed was the perimeter. Keeping to the shadows, the two cautiously picked their way across the tracks, weaving between slow-moving freight wagons, until they arrived safely at the fence. Glancing about to make sure no one had seen them, Ryder helped Afari to slip through a gap in the mesh and both melted silently away into the darkness.

30

In the secure conference room deep in the bowels of his Jerusalem offices, Prime Minister Barak, together with Defence Minister Binyamin Marok and Commander-in-Chief of Israel's Navy, Major General Nemen, stood looking at a large wall map of the Middle East.

"If the American scenario is to be taken seriously, the submarine would be somewhere here," Nemen said, pointing to a spot in the Persian Gulf just west of the Strait of Hormuz.

"I'm taking this very seriously," said Barak. "Those satellite photos clearly indicate something is going on. *Tekumah* has confirmed two Kilos have left the base, also that a Kilo may be heading into the Gulf. Our own people in Bandar have confirmed all Kilos are out. Two heading south, but where is the third?"

"As the Americans point out," said Marok, "they could be scattering in anticipation we will retaliate."

"Wise move," Barak said with a cold smile. "A second strike could come any time. What type of missiles would she be carrying?"

"Chinese JL-1s, say the Americans, with a range of a thousand miles," the General replied.

"How many?"

"Four."

"Warheads?"

"Multiple types, each can deliver seven nuclear devices."

"So, from the northern end of the Gulf, they can reach our cities?"

"Yes, Prime Minister, they can," replied Nemen grimly.

"This submarine poses a real threat if in the Gulf," said Barak.

"We cannot do much to prevent a land-based strike, but we can at least attempt to eliminate a sea threat," offered Marok.

"If the Americans are right, how long would it take for the sub to be in position?" asked Barak.

"Approximately forty-eight hours moving slowly at depth to avoid detection," replied Nemen.

"She's been out ten hours, that leaves thirty-eight," said Barak looking up at the map and folding his arms. Several seconds later he turned to the General. "Send *Tekumah* into the Gulf, find out if the sub is there and destroy if found. Hold Grand Slam for the time being unless we are attacked again."

The telephone rang. The prime minister picked up the receiver and listened for a few moments. "Send him in," he said and replaced the receiver. "It's Dagan; he wishes to see me urgently. The matter apparently cannot wait."

"Shall we stay?" asked Marok.

"Yes, if appropriate. We'll see."

The door opened and Meir Dagan, short and smartly dressed, entered.

"Take a seat," said Barak to the chief of Mossad, pointing to a chair at the table opposite his. "Should Biny and the General stay?"

"Yes, what I have to say will affect them too," replied Dagan, grim-faced, forty-five years of age but looking ten years older with grey receding hair and bulging eyes under dark, bushy brows.

"Do you want the tape on?"

The Mossad chief nodded. All meetings between the prime minister and his spymaster were usually taped. A military stenographer typed up the transcript and a copy was placed in the secretariat safe with another copy sent to the Mossad chief.

Barak pressed a button beneath the table to activate the recorder and turned to Dagan.

"Now, what is so urgent?"

Dagan came straight to the point, "We are about to be attacked again with nuclear missiles."

"By who?" shot Barak.

"Iran."

Barak, Marok and the navy chief glanced fearfully at each other.

"Submarine launched missiles?" Barak asked.

"Yes," replied Dagan, somewhat surprised. "How did you know?"

"The Americans suspect an Iranian Kilo sub is in the Gulf to do just that, using Chinese JL-1s that could carry nukes," replied Barak. "Where did you get your information?"

"I prefer not to say. It may compromise the source."

"Then how are we to authenticate it? I have already ordered one of our submarines to find and destroy the Kilo. It would be good to know I am justified in doing so," said Barak sharply.

Dagan sat silently for several seconds unsure if he should reveal his source, then, reluctantly: "Please, turn off the tape."

Barak did. "You sure you want this?"

Dagan nodded. "We have a highly placed contact in the armed forces."

"Why did he not inform us of the first strike?" asked Marok.

"It did not involve the Iranian Navy; now it does," Dagan fired back. "This strike has been hurriedly arranged for unknown reasons."

"Does your source know why the first strike was not followed by another?" asked Barak.

"No. All he knows is that the Iranians believe a window of opportunity must not be missed," replied the Mossad chief. "Two Kilos have been sent out into the Indian Ocean as decoys and a third is now somewhere in the Gulf with orders to fire nuclear missiles at Jerusalem, Tel Aviv and Haifa."

Again, fearful glances, Dagan continued, "The Kilo has only

recently been converted, launch tests have yet to be carried out and the crews, although experienced, are barely into the launch training programme. Chinese instructors are on board to manage the firing process."

To have the American suspicions confirmed presented a shock to the three men. All they could do was stare at the Mossad chief.

Barak broke the silence, "Inform *Tekumah* immediately to destroy the Kilo. Reinstate Grand Slam and alert all our anti-missile batteries to prepare for an imminent attack." He stood up. "Thank you. Please excuse me, I have to attend a function – everything must still look normal." He paused, a false smile creasing his haggard features. "We have no alternative but to await events."

With that, the meeting came to a close.

31

The port town of Bandar Abbas was the main commercial maritime outlet for much of southern Iran, and also a major base and headquarters of the Iranian Navy. It was also one of the most important strategic centres in the Persian Gulf and Sea of Oman. Once a British outpost, the old fishing town was sold off to various Arab potentates from 1740 and subsequently controlled by Muscat until 1868 when the town with its sprawling streets, alleyways and bazaars reverted back to Persian rule. From a population of 17,000 in 1955 it now had almost half a million occupants commensurate with a major commercial port city. After leaving the rail yard situated just north of the base, Ryder and Afari spent half the night hiding in scrub on the outskirts of a small residential area, and the other half weaving their way through almost deserted suburban streets until they found themselves outside the naval base on Suru Spit, two miles west of the city centre. Ryder, from his recollection of the city on a short visit several years ago, concluded that the two small commercial harbours on the highly exposed central waterfront were too far away to make an attempt at hijacking a dhow or maybe a small launch, especially in Afari's condition. To make their way through such a densely populated area to the harbours certainly did not appeal. The base seemed a better option, despite the added risk, but it was close and he was more likely to find a suitable craft to take them fast across the Strait. If the base was too well guarded then they would have no alternative but to take the waterfront option.

From a hideaway in scrub on the south-eastern perimeter of the base, he scanned the complex through binoculars, noting empty dry docks, clusters of administration and storage buildings, together with several naval craft moored in the eastern arm. However, what interested him most were three coastal patrol boats moored at the extended quayside almost directly across from where they hid. To get at them they would need to cover more than seventy yards of open ground, scale a high wire-mesh perimeter fence and then cover a further fifty yards of open ground to sheds on the quayside. To move swiftly and hope to avoid any guards that may be patrolling the immediate area would be paramount. Ryder worried the exertion needed might be too much for Afari.

"One of those boats would get us across," he handed her the glasses and she scanned the quay. "It won't be easy getting to them; will you be up to it?"

"I have come this far; I'm not giving up now when so close." She handed back the glasses. "I can make it, but if you think I'll hold you up, then you go; I'll find some other way out."

Even though he could see she was in pain, what choice really did he have? No way was he going to leave her here. "Okay, we'll go," he replied then scanned the perimeter again. The 8-foot-high fence topped with strands of razor-wire looked new and without mesh cutters would be impossible to penetrate. He moved glasses along the perimeter line and stopped where the fence joined a short run of brick wall to the right of their position. The wall was the same height as the fence and had glass shards bedded in mortar along the top. Where the two met, he could see what looked to be a temporary connection. He turned to Afari, "Maybe we won't have to climb that fence; looks like repair work is under way to the brick wall where it joins the fence. Could be a weak point and we might just be able to pull the mesh away and squeeze through."

"That fence and wall is very exposed."

"We'll wait for nightfall before making the attempt. In the

meantime, get some sleep." He hoped a few hours rest would build up her strength; she'd need it to cope with the ordeal.

The day passed quietly. Ryder spent the time, in between naps, surveying with binoculars every part of the inner basin and in particular the harbour, its entrance, and the outer bulwarks. He also covered the perimeter road they were to cross and felt concern at the frequency of armed vehicle patrols passing, hoping there would be fewer when darkness fell. He did not see any movement around the patrol boats, but that didn't mean they would not be guarded at night. Afari, come nightfall, had improved and said she was good to go. Looking at her drawn features and pallor, he wondered, but could see the determination in her eyes.

Patchy, low cloud scudded across the sky and patrols had become less frequent. They prepared to move out. Ryder decided to discard all equipment and weapons, except for knives. No point now in carrying anything that might hamper the dash for the boats. Should they fail, there would be no going back now anyway. They waited for a patrol vehicle to pass, made sure no one else was in sight, and crossed the road to the open ground. Slinking into the shadow of the wall, he was relieved to see that the temporary connection had been poorly done and began to chip away with a knife at the mortar between the bricks. Within minutes he had freed the metal fence anchor and pulled back sufficient mesh to allow them to pass. Sliding into the gap, adrenaline increasing, he helped Afari through and replaced the mesh. Then, without hesitating, they both scampered across the open ground, Ryder expecting searchlights any moment to illuminate their run and bullets to rip all around. Afari stumbled twice but rallied quickly with his help and eventually they reached the main building alongside the quay. Breathless, backs clinging to plastered walls, they skirted the structure in the shadows and arrived twenty yards from the quayside opposite the patrol boats riding high on an incoming tide.

Ryder eyed the nearest patrol boat, a 40-foot-long, sleek vessel, tugging gently at its stays and appearing to be unmanned. Festooned with radar equipment, a dim red glow emitting from the central control cabin and he could just make out the profile of a 20mm deck-gun aft. This was their ticket out and he prayed the tanks were sufficiently fuelled to get them over the Strait.

The extended quay seemed deserted, but on the other side of the harbour basin, activity could be seen. Ryder hesitated before heading for the short bridge leading to the outer quay structure and the moored boats.

Suddenly, a guard stepped out onto the inner quay from the shadows between the buildings to his right and began to patrol the area in front of the building where they hid. He'd been lucky; had he moved a second sooner... Both drew sharply back into the shadows; no way now could they reach the vessels without being seen.

Should he wait to see if the guard moved on or eliminate him? He chose the latter; it was too risky to wait. Indicating for Afari to remain concealed, he slipped away behind the building until he was in the same position from where the guard had first emerged.

The guard turned at the bridge structure. Ryder unsheathed his knife and waited. The kill had to be swift and silent. He steeled himself.

The guard reached the corner of the building.

Ryder made his move, covering the short distance silently and fast. Grabbing the unsuspecting man from behind, clasping one hand over his mouth, he plunged the knife deep into his heart, killing him without a sound. Hurriedly he dragged the body back into the shadows and returned to Afari.

Making sure all was clear they crossed the short bridge which led to the outer quay. Here he helped Afari up the gangway of the nearest craft and made her as comfortable as he could in the central control cabin. After checking the instruments, relieved they were similar to the boat taken when fleeing Iraq, he checked the fuel gauges and was more than disappointed to see the tanks were less than half full – would it be enough to get them over the Strait?

Instantly he thought about checking the other two boats but gave that away – no time; it would have to do. He then went down to the engine room, found it clear and headed fore and aft to sever the mooring ropes. Back in the cabin he checked the control instruments once more and pressed the starter. The throaty roar of the diesels filled the cabin, the deck shuddered beneath his feet and slowly he opened the throttle. The craft pulled away from the quay, heading towards the green lights marking the entrance to the harbour. At that point he allowed himself to believe they might make it after all and he turned on the navigational lights; everything had to appear normal as he passed through the inner basin.

Two hundred yards out, he steered carefully between other moored vessels, veered a few degrees to port, and began the short approach to the harbour entrance. In only a matter of minutes they would clear the basin, pass through the bulwarks, and would soon be out into the open sea.

Suddenly, a voice from the radio startled Ryder, requesting identification and destination. Should he reply? He decided to chance it, if only to gain time. He gave the number of the craft and told the voice in Farsi his orders were to patrol moored cargo ships out in the bay.

The voice came again, only this time it requested the name of the captain and confirmation of the orders. From the tone Ryder knew immediately he had made a mistake. The voice came again, ordering him to return to the quay. There was nothing for it now, but to dash full speed for the open sea.

Alarm klaxons blared on land. He turned to look at the quay where the other two patrol boats were moored, now illuminated, and saw sailors running along the quay towards the vessels. With navigational lights now extinguished and throttle fully opened at a maximum speed of thirty-five knots, he swept past the harbour entrance, through the outer bulwarks and breakwaters and on into the open sea. Heading the boat at the gap between the large island of Qeshm on starboard and the smaller islands of Hormuz and

Larak to port, Ryder knew, once beyond these islands, he would be in international waters amongst the busy shipping lanes of the Hormuz Strait. If they could make it more than halfway towards Oman's Musandam Peninsular on the other side they would be in sovereign waters and safe. Even with half-empty tanks, he dared to hope again that they might just beat the odds, but quickly changed his mind when 20mm cannon shells from two pursuing Iranian patrol boats churned the sea in his wake.

While he fought to keep the patrol boat one step ahead of the pursuers, Afari tried desperately to raise help on the radio transmitter following Ryder's instructions to continuously repeat in Hebrew the code-word 'Abyss' and the mountain co-ordinates in a forlorn hope the Israeli warship Shiron had referred to may still be in the vicinity.

The trio of boats raced past the islands and were soon out into the Strait and choppy water. To avoid the cannon onslaught, Ryder swerved the craft in a zigzag pattern across the silvery expanse, but the pursuing boats slowly gained and began to inflict serious punishment, peppering the superstructure with bullets and tracer streams. Not only had he to worry about the barrage coming from the rear, he also, in the darkness, had to concentrate to avoid the possibility of colliding with one of the many ships plying the Strait in his path. The experience of the Iranian crews began to tell and it was only a matter of time before they would be right on the stern unless firepower could be effectively returned to hold them at bay.

Ryder, acutely aware of the mounting danger with the hail of bullets striking the bouncing, swerving hull and superstructure, shouted for Afari to take over the wheel. He had no choice now she had to do it despite her condition; if nothing was done to stop the onslaught they would not make it anyway. She stopped transmitting and staggered to the wheel. He told her to hold the course they were on and to keep the throttle wide open, before he left the cabin and edged his way along the starboard side towards the gun on the aft deck. Fortunately, the main onslaught was coming from the port beam and port quarter. He reached the gun, opened the ammunition box attached to the side and, with some difficulty, fed in the belts before rapidly returning fire with the 20mm cannon, shells from the pursuers whistling and ricocheting all around. His relentless firing from behind the protective metal shield raked the decks of the trailing boats with such accuracy it forced them to drop away, reducing the ferocity of fire and giving him and Afari much needed respite from the attack.

32

Tekumah was now on her firing station at a depth of 200 feet in the centre of the Strait on a line between the island of Larak and Kamasan at the tip of Oman's Musandam Peninsular, awaiting orders to put Grand Slam into effect. Tension ran high among the crew since Commander Lehmann had notified them of the purpose for preparing and arming the missiles. They knew the horror they soon would unleash and the consequences it may have on their homeland. All systems had been checked and rechecked and the crew now waited nervously for the order to fire.

"Captain – comms: Receiving urgent, bizarre signal in Hebrew calling for assistance. A female voice is continually repeating the name 'Abyss' and provides co-ordinates of a mountain in the southern Zagros range."

The commander looked up from the chart table. "Are you certain it's not a TV channel?"

"Comms, affirmative sir."

"Position?"

"Captain – sonar: small surface craft bearing three-five-zero. Range 1000 yards. Course: two-one-zero."

"That will take it directly across our bows. The co-ordinates, what are they?"

"Captain – comms: 30.34N, 54.52E."

The CO stiffened; they were those for Target 2. The adrenaline increased.

"Captain – comms: have that transmission relayed in its entirety to Centre – *now!* Request most urgent response."

"Comms, aye."

"Captain – weapons: continue countdown."

"Weapons, aye."

"Go to periscope depth."

"Aye, sir."

★ ★ ★

Afari, with throttle fully open and barely able to keep her grip on the wheel, steered the badly damaged patrol boat as best she could across the busy shipping lanes, relentlessly pursued by the Iranians. Most of the control cabin had been shot away and a large hole had been made in the stern at the water line allowing seawater to pour through, greatly reducing speed. It was a miracle the boat had not yet sunk and they were both still alive. Ryder kept up the accurate fire but ammunition was running out; soon they would be at the mercy of the pursuers. As the clouds parted and a quarter-moon lit the waves, the fuel alarm bell suddenly rang; tanks were all but empty and to cap it, ammunition had expired too. Ryder rushed back into the cabin, took the wheel from an exhausted Afari, and in desperation searched for salvation; his only hope: several large illuminated ships bunched together in convoy not far away in the distance. Without hesitation, he swung the wheel hard to starboard and headed as fast as the boat would allow towards the ships until he finally plunged in amongst them praying the looming presence of these vessels would deter the Iranians from closing in.

★ ★ ★

"Up periscope," ordered *Tekumah's* commander.

A hiss of hydraulics and seconds later he was looking through the night-scope scanning the waves. To port he saw several ships clustered together at less than 1000 yards and to starboard three small craft speeding towards them. The leading boat was low in the water and appeared to be in a damaged condition.

"Confirm leading craft as source of the transmission."

"Captain – comms: confirmed."

"Captain, roger."

"Captain – comms: signal from Centre – translating."

"Captain, roger," replied the CO tensely, his whole body taut awaiting the contents of the signal.

"Maintain countdown."

"Weapons, aye."

"Captain – comms: signal translated."

"Bring to the conn!" the CO almost shouted; tension now really beginning to bite.

Shortly the communication officer arrived and handed the captain an envelope which he hurriedly opened and read:

OO30FEB25TELAVIV.
FROM COMCHIEF NEMEN CENTCOMSUBIND.
TO SUBCOM TEKUMAH GULF OF OMAN.
GIVE EVERY ASSISTANCE TO PURSUED SURFACE CRAFT.
IRANIAN KILO-CLASS SUBMARINE SUSPECTED IN PERSIAN GULF ON
HOSTILE MISSION AGAINST ISRAEL POSSIBLY ARMED WITH CHINESE
JL-1 NUCLEAR MISSILES. YOU ARE TO SEEK OUT & DESTROY.
MISSILES EFFECTIVE BEYOND LATITUDE FIFTY-TWO DEGREES. KILO EXPECTED TO REACH LATITUDE WITHIN THIRTY HOURS. GRAND SLAM TO REMAIN ON STANDBY. REPEAT GRAND SLAM TO REMAIN ON STANDBY.
CONFIRM UNDERSTOOD.

The commander handed the signal to his XO, grim-faced, took one more look through the periscope seeing the small craft not far away now, almost above them, wallowing helplessly on the starboard bow, then ordered:

"Down periscope, go to surface, all speed."

"Aye, sir."

★ ★ ★

Ryder felt the taste of fear; the combination of exhaustion and stress had all but overcome him. The boat failed to make the protection of the convoy and had begun to sink in the 3-foot swell. He could only stare in despair at the Iranian boats as they quickly closed in, guns now silent, powerful searchlights raking the wreck. It was obvious they wanted to take the occupants alive. Afari waited, slumped in the waterlogged cabin, while Ryder clung to the far side of the half-submerged boat.

Suddenly, the sea surged and boiled around them. From out of the depths, less than fifty yards away, rose the huge bulk of a submarine, first the sail then the sleek black hull, its top surface levelling off, glistening, just above the silvery waves. The sail silhouette, menacing in the moonlight, towered high above them. The Iranian searchlights faltered then ran erratically along the length of the hull as armed sailors poured from the forward hatches. With water lapping at their feet the men promptly slipped inflatables into the waves, clambered in and made for the sinking boat.

Shots rang out from those still on the hull of the submarine, shattering the searchlights. The Iranians returned fire, more as a gesture rather than to inflict damage, before veering away and making a hasty retreat.

Plucked from the sinking boat as it went down, Ryder and Afari were ferried to the submarine, lifted to the hull and taken down into the warm bowels of the warship. Not wishing to stay on the surface any longer than necessary Commander Lehmann ordered *Tekumah* to submerge and within minutes the submarine disappeared silently beneath the waves.

33

In *Tekumah's* control centre, Commander Lehmann stared incredulously at his XO after his return from questioning Ryder and Afari in the sickbay.

"Missile base? You're saying, Lieutenant, two missiles were fired from the mountain we are to target before it blew. Holy mother, were they meant for our homeland?"

"More than likely, sir."

"That explains the order to target the mountain and Tehran, and now to destroy the Kilo probably sent to finish the job." Lehmann shook his head.

"Could we be at war with Iran?"

"Maybe, Joseph," the commander shrugged, cursing under his breath. No communication with Central Command was permitted under the current attack conditions. "When we go to the surface have what they said put on the SAT and we'll ask the question." He paused to look at the data monitors. "Was the mountain destroyed?"

"They believe so – at least in part."

"What the hell were they doing out at night in the middle of the Strait?"

"Apparently part of a mission by our Special Forces to destroy the base; they're the only two survivors. They were trying to escape to Oman. The woman is Iranian; has a shoulder wound – not serious. The man's a Brit; he's okay, just needs rest."

The commander looked down at the chart table, features grim. "If that was the Kilo we heard," he said, running his finger over the Strait of Hormuz, "my guess is she entered the Clarence Strait and is now somewhere about here," he pointed to the narrow strip of water between the Iranian coastline and the eastern end of the long island of Qeshm.

"The Strait is shallow – difficult to navigate," said the XO. "The narrows at Khuran even more so," he pointed to the western end of the island. "No more than 100 feet, if that."

"Taking that course is the most direct to get to latitude fifty-two; slower, yes, but less chance of detection. If right we could cross her path about here," he stabbed a finger at the channel between the islands of Qey and Jazireh Forur, respectively ten and twenty miles off the Iranian Coast. "We'll have the element of surprise. The Iranians will not suspect an ambush; they will be too focused on the mission and try to avoid trouble."

"Not if we're blocking their path," replied the XO. "They think we're hostile, instinct will be to attack before we do."

"We'll position ourselves ready. Anyway if we're wrong we still have time to make a sweep west towards the centre of the Gulf."

"They could have reached Jazireh already with a head start of almost twelve hours," said Lieutenant Levi, looking up from the chart table.

"I doubt it," replied the CO, not taking eyes away from the chart. "The Clarence and Khuran would slow them considerably. They would not be able to make more than five to six knots, and at that rate it will take a little less than thirty hours to pass Jazireh from the base. If already twelve ahead, that leaves eighteen. We could be in the channel in ten, doing fifteen knots."

"We could also be detected," said the XO.

"A risk we'll have to take."

The XO nodded. He could see the commander had made up his mind.

The CO turned to the helm, "Make your course two-six-zero, speed fifteen knots, depth 200."

"Aye, sir: Course two-six-zero, speed fifteen knots, depth 200 feet," repeated the planesman.

The Russian made KILO-class diesel-electric submarine could run stealthily below the surface at seventeen knots, using powerful batteries that made little sound below four or five knots. Two hundred and forty feet long with a crew of fifty-two officers and men, the submarine had a range of 400 miles running on batteries, and 6,000 miles using diesels, 'snorkelling' just under the surface. Armed with twenty-four torpedoes and a cluster of short-range surface to air missiles, the KILO-class could indeed be a formidable opponent.

After an uneventful ten hours, *Tekumah* arrived in position on a line five miles north-west of Jazireh and twenty miles south-east of Qeys. Engines were cut and the computer-controlled pumps kept the submarine trimmed and steady as she lay motionless just above the seabed some eighty fathoms below the surface. The primary sonar operators listened intently to detect the telltale signature of the Iranian sub amongst the natural sounds of the ocean and vessels in the busy shipping lanes above. It was not uncommon for submarines to use noisy surface vessels to cover their tracks. If Commander Lehmann was right, the Iranian sub would pass this way sometime within the next eight hours. Orders were given to maintain a silent ship and the crew settled down to wait. The commander, concerned if he had made the right decision, invited his XO to join him in his cabin.

"Supposing they didn't enter the Clarence, instead headed directly south into the Strait of Hormuz?" he asked, more to himself than his number two.

"The towed array would've alerted us. What we got may have been the Kilo, but then again it may have been an American sub. We've detected the signatures of three so far."

"She could have hugged the southern coastline of Qeshm – made greater speed."

"Still could only make four or five knots, otherwise the passive would have picked them up."

"Passive sonar does not work well inshore, as you well know."

"Accepted, but it would be less attractive going south, even hugging Qeshm. US subs would be on a line anywhere between Bahrain and Hormuz using active sonar," reassured the XO.

"It's possible that it may have headed south once out of the Khuran channel, passing between any of the three islands below Jazireh."

"It would take much longer to reach the release zone that way," countered the XO.

The captain nodded slowly. "I guess you're right. It seems logical to take the Clarence and Khuran channels, then on past Jazireh Forur," he said, still trying to clear himself of doubt, justify his decision, but seemed less convinced he was right.

The executive officer nodded agreement and went on briefly to discuss technical aspects of the submarine's performance before he eventually left.

★ ★ ★

In the control room several hours later the commander and his XO waited. If guesswork was right, the Iranian sub should now be well in range of the passive sonar, but so far the sweep had proved negative. Maybe there was no Iranian sub in this part of the Gulf after all.

Captain Lehmann turned to his XO. "She should be showing by now."

"Unless she's on the surface and lost in traffic," offered the XO.

"The surface would definitely attract attention."

The CO was suddenly tempted to go to periscope depth, but thought better of it. Any move could give their position away. "She's down here somewhere and travelling at a very slow rate of knots."

"Go active?" asked the XO.

"No," replied the CO sharply. "That will alert. Surprise must be kept. We'll hold here for another hour then head south-west."

The hour passed slowly. Those in the control centre waited silently for the commander, hunched over the plotting table, to give his orders. Finally he looked at his watch, straightened up and turned to the helm.

"Make your course two-four-zero, speed five knots, depth 200."

"Aye, sir," replied the planesman, repeating the order.

Shortly, *Tekumah* began to rise and head slowly south-west.

Suddenly, "Captain – sonar: contact bearing zero-six-zero. Speed six knots. Range seven miles. Checking profile."

The CO and XO glanced at one another and quickly moved to the conn, looking intently at the bank of screens displaying tracking data of the approaching sub.

"Could be our baby," said the XO.

The CO half smiled.

"How did it get so close without our knowing?"

"Creeping at a very low rate of knots," replied the CO, not taking eyes off the screens.

The alarm on the Acoustic Intercept Box sounded.

"Captain – sonar: active scan!"

"Jesus, they've pinged us!" exclaimed the XO.

"We moved too soon," the CO replied, calmly.

"You were right, and we're in their path!"

The commander nodded and turned to the helm. "Left full rudder, come right around, steer course zero-four-five. Make your speed twelve knots." He wanted to be facing the sub on the starboard quarter.

"Captain – sonar: profile reading: signature, KILO-class 6-2-3."

This was it. The control deck hushed. *Tekumah* had turned and was now facing the oncoming Iranian submarine.

"Rig for attack; ready tubes one and two in all respects. 48 ADCAPS," ordered the CO crisply.

"Weapons, aye," replied the weapons officer before repeating the order.

In the torpedo bay the MK-48 ADCAPS were duly readied. On leaving the tubes they would send back data via fibre optic cables that reeled out behind. If the cable broke the torpedoes would hopefully still hit the target using the on-board pre-programmed guidance system.

"Hold course for tracking solution. Use passive approach, low speed until 1,500 yards, then go active," ordered the CO, voice taut.

"Weapons, aye."

"Captain – computer: tracking complete."

"Captain, aye."

"Captain – sonar: torpedoes: three incoming. Bearing, zero-five-zero. Range 4,000 yards. Bearing steady," came the slightly agitated voice of the operator.

The CO remained cool, mind calculating the level and type of evasive action.

"Release decoys. Down ten; full ahead. Level at 400," he ordered, praying the torpedoes were not active homing.

Tekumah immediately angled down through the water at 10 degrees to the horizontal at maximum speed, at the same time ejecting noisemakers and bubble generators to create an acoustic barrier to reflect the radar energy of the incoming torpedoes.

"Captain – sonar: bearing still steady."

After two of the longest minutes: "Cut engines; free fall."

"Aye, sir."

Everyone held their breath.

Seconds later they all heard torpedoes pass overhead and fade quickly away.

"That was real close," said the XO, sweat clearly visible on his brow.

Retaliation must be immediate.

Suddenly, a loud bang reverberated through the submarine. *Tekumah* shuddered violently and lurched sidewards, sending many of the crew sprawling.

"Jesus!" shouted the XO, gripping bulkhead over. "What the fuck was that?"

Tekumah steadied.

"Torpedo!" exclaimed the CO, holding grimly to the edge of the plotting table and looking urgently around the control deck. "Dud – has to be." He reached for the intercom "This is the Captain. All sections report damage… I repeat: all sections report damage."

"Pre-programmed gyro?"

"No question – and a dud. Count ourselves lucky. Had that been a MK-48 we'd be on our way to the bottom – doomed."

"Thank God the Iranians are still using gyros." The XO referred to the previous generation of torpedoes using gyroscopic guidance systems with often unreliable explosive mechanisms.

"Captain – weapons: torpedo bay. Several men badly injured, damage superficial. No water penetration. All six tubes registering faults; outlets one, two, five and six jammed, three and four registering external obstruction."

"Captain, aye. Lay to the seabed; rig for silent ship." The only thing he could do now was go to the bottom, wait until the damage could be fully assessed and pray no more torpedoes came their way.

"Captain – engine room: no damage. All systems fully shut down."

"Captain, aye."

"Captain – comms: no damage; all systems on stand-by."

"Captain, aye."

The rest of the ship reported negative damage.

"Captain – sonar: hostile silent, last bearing, zero-six-zero. Range 4,000 yards. Speed zero."

The CO looked urgently at his number two. "She's waiting for us to move."

Both knew if their torpedoes could not be fired they would have to wait in the hope the Iranian submarine would eventually leave to complete its mission. Unfortunately, *Tekumah* had soon to replenish batteries.

"How long before we need to surface?" the CO asked, slight tremor to his voice.

"Three hours at most."

"Ready tubes three and four," ordered the commander, voice now steady.

"Weapons, aye."

Then to his XO: "Prepare dive team for external inspection."

"Aye, sir,"

Lieutenant Levi left the control deck to return several minutes later.

"Dive team are all badly injured. They were in the torpedo room at the time."

"Backup team?"

"Sir, they were reassigned."

Grim-faced the CO remembered and shook his head, "Any of the crew with dive experience?"

"None, sir."

The CO looked resignedly down at the plotting table.

"Maybe the Brit can dive," offered the XO. "Part of Special Forces training, I'm told."

The commander eyed the XO with some scepticism.

"Well, go ask him!" he all but shouted.

Ryder was on his cot talking to one of the medics when Lieutenant Levi arrived at the infirmary bay.

"Can you dive?" the exec officer asked him straight out.

He nodded.

"Good. Please join me in my cabin."

Ryder nodded again, raised eyebrows at the medic, wondering what was up, and followed the XO to his cabin.

When they arrived, the officer gestured towards the only other seat in the small cabin, and came straight to the point. "We have a problem and need your help." He then went on to explain what had happened and the danger it presented.

Ryder was taken aback.

"We need to know the extent of the damage. Will you inspect the hull?"

"What about your own divers?"

"All three are concussed."

"How deep are we?"

"Five hundred feet; we're on the bottom."

He'd never dived deeper than 200, and his last refresher had been several months ago. He doubted his ability to undertake the task.

"I've no experience at this depth… put me out there and I probably won't get the job done."

"Our divers are out of action; no one else is available," pushed the XO.

"I understand, I understand." He could see the fix they were in; it looked as if he would have to do it. "Just give me a little time to—"

Just then the cabin door opened and Captain Lehmann entered.

"Well, can he dive?" shot the CO.

"Yes, but seems reluctant."

The commander fixed him with a steely gaze and said in a strong, even tone, "Unless we return to the surface within the next three hours, everything will shut down and all of us will eventually die, including you. And if we move before the Iranian sub sitting out there leaves, we'll again all be dead. That sub is carrying nukes and is going to start World War Three. So you see, Mr Ryder, we all have little choice; we need to know if we can fire our torpedoes. You are the only man with diving experience available right now to find out. You either do it or we die." His stare bored into Ryder.

Can't get more to the point than that, Ryder thought. If they were all going to die one way or another, he might as well go out with a bang. "Show me the exit," he replied with trepidation.

One hour later, after a briefing by members of the crew and donning the Israel Navy's standard issue frogman outfit, Ryder waited apprehensively for the forward escape compartment to flood. Soon the external hatch opened and he glided out into the misty, grey waters. Keeping close to the black hull spread out massively below him like a huge beached whale, he edged towards the bow. Even through the wet suit he could feel the cold and his muscles beginning to stiffen; he hoped they would loosen once the adrenaline fully kicked in.

Shortly he arrived at the bow. The whole nose cone had been shredded; strands of metal hung everywhere. The torpedo had taken the hollow bow casing right off, leaving a shattered, tangled mess. Ryder shuddered at the thought of what might have been had the warhead exploded. He closely inspected the torpedo outlet covers, fully exposed on the now blunted bow structure; all but two looked distorted and firmly jammed. Instead of going back to report, he decided to attempt clearing away the shards obstructing the two undamaged outlets, and began to pull at the metal pieces. Some strands bent away relatively easily but others he could not budge. He struggled for what seemed an eternity, burning up valuable oxygen and he became increasingly concerned at the rapid depletion of air in the tanks. He would make one last effort. Bracing feet firmly against the hull he pushed and pulled as much as his strength would allow and eventually the strands began to move.

He had just about removed the last obstruction when suddenly a strong current surge pushed him hard against an extended strand of steel which, like a knife, cut into his right shoulder. Cold rushed in and blood gushed from the wound. Ryder almost blacked-out from the pain. He quickly rallied, instinct screaming to get back to the hatch as fast as he could. After one last glance at the openings through blood-clouded water, he swam around the bow and made his way painfully towards the hatch, breathing laboured from lack of air in the tanks.

As he reached the hatch, tanks now almost empty, he could feel himself slipping into unconsciousness. With a superhuman effort, delving deep into reserves, he entered the escape compartment, closed the hatch and collapsed as the seawater began to drain. He slipped further into unconsciousness, everything became distorted, noise distended, and finally a bright white light appeared. Then all thought slipped away.

34

In the torpedo bay, the crew hurriedly opened the escape hatch and Ryder's limp body slumped heavily to the deck, blood everywhere. A crewman quickly checked his pulse, felt almost nothing, and tried desperately to revive him. Another attempted to stem the flow of blood, applying direct hand pressure to the wound. At the same time others removed Ryder's tanks and suit exposing the deep gash from shoulder to upper chest before rushing him away to the infirmary.

On *Tekumah's* control deck, the commander paced back and forth waiting for the hull damage report.

The executive officer arrived from the torpedo bay.

"Damage?" snapped the CO.

The XO shook his head, "No report, sir."

"No report! What happened?"

"The Brit is cut bad; losing a lot of blood. How he got back into the escape hatch is a miracle."

"Any of the outlets cleared?"

"Sensors are registering no change. Malfunction systems are now being checked again."

The commander reached for the intercom. "Infirmary, this is the Captain. Is the diver alive? Can he speak?"

The medic at the other end replied, "No, sir. We're doing everything we can."

The CO stared despairingly down at the plotter.

Suddenly, "Captain – weapons: tubes three and four are clear."

Lehmann's head shot up, casting a relieved glance at his number two. He sprang at the comms button. "Captain – sonar: ping the Kilo, we need a fix."

"Aye, sir."

The XO looked inquisitively at his captain; to ping the sub would expose their position.

Lehmann saw his concern. "We have to risk it. If we can get two away now and run, at least we have a chance before they fire again."

The XO nodded; the CO was right.

"Captain – sonar: go active."

"Aye, sir."

Sonar made the sweep and immediately a fix was made on the Iranian sub.

"Prepare full ahead!" Lehmann yelled

"Aye, sir."

★ ★ ★

In the infirmary, the medic was having difficulty in stemming the flow of blood. Ryder's heart had stopped and a lot of blood had been lost. He worked frantically pumping in stimulant drugs, clearing the airways and applying cardiopulmonary resuscitation. Bags of fluids were being intravenously fed into veins as quickly as possible. Finally, he punched Ryder's chest; the heart monitor flinched but did no more. He punched again. The monitor did not register; Ryder was not responding.

★ ★ ★

In the submarine's control centre the captain focused on the problem at hand.

"Make tubes three and four ready in all respects."

One level below, the torpedoes were readied.

"Weapons – Captain: tubes three and four made ready."

"Very well, tracking evaluation when you have it," ordered the CO calmly, not looking away from the plotting board.

"Captain – sonar: target bearing zero-six-zero-two, range 3,000 yards. Tracking confirmed. Firing solution resolved. Computer set."

"Stand by tubes three and four – fire by sonar."

A calmness fostered by the tension and focus of the crew engulfed the control deck.

"Fire three!"

"Three fired."

"Fire four!"

"Four fired."

Tekumah quivered as the two self-propelled heavyweight MK-48 ADCAPS shot out of the tubes and raced away into the depths and began searching for the Iranian sub.

★ ★ ★

A tray of instruments slid off the edge and crashed noisily to the infirmary deck and everyone swayed at the lurch from *Tekumah's* torpedos leaving the tubes. An audible gasp came from Ryder, but the heart monitor indicated he was dead. The medic leapt to Ryder and pumped again at his chest.

Instantly a hesitant and precariously faint pulse returned on the monitor.

"He's coming back," the medic said calmly as he ran two large bore needles into Ryder's arm and readied a replacement IV. The pulse soon strengthened, blood pressure increased and Ryder began to breath regularly and slowly revived.

"He'll need blood – and quickly," said the medic squeezing the plastic bag on the tripod to push the IV fluid in quicker.

The other crew members assisting nodded in agreement. The medic then began to stitch together the sliced deltoid and pectoral muscles.

Meanwhile, in the control room the tension was palpable.

"Captain – weapons: torpedoes under guidance."

"Captain, aye: arm weapons."

"Captain – weapons: torpedoes armed."

Only the sound of electrical motors, beeping computers and the ventilation system could be heard as the two torpedoes sped through the water searching passively at forty knots for the target.

Seconds later, the MK-48s picked up the Kilo.

"Captain – weapons: torpedoes 1,000 yards from target. Switched to active; still holding."

"Captain, aye."

"Captain – weapons: torpedoes contact active."

"Release weapons," ordered the CO, voice void of emotion.

"Weapons, aye."

Seconds later the Iranian sub, realising the Israeli sub's torpedoes were homing in, released all anti-torpedo devices in sheer desperation and panic, at the same time blindly firing the last of its small arsenal of gyro torpedoes.

Tekumah's torpedoes were deflected, one out into the deep, the other searing obliquely along the upper hull of the Kilo, damaging the missile outlet covers and glancing off the sail without the 650 pound warhead exploding.

"Captain – weapons: torpedoes have not found the target."

They all froze as the Iranian torpedoes passed close overhead.

"Captain – sonar: target lost."

"Captain – weapons: reload tubes three and four."

"Weapons, aye."

"She's gone to the bottom, damaged maybe," said the XO.

"Captain – helm: cut engines; lay to bottom. Rig for silence."

"Helm, aye."

"Captain – weapons: tubes three and four jammed."

The captain gripped the edge of the chart table and closed his eyes for several seconds then, "We have to surface and risk the gyros. If we move fast enough we could get away before they can line us up. We—"

"Captain – sonar: target bearing zero-six-zero-four, range 2,000 yards and moving away, speed fifteen knots."

"We've damaged her, she's running!" exclaimed the XO.

Visible relief showed on the commander's face. "Follow, I want to be sure she's heading for base. Course: zero-six-zero-four. Depth 300. Speed fifteen knots."

"Aye, sir."

★ ★ ★

In the infirmary, the situation with Ryder was improving. Rallying, he mumbled from the operating table, fighting intense pain, not sure if he was alive or dead.

The medic knew he needed morphine but it could kill him after losing so much blood. The drug would reduce heart rate and slow respiration, a condition that could be fatal with an already very low blood pressure count.

"What blood type are you?"

Ryder winced, "O pos… O positive," he got out, slowly becoming more aware of his surroundings.

The medic turned to his assistant. "Check crew records; see if we have a compatible donor for O positive or O negative, otherwise this man's chance of survival is marginal." A group O positive individual could only receive blood from a group O positive or an O negative donor. Any other grouping could prove fatal.

The man hurried away and within minutes returned.

"Lieutenant Levi is O negative."

"Good." The medic reached for the intercom, "Captain – infirmary."

"Captain, aye."

"Sir, the Brit has revived, but is in urgent need of blood. Lieutenant Levi is compatible. Can he come to the bay?"

The commander passed the intercom to his number two and the medic again explained the position.

The XO glanced at his captain who indicated with a nod he could go. The lieutenant took leave of the deck and headed for the infirmary.

The transfusion was completed in less than half an hour, in which time Ryder, now fully aware of his surroundings and improving, explained to the executive officer, in halting terms through the haze of pain, what had happened outside the submarine. When he had finished, the XO went straight to his cabin, typed up what had been conveyed and returned to the control centre where he handed over Ryder's report to the CO.

Tekumah, unaware the Iranian sub had used up her small compliment of gyro torpedoes and that she was unable to fire her missiles, followed the Kilo at a discreet distance all the way back to Bandar Abbas, ensuring she entered the base before heading back out into the Strait of Hormuz. Commander Lehmann sent the following signal to General Nemen:

IRANIAN KILO-CLASS SUBMARINE, 623 ENGAGED AND DAMAGED IN PERSIAN GULF. TEKUMAH SUSTAINED SERIOUS DAMAGE IN PROCESS. TRACKED SUBMARINE BACK TO BANDAR ABBAS. CONFIRM GRAND SLAM STANDBY.

The signal arrived on General Nemen's desk in Tel Aviv within the hour. It was conveyed immediately to Prime Minister Barak in Jerusalem. His reply sent through General Nemen and received by Captain Lehmann three hours later read:

GRAND SLAM CANCELLED. REPEAT GRAND SLAM CANCELLED. YOUR ACTION HAS AVERTED

IMMINENT DANGER. RETURN TO BASE. IMMEDIATE EFFECT.

The commander smiled inwardly, read the reply over the speaker to the ship's crew then turned to the helm. "Make your course zero-eight-five. Make your depth 150 feet. Speed fifteen knots." To the rest of the crew on the control deck he said: "Gentlemen, we are going home."

35

Ryder lay in his room in the private wing of the nursing home used by convalescing government employees in West Sussex. By his bed sat George Conway, neatly presented in pinstriped suit and looking every inch the city gent.

"When they going to let me out of here, boss? I'm going nuts."

"Back to your old self, I see. Good, but it will be at least another week. That was a bad injury. I told them you're as tough as old boots but they wouldn't let you out sooner, old chap," he smiled. "Another scar to add to the list; the ladies will indeed be intrigued."

Ryder managed a bland smile and touched his bandaged shoulder, "Beginning to itch – good sign."

"You're lucky, another inch deeper… " Conway trailed off.

Ryder worried this might see him discharged from the unit and given a desk job back at the 1st Para's battalion headquarters at St Athan; worse still, total discharge from the service altogether.

"They say it's healing nicely," said Conway with a look of confidence. "When fully healed no impairment is expected and you should be okay to start getting fit again then back to work."

He was relieved, but wasn't about to show that to the boss. "Well, thanks. Six months' convalescent on full pay would be appropriate."

"In your dreams, Frank; when you take the Queen's shilling…" Conway stopped short, forcing a grin.

"Nice to be wanted; the 'Queen's shilling' could be increased for the risks I take. You know what I mean? Oh, and by the way: so much for a working holiday; if that's your term for what I've just been through I'd hate to think what would happen on a real mission."

Conway forced another grin then adopted a serious face. "The opportunity you and the others took to look for that base undoubtedly saved many lives. A job well done, Frank; the Israelis couldn't thank us enough. They owe us big time."

"How's Afari?" Ryder felt the Iranian deserved to be rewarded for what she did. "She's one brave lady." He hoped he might see her again under better circumstances.

"Mending okay; she'll be given a new life in America. Families of the other four have been spirited out of Iran, too. I tell you, Frank; the Yanks were stunned by that sergeant's treachery. We asked Mossad to find out what they could about him; their people in Iran dug deep and found out he was a Savama (Iranian Secret Service) agent, and had been for many years. His father was killed when the US Navy attacked two platforms in the Rashadat oil field back in 1987. He was six when it happened. Apparently, when old enough, he was sent to America as a sleeper with an airtight cover and orders to join the US military. Now, of course, we know he worked his way into the Special Forces and fed his masters information on everything that would help the country of his birth. We sent a few other names they found to our Cousins and I suspect anyone in the US armed forces with eastern heritage should now be very worried indeed."

"Did he compromise the operation from the start?" It still bothered Ryder that there were so many troops at that checkpoint outside Tabriz.

"Highly unlikely, but we'll never really know. The Americans have a policy that black-op missions are kept to 'need to know' and the operatives involved are usually in lock-down before getting underway, so it seems he would not have had time." Conway changed the subject, "I'm told two Americans and the Israelis have been posthumously awarded for their part."

Ryder raised eyebrows.

"Before you ask, Frank," Conway shot. "You know the rules: no gongs. But we will increase your exit benefits."

That's if I'm still alive to enjoy them, he almost said.

"What you and the others achieved was extremely important; the lives lost were not in vain. If all the missiles had been fired Israel would not exist now as we know it; we would all probably be in the throes of a Third World War."

Ryder reflected on how fortunate he'd been to have survived this time; his luck must surely run out one day. The State had trained him to be a killer, autarchic in manner and confident but it was times like this he felt so vulnerable, so uncertain about his life and to what end it would finally take him. He lived on the edge and the danger of his life abruptly ceasing was never far away. His vocation blurred the difference between 'amoral' and 'moral' and he felt the pent-up rush of emotions generated by this taking a little piece of his courage and confidence away in the aftermath of particularly tough missions. Treated the way he had been in that Iranian prison and his injury made it worse this time, but his sense of relief at overcoming the odds gave him some level of comfort. As always, he knew he had to ride with it or let it go before he could return to normality, if there was such a thing in his chosen way of life.

"How much damage to the base?" he asked, pushing away these pessimistic thoughts.

"Don't know for sure, the Iranians are tight-lipped about the whole thing, including the damage to that dam, but what we can gather from our networks and satellites, and the Cousins of course, is that it will take years to reinstate. However, now the base is exposed, it's thought unlikely to be recommissioned. Regarding the dam, the tunnel entrance is still heavily blocked; looks as if a large chunk of mountain slid down. As for the power grid, it seems the American placed the charges well, that part of the complex looks a mess. I would imagine it will take some time to get the region back on full supply."

"Good, at least some compensation for missing out on the original mission."

Conway gave a wry smile, "You could say that, yes."

A nurse entered the room and told the Omega chief it was time to leave. Conway protested, but to no avail, and finally gave in.

"Rest up, Frank... Oh, by the way, I'll be expecting the full debrief soon," he said as he left the room.

Ryder hated writing reports, so bloody difficult to remember details after the event. He could not help thinking as Conway closed the door: what he'd give now to be on the Harley winging his way up to London to the Prince Albert for a pint and a ciggy.

The nurse lent over the bed to ruffle the pillows. He smelt her perfume; she was pretty. He seemed to have a thing about nurses, reminding him to give Sarah, from Clapham, a ring as soon as he was out of this place and pick up from where they hurriedly left off in Seville. Then on second thoughts – must be the perfume – he cheekily placed his free arm around the nurse's narrow waist; pessimistic thoughts long gone.

"Now, now, enough of that; what would your wife think?" she said primly, gently removing his arm.

"I don't have a wife."

"Oh," she said, looking at him more keenly.

"Perhaps you would do me the honour of allowing me to take you to dinner?" he said formally, never one to waste an opportunity, especially when it came to a pretty face.

"Well, Mr Ryder—"

"Frank, please."

"Well, eh, Frank, maybe when you are well enough, I'll think about it." She blushed, busily tidying the bed before taking his temperature.

Ryder smiled knowingly.

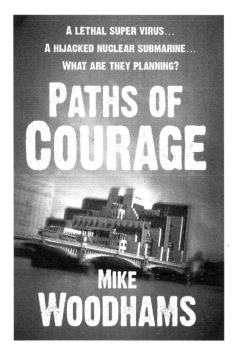

The North Koreans have created a lethal super virus…
Terrorists have hijacked a Russian nuclear submarine…
Together, they are planning an attack that
could have deadly consequences…

Using their spy networks in Seoul and Moscow, British Intelligence establish that the North Koreans are manufacturing a lethal super virus. They also learn of a planned attack on a major Western city, to be carried out by terrorists using a hijacked Russian nuclear submarine. Are these two strands of intelligence linked?

MI6 send a small team of specialists into North Korea with orders to verify if a virus does exist. Led by Frank Ryder, an ex-SAS operative, who is accompanied by Dr. Grace Seymour, an army virologist, the team search the remote central highlands to find the manufacturing facility.

Meanwhile, the British Navy's 'state-of-the-art' nuclear submarine, *HMS Ambush*, is ordered to find and destroy the hijacked Russian submarine. The crew must endure weeks of cat-and-mouse searching, but will they succeed in finding the rogue submarine before a missile and its deadly warhead are unleashed towards an unsuspecting city?

Available from www.troubador.co.uk

★★★★★ Great, action-packed thriller.

At last a new rip-roaring thriller-adventure! Interestingly, not involving the Middle East terror elements but facing down a potential terror threat from Korea. Mike Woodhams takes no prisoners in his book *Paths of Courage* as he gives us an elite team, transported into North Korea to trace evidence of a threat. A new super-virus has purportedly been manufactured, ready for an assault on the West. The SAS team is led by Frank Ryder whose job it is to ensure that the virologist, Dr Grace Seymour can investigate this impending threat and seek any available vaccine. Meanwhile, a Russian sub has been taken by the North Koreans as a delivery mechanism for the life threatening bug. The Brits' *HMS Ambush* is tracing the sub…all action, all the way.

This is a great read projecting a very gloomy picture of life inside this mysterious country where life does not count for much. It is such an energetic novel and the action is the name of the game.

Vine Voice – rhosymyndd "liz"

★★★★★ Excellent spy caper.

Mike Woodhams' book is a great thriller. A mix between Tom Clancy and James Patterson, this story moves at pace across the globe, it was difficult to put down with every chapter ending on a cliffhanger, it's a quick and enjoyable read.

Bravo Mike Woodhams.

Vine Voice – L. E. Cooper "Lindsey"UK.

★★★★★ An engaging read.

Very engaging, very well written; you get absorbed by the characters and fully invested in the plot. This is a great spy thriller novel. Laura.

★★★★★ Pure entertainment, superb.

Looking for a good old-fashioned, espionage-based action thriller, look no further. This story starts with action and does not stop until the conclusion, my type of book – pure entertainment. Omega team, an elite British black operations unit led by Frank Ryder, is given the task of tracking a deadly virus and retrieving a vaccine. To do this he has help from Grace Seymour, a scientist from Porton Down. Whilst Omega are tracking the virus, the latest British hunter killer submarine is looking for a rogue Russian Delta sub. Are the two linked? Mike Woodhams has to be congratulated for a superb book, like a 007 movie in type.

Basingstone Book.

★★★★★ Pure adrenaline action.

Paths of Courage started out fast, edge of your seat, ran that way all the way through and ended up with a huge bang. I loved this book, it is an espionage thriller written like you were there. Current events lead the way, with Frank Ryder, former SAS teaming up with a virologist to find out if North Korea has developed a lethal super virus or not. It is filled with action, and very well written. Don't waste any more time reading my review, get this book and enjoy the read. This preview copy was given to me by NetGalley in exchange for an honest review.

Mayrilynhea.

★★★★★ Great Book!

This is a well-written action adventure. I did not want to put it down. Great read – Good job Mike.
Boatman.

Photo by Firefly Photography NZ

About the Author

Mike Woodhams was born in London and emigrated to New Zealand with his family and now lives in Auckland. He has travelled extensively to all corners of the world, including China, Australia, the Pacific Islands and India, meeting many interesting and colourful characters who have influenced his writing.

www.mikewoodhams.co.uk
Contact Mike at: mwoodhams@xtra.co.nz